IN THE DARK

The Dwelling Hunter Series
Book 2

M. J. Glenn

Self-Published by Softwood Self-Publishing, Ipswich, UK.

www.swspublishing.com

All rights reserved; no part of this publication may be reproduced or transmitted by any means, electronic, mechanical, photocopying, or otherwise, without the prior permission of the author.

First published in Great Britain in 2022

Copyright © Text M. J. Glenn 2022

ISBN 978-1-8381735-2-4

Any references to historical events, real people, or real places are used fictitiously. Names, characters, and places are products of the author's imagination.

Printed and bound in Great Britain by TJ Books
Cover design by Booksmith Designs
Map designed by Frederique Tienmans

Thank you, Nathan, for your never-ending support.

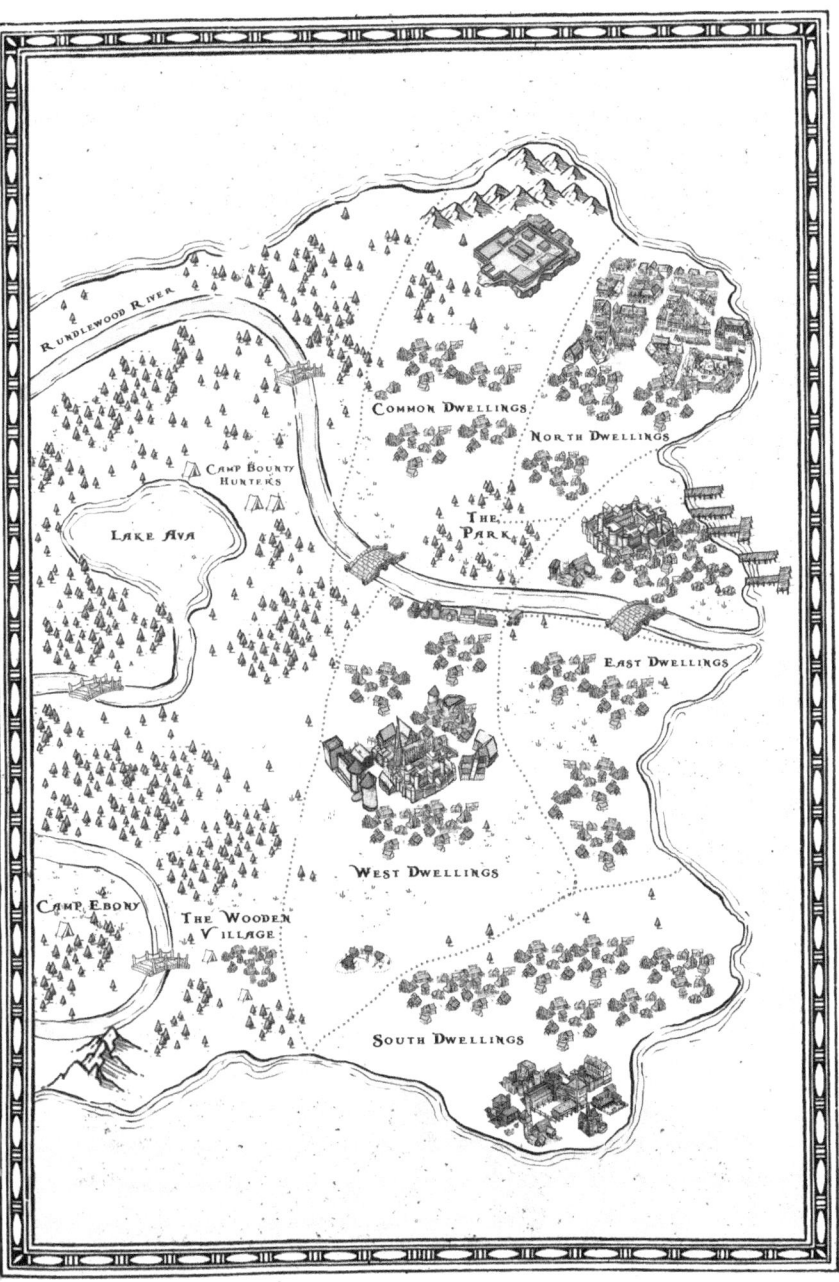

They say there's a Demon in the woods, a glare in the darkness, watching at night. They say it's as quick as the wind; a tearing, burning inferno.

It feeds on souls to look for its wick; even the FaeFolk run.

They say there's a Demon in the woods. From the shadows it came, searching the light. It has no heart, just a fiery pit. They say there's a cure that only Time can tell.

1

Mary didn't often frequent the Common Market, but today was different. Today, she was in a hood, blending in with the Commoners. Nobody could know she was in the Commons—it was not the place for a lady, especially not a Donahue. She waded through the crowds, heading to the apothecary—some said the owner of the shop was a witch, but Mary knew better. The woman just dabbled in things that others dared not imagine. It didn't make her a witch, just a bit … sketchy. All she needed was a potion for her maid—a potion to help keep the pregnancy a secret. Once she'd got it, she could go straight back home.

Mary breathed a sigh of relief when she saw the shop come into sight. She never felt safe on those dirty streets, so full of urchins and beggars. A movement caught her eye that nobody else seemed to notice. To her right, a dark figure clad in black scurried along the edges of the walkway, a hood hung low over its face. The figure looked up at her and Mary jumped. Hadn't she seen those eyes before? So much depth ... so much colour.

Ebony stared at the woman wearing the red hood, made from the finest silk and trimmed with gold fabric. Was she trying to be discrete? The woman stood out like a dove amongst thorns. Ebony could swear she had seen that face before ... but she had no time to contemplate it now. She had to find Tusting before Hunter found out where she was. She also couldn't risk being caught by the Common Custodians—the Snatchers, as they were better known—or the Black Jade gang. She had promised to give her old street gang Bounty Hunter secrets but had successfully avoided them all winter. She didn't *have* any secrets to give them, but she doubted they'd believe her.

Ebony was so used to entering the Common Market that she had to stop herself repeating old habits. She was going to the port today, in the East Dwellings. With a pang of longing for her old ways, she gazed down the street that lead to the market. Would she ever be able to enter the Commons again? In the centre where the stalls normally were hung three bodies on a gallows. Two looked to be members of a street gang. The third was a child. Bile rising in her throat, she turned and set off for the East Dwellings. She headed towards the sea, past tall houses, under bridges that reached over the streets, through archways, and down narrow alleyways and steep steps. Eventually, she could hear the sounds of the docks—ships rocking against the harbour, sea water splashing up onto the boardwalks. It was a sunny day and it appeared that every soul was out working.

Ebony weaved her way through the crowds and soon spotted Hicks, who was loading up a cart with wooden crates of fish, laden with salt, his hands gloved to hide his two missing fingers. She approached and lightly brushed his shoulder as she passed.

"Hey, watch where you're—" Hicks paused. He would recognise that cloak anywhere. His heart leapt as he watched the hooded figure disappear down an alleyway.

After piling on the last crate, he sent the driver of the cart on his way and followed the cloak into the shadows, down an alleyway that looked straight onto the sea. As he neared, Ebony lowered her hood. He beamed and launched into a tight embrace.

"Where the hell have you been?" he barked. "I thought you were dead! You could have sent a note. Or something. You could have let me know *somehow* that you were alive."

Ebony gave him a sheepish look. "I'm sorry. I should have sent word."

Hicks sighed. "No. You were right not to." Ebony looked up at him, her eyes a quizzical yellow. "The Snatchers are more vigilant than ever before," Hicks continued. Despite Ebony's best efforts, the Snatchers had only come back stronger. With Alastor Bates' brother, Donavan, now in charge, they were more akin to a militia than a police force. "You have to stay clear of trouble,"

Hicks said, shaking his head. "But where have you been? You had me worrying the last time I saw you—handing over all your belongings like that. At first, I thought the worst." He grimaced. "But then I figured you were too smart for all that. You were just caught up in something. By the way, I hid your stuff in my Nan's basement. I could take you to it—"

"Woah, woah, Hicks. Slow down."

Tusting sighed. "I'm just glad to see you alive." He grasped her shoulders and gave a warm smile that touched his eyes. "You look healthy."

"I've been living with the Bounty Hunters," Ebony admitted. Might as well get straight to the point.

Tusting's face fell. "They are *not* safe."

"They saved my life."

Tusting considered that a minute then said, "Were they the reason your life was in danger in the first place?"

"No. Not exactly," Ebony stammered. Hicks gave her a look of disbelief. "Sort of. But it wasn't their fault—it was all me. It's a long story …"

"You shouldn't trust them, Ebony."

"I know."

"They're not good company—"

"Hicks, I know. But I feel safer in their camp than on my own."

Hicks' jaw dropped. "Ebony Wick feels safer *with* people?" He chuckled darkly. "Something must have happened to shake you up that much."

"I nearly died in a fire. And I saw …" She paused, gazing into the light glistening on the sea. She'd seen a shadow with red eyes staring at her from the darkness.

"What? What did you see?"

"Nothing," Ebony replied. "I've just made some enemies who the Bounty Hunters can protect me from."

Hicks slowly shook his head. Ebony sighed, though she had been prepared for his disapproval.

"They'll get you into trouble more often than not. You shouldn't work with them."

"I'm not."

"What do you mean? Surely, in return for protection, they'll expect your help on missions?"

"They won't give me any missions. They don't think I'm experienced enough."

Hicks guffawed. "You've survived alone long enough. I think you can handle a spot of bounty hunting!" Ebony nodded but couldn't catch his eye. "You've got to stay with them to be protected but they're not giving you any missions. So you have no money of your own?"

Ebony looked at her feet. "I help in the kitchens, sometimes hunt for food." She shrugged. "They've given me food and warmth over the winter. But no, I'm not being paid."

"Sounds like a pretty raw deal, to me."

Silence fell between them. He was right, of course. But she was safe with the Bounty Hunters. They looked after her—better than she could look after herself, anyway. She had been so stupid, letting herself get caught by the

Foryx. Her impulsiveness had led her into another fire. Their protection wasn't all that Ebony wanted from the Bounty Hunters. She had friends there, but she didn't think Tusting would understand how she could be friends with people she couldn't quite trust. And she couldn't say a thing about the family connection. Despite her endless fights with Hunter, they agreed on one thing—their blood relation must remain a secret.

"So, about my stuff …"

"Yeah, I hid it all in my Nan's basement. I'll take you there."

"Don't you have to work?"

"Nah, my shift is almost finished anyway. Come on, come see my Nan's."

Ebony smiled, seeing the excitement in his eyes. Tusting had been pleading with her to stay at his Nan's house for years, but she had always refused to even visit.

"Lead the way," she said, gesturing for him to start walking.

He beamed and, turning on his heel, strode away from her. "This way, m'lady."

"I am *not* a lady!" Ebony snapped, though she couldn't help laughing at his cheeky grin. She had missed him over the winter.

As they left the alleyway, Ebony scanned the port for any sign of Snatchers. Hicks couldn't be seen talking to her—or sneaking into dark alleyways, for that matter. She hated to put him in danger like this.

They didn't have to walk far. The house was in the East Dwellings, though the sea was hidden by the winding pathways, lined with small houses. In the distance, they could hear a dog barking and children playing in the streets. Tusting stopped short and gestured towards a wooden door with a brass knocker. He fetched a key out of his pocket.

"Been keeping this handy in case you showed up," he mumbled as he went to unlock the door.

Ebony followed him into the house. It smelt musty,

like no one had cleaned it for years. In fact, it looked as if nothing had been touched for a long while. They stood in the hallway, which led to a small kitchen and a living room. A set of wooden steps led upstairs.

Tusting glanced at Ebony and looked to his feet. "Nan died a long time ago ... but I can't bring myself to change a thing. She brought me up in this house."

Ebony wondered why his parents hadn't brought him up but didn't want to pry. His eyes looked sad enough already. Tusting seemed to snap out of his reverie as he ambled into the living room and returned with Ebony's sack of goods.

"Well, here it all is, safe and sound." He smiled as he handed it over.

"Is my blue ring in there as well?"

"Oh yes! I kept that hidden somewhere ... hang on a minute."

Hicks leapt up the stairs, taking two steps at a time, and when he returned, he unfolded his hand before

Ebony, her ring on his palm. She carefully picked it up and gazed at it, now understanding the sensation of déjà vu that washed over her. She must have known this ring as a baby.

"This was my mother's," she mumbled. When she'd found it in the cart, she'd had no idea it had belonged to her mother. Such a strange coincidence that it should make its way back to her ... She tucked the ring safely into her jacket pocket.

"Want a cup of tea or something?" Hicks asked. "Or perhaps a drink at the Cloak and Dagger?"

Ebony shuffled her feet. "Thanks for the offer, but umm ... I'm not really supposed to be in town, and if I'm discovered ..." she sighed. "I should really be getting back."

He raised his eyebrows. "They're not letting you come into town?"

"Too dangerous. Snatchers and all ..."

"You know, I would offer this place to you any day if you needed it. But now ... the Snatchers have changed,

Ebony. They're not just taking urchins anymore. I've heard rumour that they've got a hit list and will take anyone linked with people on it."

"I know. I'll be okay. I just need to get back into the safety of the woods."

She turned to leave.

"No, wait. I could get you a job," Tusting said so fast, Ebony thought she might have misunderstood him. "You'll get all the profits, and the Bounty Hunters don't have to know a thing about it."

"You're kidding? You can't put yourself at risk like that."

"I know a guy who's looking for some help."

"I just—I can't really take on anything at the moment. But thanks."

Tusting frowned. "Keep in touch, yeah? I care about you, you know …"

"I know," she smiled. "See you soon."

She hauled her sack onto her shoulder and reached

for the door handle. The spring sun made her stop and cover her eyes for a moment before she made her way back towards the Commons.

She reached the market without being detected by a Snatcher; so far so good. But the bigger challenge would be getting over the bridge. She'd managed it in the early hours of the morning, but that had been a few hours ago. The Snatchers had become cleverer; they knew the best places to get in and out of Rundlewood Forest. Maybe there was a better way out than over the bridge? There probably was, but she didn't want to risk getting lost or taking too long. No, she'd have to go the tried and tested route. She took a deep breath and headed towards the bridge.

As it came into view, she narrowed her amber eyes. The bridge was empty. Not a soul in sight. Was it a trap or just a stroke of luck? She took a tentative step out of the shadows and into broad daylight. She took another few steps towards the river, mentally checking her weapons:

a dagger in her boot and another at her thigh. Her heart raced and she slowly inched closer to that slight incline. It was now or never. She would make a run for it. Grasping her sack as tight as she could, she began to run toward the bridge.

But on the other side, a figure emerged wearing a red uniform. Ebony swore and swerved around, but there was another behind her. The Snatchers closed in as Ebony contemplated her options. She could try to fight her way out—but she didn't think she could handle two at once. She could try to run, but they'd likely catch her. She was cornered, and both had swords at the ready. *Swords?* Ebony's eyes widened. They'd only ever used truncheons before.

"Hand over the bag," one of the Snatchers said, a spindly man with only a few wisps of hair left on his head.

"Why do you want this old thing?" Ebony replied. "There's nothing valuable in it." It wasn't a lie.

"Put it on the ground and put your hands up in

the air where we can see them."

With a grimace, Ebony did as she was told. She would find a way out at the last second, she was sure of it. Her heart raced and her palms grew sweaty. Would she be able to wield a blade?

"We have been looking for you for a long time, Ebony Wick. That's right, we know your name." The other Snatcher was a burly woman, her light brown hair tied back in a tight ponytail. "We know everything about you."

"You can't know *everything* about me. Not even I do!" Ebony actually laughed.

The bigger Snatcher reached out to grab her arm just as a whooshing sound whipped past Ebony's ear. An arrow embedded itself in the Snatcher's hand. She howled and looked up with a face full of fury. Ebony swerved and ducked as the other Snatcher swiped at her with his sword. She grabbed the dagger from her boot and drove it into his leg as someone came running past her and tackled the female.

The spindly man fell to his knees and lay cradling his leg. He wouldn't be going anywhere in a hurry. Ebony lunged for her sack and saw Halsey, one of the Bounty Hunters, drive a knife through the woman's chest. She choked, her eyes wide, and fell to the floor.

"Run, Ebony! There are more coming!" Halsey yelled. He grabbed her wrist and launched her off the bridge. Still grasping the bloody dagger in her hand, she raced after him towards the woods.

The world darkened as they pelted through the lining of the trees, running until they could no longer see the Dwellings behind them.

2

"How did you know where I was?" Ebony snapped, her breath coming in short gasps. They had paused to take a breath, both of them leaning against a large oak tree.

"I—Hunter …"

"Hunter told you to spy on me."

"Not exactly. He told me to keep an eye on you."

"I managed on my own for years. Why does he think I can't manage now?" *Because I almost got myself killed in a fire and he had to rescue me.* Ebony pushed the thought to the back of her mind.

"Well, clearly you can't. The Snatchers have changed, you know that."

Ebony scowled and stood up. "Race you home," she said and set off through the trees.

"Hey! You've got a head start!" Halsey cried as he struggled to his feet.

It didn't take long for her to reach camp, which

was a hubbub of activity now that winter had passed.

Ebony spied Darrel hanging up some of the camp's endless washing while chatting to a pretty girl with long, blonde hair. Sarah, Darrel's latest fancy. How long would it take for this girl to grow tired of him? He always picked women who wanted dangerous men, not responsible, gentle men like him.

There was a crowd of men sparring in the middle of the yard. Ebony yearned to join them, but they'd never really accepted her as one of them. *'Can't hit a girl'* they would say. But Ebony suspected they just feared her. Her colour-changing eyes marked her out as *different*, and this camp was rife with rumours of the Demon in the woods.

As Ebony appeared in the clearing, Daya, the camp's healer, approached. "Where have you been? Hunter has been worried sick!"

"I had to collect some things," Ebony said, showing Daya her sack.

"You know he doesn't want you going into town."

"He doesn't want me going anywhere."

"He's only trying to protect you."

Ebony scoffed. "He had Halsey follow me through town. I was safe the whole time."

"Where is Halsey?" she asked.

"He was just behind me. Guess I beat him here." Ebony gave a cocky smile. Daya frowned and peered at her suspiciously. "He should be back any minute," Ebony said.

Daya paused, then said in a serious tone, "Hunter wants to see you."

"Of course he does."

Ebony rolled her eyes and followed Daya to Hunter's tent; to her uncle, leader of the Bounty Hunters. Only a select few knew he was her uncle, of course. Keeping it quiet was about the only thing they agreed on.

Daya motioned for Ebony to enter the tent before walking across the yard, back to the Healer's tent. Hunter stood at his large, wooden table, surveying the map of the

Dwellings and Rundlewood Forest, which was engraved into the tabletop. Little clay balls marked the territories of the street gangs. The forest was populated with two clay balls, marking the Bounty Hunters and the Foryx Clan.

"I told you not to go into town," he said sternly.

"I don't have to take orders from you."

"Yes, you do. You decided that when you joined the Bounty Hunters."

"You don't let me go on any missions, you don't train me—you don't let me go anywhere or do anything. I'm not a Bounty Hunter!"

"Someone is targeting our family, Ebony. We can't risk them finding out about you," Hunter said. Ebony had lost track of the number of times he had said this over the last few months.

"You had Halsey spy on me. You clearly don't trust me."

"Last time you took off on your own, I had to save you from a burning barn that you'd put yourself in!

Forgive me for trying to keep you safe," Hunter snapped, looking up at her at last, worry etched across his face.

He was right. She *had* put herself in danger. And for what? To prove Hunter's loyalty to her? She sighed. "You might be able to keep me safe from our enemies, but I'm going mad being cooped up. I need to be active. I need to *do* something. You won't even tell me anything more about my family."

"Fine," Hunter said through gritted teeth. "Your Uncle Ned—my half-brother—died in a house fire with his wife last year. I rescued their last surviving daughter, your cousin."

"What's her name?"

"It's best her identity is kept a secret. The more people who know about her, the more danger she is in. I can't risk telling you any more than that."

She huffed in response. "How did my parents die? You were the one who found them dead."

"Terra and Michael were attacked by … something.

I don't know what."

"What were they like as people?"

"Your mother had colour-changing eyes just like you."

"Her eyes don't say much about her. What was Terra Wick's personality?"

Hunter sighed and couldn't catch her eye. He was lying about something, she was sure of it. "Look, I told you how I … how I discovered them. Frankly, I don't like bringing it up." He shrugged. "There's nothing more to say until I find out more."

"Until *we* find out more."

"Well … with the Snatchers doubling their efforts …"

"What about our agreement? I join the Bounty Hunters if I can help you find out more."

Hunter turned away from her. "We'll see."

Ebony balled her fists and stormed out of the tent. He was *so* infuriating. Maybe she didn't want a family if they were all as stubborn and irritating as him.

"Ebony Wick," a voice said, making her jump. "The Devil in disguise."

Ebony took a deep breath and turned around with a look of contempt. "If you're not careful, I'll summon my friends from the darkness," she cajoled as Darrel strode towards her.

"Halsey tells me you took a bit of a gamble this morning."

"He made it back, then?"

"He was a bit puffed."

"I just had to collect a few things, that's all." Darrel followed her to her tent, where she deposited her belongings. She'd go through them later when it was too dark for anyone to see.

"Want to help me whittle some arrows?" Darrel asked.

"Sure, why not?" She had nothing better to do.

The pair meandered over to the fire, where Darrel continued his whittling lessons with Ebony.

"How did you and Halsey meet?" Ebony asked.

"Here, in the camp, when we were about seventeen. Hunter introduced us. I joined a few years later than Halsey."

Ebony raised her eyebrows. She couldn't imagine them that young. "What was Halsey like back then?"

Darrel sighed. "Well, his brother had just been murdered, so he was pretty angry with the world."

Ebony looked to her feet, her chest tightening. She didn't know what it was like to even *have* a brother, let alone lose one. Was she wrong to feel jealous?

"He and his brother were very close."

"I didn't know," Ebony said. "I guess you filled his shoes?"

"Halsey and I didn't really like each other at first. He was always brooding and moody."

"What was Hunter like?"

"Cocky," Darrel laughed.

"What's changed?" Ebony grinned.

"He's a good leader. Well … most of the time." Darrel lowered his voice. "What actually happened to you at the Foryx camp? Hunter won't talk about it." Ebony stared straight ahead at the bonfire. "You don't have to tell me," Darrel said, but Ebony could tell he was desperate to know.

"It's hard to explain."

"All I know is that Sam betrayed us and locked you in a burning building. But I don't know why."

"He wanted to test the lengths that Hunter would go to for me."

"Pretty far, I reckon."

Ebony pursed her lips. "I'm starting to think I'd like to test Hunter, too."

They spent the morning by the fire, whittling and chatting, Lennox, Halsey, and Daya stopping by when they had a moment. Around lunch time, Ebony noticed Hunter stalk out of the camp and into the trees.

The mess hall was full of chatter as Ebony, Darrel,

and Sarah ate together.

"You made this?" Darrel asked Ebony incredulously, stuffing his mouth with sausage wrapped in bacon.

Ebony smiled. Since Hunter wasn't allowing her to train or go on any missions, she'd had to find a way to be useful, and the women in the kitchens were only too glad of her help. "First time I've had so many ingredients to play with."

"'Oo taught youta cook?" Darrel asked, trying to talk at the same time as eating mashed potato. Sarah gave him a disapproving look.

"A matron in the Clink," Ebony replied.

"Have you seen Hunter?" Halsey asked, taking a seat beside Ebony. "Daya is all a dither, says she needs to speak to him."

"He's not back yet?" Ebony swept her gaze across the camp, trying to catch sight of that tell-tale ginger ponytail.

"You saw him leave?"

"Yeah, he left camp a while ago."

"What was he wearing?"

"Mother, I don't remember!"

Halsey laughed. He liked her unique turn of phrase. Ebony was the only one in the camp to follow the Fae religion.

Daya sat nearby, looking agitated and shooting Ebony furtive looks.

"What is up with Daya today?" Ebony asked.

"'oo knows," Halsey shrugged, his mouth full of potato.

"Worried about Hunter, I guess?" Darrel said. "He's changed a bit recently …"

"But he often disappears like this. Isn't she used to it by now?" Ebony replied before helping herself to a sausage. But Darrel was right. She hadn't seen Hunter's smile for weeks.

"Maybe she knows something we don't?" Halsey suggested.

Ebony rose from her seat.

"Where are you off to?" Darrel asked.

"To find out what Daya knows."

Darrel grabbed her wrist.

"Don't. Just let her be."

Ebony frowned but sat back down, then noticed Halsey staring at something moving outside the food hall. Hunter stalked in and headed for their table.

"Can I see you in my tent?" Hunter barked. The group rose to their feet, Halsey hurriedly eating the rest of his dinner. "Not you, Ebony ... or Sarah," Hunter added, before turning towards Daya. The two men followed in his wake.

Ebony's chest twisted into a knot as she sat back down, awkwardly smiling at Sarah who still sat before her. She strained to hear what they were saying over the clatter of knives and forks, but they soon strolled out of the hall.

An hour later, Ebony watched as all of her friends left Hunter's tent, chatting amongst themselves. Ebony had spent her time sitting by the large campfire in the middle of the training yard, desperate to get closer to Hunter's tent to hear what they were saying. But she knew people would notice her sneaking about and report her. She hated feeling left out.

Halsey and Darrel began heading towards the fire. Ebony peered through the darkness, trying to glean some information from their expressions. They were whispering to each other as they approached.

She couldn't bear it. She stood up abruptly and marched towards Hunter, who was doubled over the table in his tent.

"So, what was that all about?" Ebony asked, trying to keep her tone casual.

Hunter looked up at her, a worried look on his face. "Not your concern."

"Was it about the Fae War?"

Hunter frowned. "No, it wasn't about the Fae War, and it is still not your concern."

"If the Fae attack, I could help."

"We've got it covered."

Ebony shook her head. "You're underestimating them. If they attack, they could wipe out this entire camp."

"I said, we have it covered," Hunter snapped.

Ebony gave an exasperated sigh.

"How come they all get to know about your secrets and I don't?"

"They're all highly trained Bounty Hunters and you're not. Honestly, Ebony. You act like everyone is purposefully trying to hurt you all the time." He lowered his voice and said in a whisper, "Just because we're family, it doesn't mean I'm going to treat you differently. You're a new recruit, and you'll be treated like one."

Ebony paused and looked at the ground, shifting her feet. He was right, of course, but she still didn't like to be kept out of the loop.

"Eb, I need to get some sleep before ... well, before tomorrow."

"What's tomorrow?"

"Not your concern."

Ebony gritted her teeth. She hated that little catch phrase of his. "What's the point of me being here if you're never going to use me?" she snapped and left his tent before he could reply.

It was getting dark as she lit her oil lamp and unloaded her sack of belongings. She rummaged through the loot and tools she had once used to build her old camp and breathed a sigh of relief as a familiar blue ring rolled out of her jacket pocket and onto the floor. She picked it up and slipped it onto her finger. She would never take it off again. It was all she had of her mother.

She put everything else away—she would find a chance to sell a lot of it at some point—and climbed into her hammock after turning off her lamp. She pulled a small slip of parchment from her pocket and stared at it until her eyes adjusted to the darkness.

'Blank Child: 17:2416'.

Hunter had given this to her the day she'd moved

into the Bounty Hunter's camp. He'd been given it by a matron when he'd delivered her to the Clink. That was all she was to the orphanages of the Commons: a number; a child without a name. But they'd known the family name—Wick. So why did it say 'Blank Child'? Wouldn't they have included her surname? She made a mental note to ask Hunter about the day he'd given her up and put the paper back in her pocket.

She was in a barn—a burning barn. A voice was screaming—was it her own? Screaming for help. The gag around her mouth made her choke as the room grew dark with smoke and turned to ash before her eyes. She sat on the blackened forest floor, all the trees burnt to the ground. The forest was ash. She could feel it behind her—a presence—something looming. Did she dare look? Stumbling to her feet, she slowly turned around. A castle loomed over her—dark, twisted turrets and a black sky. A long bridge stretched before her, the world around her decaying. She wanted to follow the path over the water.

Something inside her ached to take one step forward. Out of the corner of her eye, in the darkest of shadows, two red orbs glared, unblinking.

Ebony awoke, screaming into her pillow.

"Hey, Ebony. Ebony, calm down." Daya was at her side. She rolled over to face the Healer, who stroked her hair from her eyes. "You're okay now. It was just a dream. You're safe."

Ebony gasped for air, struggling to breathe.

"But it—it was there…" she mumbled.

"It was just a dream. It's okay now."

Her hands shook but her breathing slowed. "I'm sorry. This is why I sleep alone."

"You often get nightmares, don't you?"

"All the time."

"What do you dream about?" Daya asked, curiosity in her eyes.

Ebony tried to remember, but the dream was

slipping away like water through her fingers. "Umm, I don't know. It was dark."

Daya chuckled lightly. "See? Just a dream. You'll have forgotten it by morning. Go back to sleep."

"No. I think I'll take a walk. Clear my head." Ebony hoisted herself out of her hammock and retrieved her dagger from under her pillow. "Thanks, Daya," she smiled.

Tucking her dagger in her boot, Ebony trudged away from the camp. She always felt safe in the trees. It wasn't long before a wandering light came to rest on her shoulder—a little silver fairy, cleaning its wings.

"Bless the Mother," she whispered and carried the fairy with her as she walked.

She returned to camp after first light, laden with meat. She had caught several rabbits and some fish from Lake Ava. The fairy had left her as she was re-entering the camp's boundaries.

"Morning, Gene," she said as she entered the back door to the camp's kitchens. Gene was a short, plump, motherly woman, who ran the kitchens for the Bounty Hunters' camp. She had a sharp eye and wavy ginger hair that she always had pinned into a plait on her head.

"Bless you! We're out of fish. Want to help us cook again this morning?"

Ebony smiled. "Sure."

She spent the morning preparing breakfast with Gene and her small team of cooks before joining Daya and Halsey in the mess hall.

"How are you feeling?" Daya asked, far too loudly for Ebony's liking.

She raised her eyebrows. "I'm fine. Just a stupid dream."

3

Ebony started to hear voices from the other side of the camp as she watched her friends leave Hunter's tent, worry etched on their faces. Even Daya had been included in the meeting, though she wasn't a proper bounty hunter either.

Tusting's words rang in her ears, as they had done all night. *I could get you a job. You'll get all the profits, and the Bounty Hunters don't have to know a thing about it.* She had spent all winter waiting for Hunter to train her, give her a mission. But it was too icy to train. Too dangerous to go into town. They didn't have enough horses. She wasn't ready. Each week, he had found a new excuse. Maybe it was time to give up on waiting? Maybe she *was* better off working alone? Should she trust her instincts?

Daya stalked past the fire, determination in her eyes.

"Hey, Daya!" Ebony called, running to catch

up with her. Daya turned on her heel, irritated by the interruption. "What's going on?" Ebony asked.

"If he hasn't included you in it, then it's none of your concern."

"Can't you tell me *anything* about it? You've let me in on some things before …" Ebony gave her a sly smile, her eyes a vibrant pink.

"This is different."

"Why? Why is it different?"

Daya just shook her head and walked away with a frown.

Even her friend was keeping secrets from her. When Daya had been told that Hunter was Ebony's uncle, her demeanour had completely changed. The scowling had gone, replaced by kind eyes and a warm smile. A frown on Daya's face was bad news, and it made Ebony's stomach twist uncomfortably. Had she unwittingly done something to anger her friend?

Minutes later, Halsey, Darrel, Alby, Lennox, and

Hunter disappeared into the trees, just like they had done on her first Bounty Hunter mission last year. Except, this time, she wasn't with them.

Ebony couldn't bear it any longer. She marched back to her tent to collect her weapons and, within minutes, stepped into the trees. It didn't take long for her to catch up with her peers.

As quietly as she could, she followed the group through the forest, doing her best to hide in the shadows. Ebony followed them on a path she recognised into the West Dwellings. They were headed for Alastor Bates' house. Well, it *had* been his house until she and Sam—her gut twisted. She didn't want to think about Sam. She still didn't know how he'd managed to kill so many men and escape unscathed.

The group paused outside Bates' old house, and Ebony hid behind the stone wall of one of the nearby front gardens.

"The back gate is locked again. We need Ebony's

lock pick," Darrel whispered.

"No. She is not ready for a mission like this," Hunter snapped.

"Says who? I think she's more than ready," Halsey said. Ebony smiled to herself, making a mental note to compliment him later.

"*I* say," Hunter replied, as quietly as he could. "She is not ready, and that is my final word. We'll just have to do this without her."

Ebony chuckled to herself. It was typical of Hunter to know her capabilities yet still ignore them.

"Darrel, did you explain to Alby why we're here?"

"Umm … sort of. He didn't really get it. And neither do I, to be honest. Since when were we detectives?"

"I know, it's an odd job. We've not been asked to do this sort of thing before. But Peregrine Poulter pays well." He shrugged. "Alby, we've been asked to find out who killed Alastor Bates."

Ebony took in a sharp gasp and covered her mouth

with her hand. Hunter knew that she had killed Bates. She had told him herself. But he hadn't told the others. He had protected her.

"We don't need to find a *thing*? Or a person?" Alby asked.

"No. This is different."

"We're not even rooting for dirt on someone?" Lennox asked, bewildered.

"No. None of that. This time, we're finding out the truth and letting people know."

"What people?" Halsey asked.

"Well, Peregrine Poulter. But I expect he doesn't intend on keeping it a secret."

The group fell silent for a minute.

"Do we know anything about it so far?" Halsey asked.

For the briefest moment, Hunter paused. Ebony's heart hammered in her chest. Surely, he wouldn't say anything about what he really knew?

"No. I don't know anything," he said. "I thought we could start here at the house. Take a look inside and try to work out what might have happened."

"But he died months ago. The place would have been cleared since then," Lennox said.

"Do you have any better ideas?" Hunter retorted. Lennox didn't reply. "Right. First, let's take a look at everything nearby. Maybe there's a passageway from one house to the next?"

Ebony froze. They were going to find her crouching behind this wall if she didn't move quickly.

"We need to be super quiet," Hunter continued. "Nobody can know we were here."

Ebony left her hiding place and crept through the shadows, heading back towards the forest.

When Hunter returned to camp, Ebony was waiting for him in his tent, sitting on one of his wooden chairs, her legs rested on another.

"What are you doing in here?" he barked.

Her head snapped up. "I need to talk to you."

"What is it now?" he said, rolling his eyes.

"I overheard you briefing the others. I know what your mission is about."

Hunter's stood stock still, his fists clenched by his side.

"How dare you?" His eyes were wide. "I told you it did not concern you."

"You lied. It *does* concern me. Quite a bit, actually. You're trying to track down Bates' killer." She pointed to herself, careful not to say it out loud in case someone was listening.

Hunter took a deep breath. "I have it under control."

"What if they find out?" she whispered.

"I said, I have it under control," he repeated through gritted teeth.

"I could help you, though. If I'm in on it, they'll never guess. I can lead them astray."

"I can do that perfectly fine on my own, thank you." He turned away from her and shook his head. "I can't believe you … no respect for orders, no respect for hierarchy—no respect for me!"

"Respect has to be earned, Hunter Sparrow," Ebony snapped.

"Then earn it, Ebony Wick."

"You never give me the chance!"

Hunter's teeth ground together. "You are so frustrating."

"And you are so arrogant. Let me prove myself to you."

Hunter shook his head. "Not on this one. It's too dangerous. It was stupid enough killing Bates in the first place. How did you even manage it?"

"If you're so good at what you do, you can find out by yourself." With that, Ebony turned on her heel and headed towards her tent. She didn't need the Bounty Hunters to prove herself. Hicks would be able to help her find work.

Ebony watched Lennox stroll across the clearing, beaming at a noisy group of four men who had been swimming in the lake. They were kicking at something on the ground and pushing each other around. With a lurch, Ebony realised what they were doing. With startling red eyes, she stormed towards the group. They actually looked nervous as she approached and gaped at the desecrated fairy ring by their feet.

"In the Mother's name, stop that!" Ebony yelled. "Do you even know what a fairy ring is?" The men fell silent and stared at her flaming eyes. Many of the Bounty Hunters were still wary of her—the Demon with colour-changing eyes. "It marks the death of a fairy."

Rynn had just pulled himself out of the lake, his shoulder-length black hair dripping and straggly. He shrugged and Ebony turned her stormy eyes on him.

"The more of them dead the better," he said with raised eyebrows.

"How dare you," Ebony seethed. "The Fae are the most ancient creatures in this forest."

"The Fae are pests."

"I've seen them kill a man," Ebony snapped. "They do not take lightly to insults."

"I'd like to see them take on Jared," Rynn guffawed, and the others nervously laughed with him. "He's so big, he could squish them between his fingers."

Ebony laughed darkly. "I saw them kill a man bigger than Jared." She took a deep breath. "Put the ring back as you found it."

"Why should we?"

Lennox looked at Rynn with wary eyes.

"Because if you don't, you'll have me *and* the fairies to contend with. This is *my* religion too."

"I'm not scared of you, Demon," Rynn spat. "You're no better than a Human."

Ebony heard a collective gasp, but she refused to take the insult to heart.

"Just put it back, Rynn," Lennox mumbled.

"I don't know how," he admitted.

Ebony scowled at him. "I'll do it."

As she got to work collecting the scattered remnants, the men slowly walked away, heading back to their duties in camp. Ebony made a ring from spring flowers and twigs, then, using the mud from the lake, she painted a circle on her chest and sat in the ring, thinking about all that the fairies had done for her. She missed them—sitting with them as she ate, bathing with them in the river, hunting with them at her shoulder. They only ever appeared when she was in the forest alone.

When she returned, every Bounty Hunter was crammed into Hunter's tent. Everyone except the staff and Ebony. Anger roiled in her stomach and burned at her eyes as she watched them all jostling for space. She knew what they would be talking about. The hunt for Bates' killer. Even if she wasn't allowed to be part of the mission, she knew Hunter wouldn't let her secret be revealed. They'd catch Sam if they were lucky and be done with it.

She sighed. She didn't belong here. They hadn't accepted her like Hunter had promised they would. She thought she would get used to seeing people flinch every time her eyes changed colour, but their fear of what they called 'magic' ran deep. Besides, Hunter had no more answers for her. He knew less about their family than she had thought.

I could get you a job, Tusting had said. Her instincts may have led her into danger, but they'd also led her to the Bounty Hunters, to safety. But was safety enough? With a heavy heart, Ebony realised what she had to do. One winter—that was the longest she had managed 'working in a team'. Maybe that was all it was—a place to be safe over winter. But winter had passed, and she missed her old way of life. Her den, her campfire, her freedom.

Nobody was thinking about her now, occupied with their all-important meeting. Nobody would notice if she disappeared and didn't come back. She needed independence—freedom. She needed the job that Hicks had offered.

As quietly as she could, she gathered her weapons and hooded cloak from her tent. She would come back for her other supplies later. On the outskirts of the clearing, she stole into the trees and, after one last fleeting look at the place she'd hoped to call home, made her way towards The Dwellings.

4

With the feeling that eyes were watching her every move, Ebony waited until the bridge into the Commons was teaming with people and slipped into the crowd. *What would my life be like if I didn't have to sneak everywhere?* she wondered. Would she ever be able to get used to safety like that?

At the far side, a hand grabbed her wrist, and she was almost pulled off her feet into a dark alleyway. "You shouldn't be here," a gruff voice whispered into her ear, shoving her against a cold, brick wall.

"Nice to see you again, Gren," she replied without even a hint of surprise. The Black Jade gang were always going to catch up with her eventually.

"Keep your voice down!" he hissed. "Bryn wants you dead for lying to him."

"What did I lie about?" She pushed Gren's hulking form away from her.

"You said you'd give us Bounty Hunter secrets. But you've been avoiding us all winter."

"I didn't actually say that. I said I would let you know if they tell me anything of use to you, and they haven't. They don't me anything, which is actually why I'm here, and I need to get going." She turned to leave but he pushed her back against the wall so roughly she winced.

"Bryn doesn't know that we're having this chat, so we need to keep a low profile." He paused. "Look, I'm just warning you—you need to stay in the forest."

"You're putting yourself in danger by talking to me behind his back." She crossed her arms. "He can't be that bad if even you are willing to break his rules."

Gren gritted his teeth and gave an exasperated huff. "I know that fighting for survival isn't exactly a new concept to you ... I just ... I don't want your blood on my hands. So I've done my part," he said, his hands in the air as if in surrender. "I've warned you."

"Gren, I'll be fine. I always am." She turned to leave again.

"Did you kill Alastor Bates?"

Ebony froze and slowly turned back to him, his slouching shoulders silhouetted in the darkness. "If I did, why would I tell you?"

"Because we're old friends."

Ebony raised her eyebrows. "One day, I hope I have 'old friends' who don't shove me into dark alleyways and whisper threateningly into my ear." With that, she turned on her heel and disappeared into the crowd of shoppers, past the market, into the East, and towards the sea. The salty air filled her nose as she brushed past Hicks, who was hauling something heavy into a cart, and headed for their dark meeting point.

"Why are you back so soon?" Hicks asked as he reached her.

"Hi to you, too," she said, eyebrows raised.

He frowned but gave her a small smile. "It's always

nice to see you, but how did you get into town? I thought your new friends were keeping you prisoner?"

"They're not keeping me prisoner, they just …" Ebony took a deep breath. "You mentioned a job."

Tusting looked genuinely surprised. "Umm, yes. I did."

"Am I too late?"

"I'm not sure. I could find out."

"Yeah, thanks. I—" Ebony cut her sentence short at the sound of boots striding up the alleyway. She looked at Hicks, whose eyes glowered as he saw who was heading towards them. Ebony turned, that tell-tale ginger ponytail making her stomach turn. How had he found her?

"Tusting Hicks, I assume?" Hunter barked. Hicks nodded. "No time to explain now. I need Ebony to come with me."

"She's not going anywhere with you," Hicks replied.

Ebony glanced from one to the other. Hunter ignored Hicks and turned to Ebony, a strange look of desperation on his face.

"We don't have much time. It's back." Ebony looked at him with confusion. "The fire is back, Ebony. *The eyes*. She's burning like the others did." He glared at her, willing her to understand. He didn't know how much she had told Hicks, if anything at all.

"You mean …" Ebony froze. "Right now?"

"Right now."

"We have to go," Ebony agreed, then looked at Tusting, an apology in her eyes.

"Yes, we do. Follow me," Hunter said before striding back towards the docks.

Without a second thought, Ebony grabbed Tusting's hand and followed Hunter.

"Where are we going?" Tusting asked.

"To save her."

"Save who?"

"I don't know."

Hunter broke into a run, and Ebony and Hicks

followed behind, Hicks almost tripping over his feet. They ran through the streets until they reached the Common Market. They could see the smoke now, billowing above the rooftops. They launched themselves down a blackened alleyway that made them choke, the path getting thinner and thinner before abruptly ending by a door. Ebony had been here before, but last time, the building hadn't been wreathed in flames.

"She's in there, Ebony!" Hunter cried. "Your cousin!"

"You have a cousin?" Hicks shielded his mouth as he coughed.

"Not for much longer if we don't save her," Hunter replied.

Ebony was rooted to the spot. "I can't go in there," she said, her eyes wide with terror. Flame had begun licking up the walls inside. It was just like a scene from her dreams.

"I'll go in, Eb," Hunter said softly. "You keep watch

and get us out of here. The Snatchers won't be far behind us."

Ebony turned her back to the fire, feeling its heat on her legs as Hunter braved the burning building.

"What about the others in there?" Hicks asked.

"He'll save who he can."

Hicks stood deliberating for a moment. "I'm going in to help him. But later, you owe me an explanation."

"You don't have to go in."

"I do. People are *dying* in there."

Ebony nodded again but kept her eyes glued to the light at the end of the alleyway. "Be careful," she said as Hicks left her side. She heard the door close behind him.

Battling the nightmarish images plaguing her mind, Ebony kept her focus, aware of every movement—aware that the building behind her was caving in and her uncle and closest friend were still in there. Her cousin was also in there, a girl she had never met. She didn't even know her name.

"Mother help us," she prayed.

She jumped as the door slammed open. Hunter emerged, covered in soot, a girl cradled in his arms. Her blonde plaits were a mess, thick with ash, and her pale face was smeared with soot.

"Where's Hicks?" Hunter barked.

"He followed you in. Went to help the others in there."

Hunter's face turned white, and he swore. "He needs to get out. *Now*. It's in there—I saw it."

Ebony's head spun. She felt utterly useless. What could she do but simply wait for Tusting to appear?

"We have to go!" Hunter cried over the crackling flames.

"I'm not leaving him!" Ebony shouted, and her voice cracked.

"The Snatchers will be here any minute!"

Ebony's heart raced as Hunter began dragging her away from the burning building.

"Hicks!" she cried, tears sliding freely down her cheeks. She tried to pull herself from Hunter's grasp, but he was too strong. "Tusting!" she cried.

"Run, Ebony!" That was Tusting's voice.

Ebony glimpsed a figure emerging through the door frame, two bodies in his arms. They were alive. They scrambled away from him, and Hicks stumbled towards her. Ebony launched herself into his arms.

"I thought you were dead."

"What's going on?" a voice wheezed. They all turned to the girl in Hunter's arms. He sat her against a wall and kneeled down next to her.

"We have to go. There's something in there," Hicks said.

"What did you see?" Hunter asked.

Hicks shook his head. "There's something in there," he repeated, his eyes wide with terror.

The four of them turned to look through the downstairs window. It was unmistakable. Red eyes glared at them through the flames.

"Run," Hunter whispered.

The light at the end of the alleyway darkened. Ebony turned to see five red uniforms marching towards them. They weren't there to drag her back to the Clink. She could see their intent in their fierce expressions. They were there to kill. Hunter helped his niece to her feet and grabbed her hand, then unsheathed a sword. Ebony already had two daggers in her hands. Hunter would protect the girl and Ebony would protect Hicks. She *had* to.

Blades in hand, Ebony dealt death after death, pulling her daggers from flesh and meeting with yet another body as she spun on her heel. She hardly remembered each move as she struck. Swords clashed and an arrow grazed her cheek. The Snatchers had been training. She couldn't remember them using arrows before. And where were their truncheons? She clutched at her bleeding face as, at last, she reached the end of the alleyway. Hunter grabbed her arm and pulled her into the shadow of a nearby doorway, where her cousin sat shaking, as more Snatchers filed past. There were too many to count, and they couldn't fight them all.

Where was Hicks?

The building they had just come from crashed and crackled, but the flame didn't touch the other buildings nearby.

Where was Hicks? Ebony risked a peek down the alleyway, her eyes as grey as ash. Hicks was crouched over the two women he had saved, shouting at the Snatchers. Bodies littered the ground around him.

"We're arresting you on suspicion of murder," one of the burlier Snatchers snapped. The Snatcher hauled Tusting to his feet and tied his hands behind his back with rope.

"There are more people in there! You have to save them!" Hicks cried, but the man ignored him.

"You're the one we want, not them."

"But I didn't do anything –"

"One of our men just saw you with wanted criminals. You're coming with us for questioning. Now."

Ebony thought she might be sick. She turned to Hunter, to find her cousin had blacked out again. She looked so small and frail.

"They've got Hicks," Ebony whispered, tears streaking down her dirty face. "They blame him for what we did. We have to get him back."

"No. We have to go."

Ebony glared at him. "They'll kill him." A sickening image of Hicks on a gallows flooded her mind.

"It's too late, Ebony. The place is swarming with Snatchers."

"No, it's not too late." Ebony turned away and gripped her dagger tight, getting ready to let it fly, but Hunter pulled her into the fray of the market, holding his niece in his arms. "Let me go!" she yelled at him, but to no avail. She watched as Hicks was dragged away by the red suits, her heart plummeting. She'd framed her best friend.

How would he ever trust her again? She gritted her teeth, her chest burning with hatred, shame, loss. She would get him back, whatever the cost.

Defeated, she let Hunter pull her through the streets and into the woods, her head in a daze. Hunter cradled his niece as he ran. As soon as they had lost sight of the city, they stopped to catch their breath. He put the girl down on the forest floor. She still hadn't woken. She was breathing, but it was shallow.

"Myla, please wake up," Hunter said, shaking her shoulders. Her eyes opened slowly, and she stared at Ebony. "Are you hurt?" he asked her. She shook her head but didn't shift her gaze. "This is Ebony," Hunter explained. "Your cousin."

"Hi," Ebony said weakly, trying her best to give her cousin a reassuring smile. The girl scrambled away from Ebony as her eyes changed from grey to turquoise.

"She's not dangerous," Hunter said. "Well—she's pretty good with a blade when she needs to be, but …"

His voice petered off. "We'll take you to safety."

"Where?" the girl rasped.

"Our home."

Your home, Ebony thought. Only a few hours ago, she thought she had left the place for good.

Hunter helped the girl to her feet, but she kept a wary distance from Ebony. Exhausted, but luckily not injured or burnt, they slogged back to the camp. Daya was waiting by the fire, biting her nails with worry.

"Another fire?" she cried as they emerged from the trees. She launched to her feet and led Myla to the Healer's tent. She looked over her shoulder at Ebony and Hunter, making it clear that they were to follow her and they didn't have a choice about it.

Daya fussed over the three of them, giving them lotions for their skin and potions to drink.

"You all need to rest for a few days."

"But Myla—" Hunter started.

"I can look after her. Go to your beds. Now."

There weren't that many people Hunter would obey without question. With a sigh, he dutifully traipsed to his tent.

"Hunter—" Ebony said as he left. She had so many questions. How had he found her by the port? How had he known about the fire? Had he seen the eyes in the flames?

"Tomorrow, Ebony," Daya said. "You need to rest." She walked Ebony to her tent, her bed a welcome sight.

5

Ebony lay in her hammock, staring at the canvas ceiling. Daya had slathered ointment all over the wound on her cheek, but it stung and felt swollen. The world around her was so quiet she could hear a pin drop ... or a slight buzzing. Was it a fly or ...? Her tent filled with a dim, glowing light. She sat upright to find a small fairy hovering beside her.

"Come," he said.

"Come where?" she whispered, her eyes heavy.

The fairy beckoned her to follow him to the entrance. She clambered out of her hammock and tentatively took a step outside. It was just like it was before. Something was wrong. The entire camp was sleeping and still—too still. It was rare for everyone to be asleep at the same time. There was always *someone* on duty.

The unmanned campfire flickered in the centre of the yard, but the fairy led Ebony away from it and into the dark trees. She followed its orb of light deep into the woodland and finally stopped walking when they came to a clearing of shimmering trees. Two lights sprung from a branch and approached her. Both fairies were purple and looked old, one dressed in a magnificent green gown, the other in a red robe. Crowns made from berries sat on their heads. King Alvero and Queen Coralia. It had been months since they had first met her in her old camp.

"Ebony Wick, you must leave this place," the king said as he flew. No greetings, no small talk. The Fae spoke on their own terms.

"These trees?" Ebony replied, perplexed.

"These people," the king replied.

Ebony looked to her feet. "I know. I tried to, but …"

"Come with us," Queen Coralia said, holding out a hand. "We can protect you."

"It's not me that needs protecting."

"We *want* to protect you. We are of the same." Alvero gestured at the forest around him.

"I am honoured that you consider me to be one of

you, though I have no wings and no magic."

"You are Of the Forest," Alvero explained.

"I do love the trees," Ebony admitted.

"You are Of the Forest. You belong in the Forest," Coralia added. "Come with us and understand."

"Understand what?" The Fae fell silent and didn't reply. Ebony rolled her eyes. She could never get a straight answer out of them. "I can't leave the Bounty Hunters now. My closest friend is in danger, and the Bounty Hunters could help me rescue him."

"We understand, but they will not," Coralia said. "Come to us when you are ready."

Ebony nodded without really knowing what she was agreeing to. Ready for what?

"I have to get back. I have to convince Hunter to help Tusting."

"May the Three be with you," the king and queen said in unison.

"The Three?"

"The Mother, the Sister, The Daughter," Alvero said.

With that, the lights left the trees and floated away, leaving Ebony in darkness. She walked back to the tent and clambered back into her hammock. Hicks had been worried about her. The Fae were worried about her. Maybe they were right? Maybe Hunter *was* bad news?

She sat in a burning barn, her arms pricking with heat while she watched the walls melt away. She could hear someone screaming for help—was it her or someone else? But there was no one else around, just a burnt forest. And behind her was a castle, casting a long shadow in the dying light. Its tall turrets reached into the sky, like long, sharp fingernails. She stood on a small bridge above a river, decaying houses surrounding her. Why did she recognise this place? She gazed down into the water and saw shadows—reflections of figures. But there was no one above the water to reflect. Out of the corner of her eye, a boy peered at her from behind a blackened pillar and smiled.

"Henry?" she gasped and took a step forward.

The child cackled and ran, disappearing into shadows.

Stumbling, Ebony followed the child. Where had he gone? She crossed the bridge and found herself under an archway, Henry's silhouette just out of reach. With tentative footsteps that echoed around her, she crept forward and stifled a gasp. The path before her seemed to go on forever; a stretch of endless archways. She had to know what was at the end of them. With one last look at the bridge behind her, she turned around, but the whole world had gone dark. All she could see were a pair of red eyes and the outline of a figure.

Ebony's screams woke her, but Daya was already at her side, ready to help her out of her dreams. The Healer stroked her hair and quietened her as Ebony's heart thumped in her chest. She had seen it again. They had all seen those eyes.

How long had she been asleep? It was dark outside. The memories of yesterday's fire came flooding back to her, and she sat up straight, making Daya jump. "Hicks.

Hicks was taken. We have to get him back."

Before Daya could stop her, Ebony leapt out of bed and went to leave her tent, only to find her way barred by two large men. She stopped in her tracks. Not again. She turned to Daya, who flinched at her glare.

"He said it isn't safe for you to leave, and … well, he can't trust that you will stay."

"So he has trapped me inside a tent, *again*?"

Daya swallowed. "He didn't know what else to do."

"I'll escape the same way I did before."

"How *did* you escape last time?"

Ebony squared her shoulders but didn't reply.

"I'll go and fetch him," Daya said and sidled out of the tent.

Ebony paced up and down until she heard Daya's voice returning. It sounded like she and Hunter were fighting.

"Keeping her locked up isn't going to help," another voice snapped. Darrel.

"It is not your decision to make," Hunter replied,

then entered the tent, Daya hot on his heels. She had an apologetic look on her face as Hunter stormed over to Ebony and grabbed her by the shoulders.

"I told you not to go into town! You see why I can't make you a Bounty Hunter yet? You can't stick to even the most simple orders."

"How did you even know where I was?"

"Halsey—"

"I thought he was in the meeting?"

"Yes, that was the idea."

"How did you know about the fire?"

"I saw it on my way to you. I knew you'd be either at the docks with Hicks or …" He shook his head slowly. "You shouldn't have gone into town."

"I think it's damn lucky I *was* in town. You would never have got passed all those Snatchers without me."

Hunter growled, but then sighed. "You're right. I needed you there. But that could have been you in a burning building." Ebony touched his hand, which was gripping her shoulder so tight it hurt. His eyes were glistening and full of anguish. "I can't lose any more of my family," he said, his voice almost cracking.

"I know," Ebony replied. "Did you see them? The eyes?"

Hunter nodded, a grave look on his face.

"What are they? It looks like ... a figure, a shadow."

"I don't know. But it's always there when our family is killed. Always in the flames."

"Why our family?"

"I don't know, Ebony."

Hunter had promised her answers, but all he'd given her were more questions. "Am I allowed out of the tent now?"

He looked at her suspiciously. "Yes. But I don't want you to leave the camp, and the men know that."

"So I'm a prisoner?"

"I just want to keep you safe, and every time you go off on your own, bad things happen."

She scowled but changed the subject. "How is—" she'd already forgotten her name "—my cousin?"

"Myla?" Hunter frowned. "Her lungs were badly damaged in the fire ... Daya thinks it will be a miracle if she survives."

Ebony's heart twisted. She was about to lose yet another family member ... and she'd hardly had a chance to get to know her.

"Can—can I meet her? Properly, I mean." Ebony looked at him with pleading, bright eyes.

Hunter shuffled his feet awkwardly. "She ... she doesn't want to see you."

"What? Why?"

"She saw your eyes change colour." He looked away from her, unable to see her expression as he explained. "She thinks you're a witch."

Ebony chuckled disbelievingly. "There's no such thing."

"Well ... some think there is. You know how much

magic is feared in The Dwellings."

"But I'm not magical!"

"She thinks you are."

Ebony's eyes turned a dark blue. "She should give me a chance, at least. Let me get to know her." Ebony had given Sam a chance, and he was a *Human*.

"It will take time, Eb."

"What if ..." Ebony's voice cracked. "What if all our surviving family is scared of me?"

Hunter sighed deeply. "We have no more surviving family. Not that I know of."

Ebony's chest felt hollow. "Then help me save Hicks. He's family to me. They could be torturing him for information." Her eyes glistened. "He has done so much for me. I can't leave him."

He removed his hands from her shoulders and took a step back. "How do you think we could do that? We don't even know where he is being kept. He should have left those women and come with us."

"He's not a fighter like we are. He doesn't know how to wield a blade!" She shook her head. "He risked his life for strangers … he was framed for our kills, and this is how you repay him?"

"He didn't do it for me, so why should I help him? He shouldn't have even been there."

Ebony almost punched him. She scowled at him and bunched her fists, but she knew he was stronger than her. Punching him wouldn't help her in the slightest, however satisfying it might be.

"Get out," she growled through gritted teeth.

"Ebony, you have to understand …"

"GET OUT."

Hunter sidled out of the tent.

"I'll try to talk to him, Eb," Daya said. "I'm sure he's just angry right now."

"Hicks will die before we find Hunter's empathy."

"I'll talk to him," Daya said before leaving Ebony to stew in silence.

Ebony flung herself into her hammock, grinding her teeth so hard it hurt. The Bounty Hunters hadn't given her anything she had hoped for. Better work? Hunter wasn't allowing her to even loot a cart. A family? Hunter knew *nothing*. Ebony could probably find out more on her own. Friendship? She had a few friends here … but most people couldn't get past her colour-changing eyes.

She had taken Hicks for granted. What was he doing now? Where was he being held? She doubted they would kill him. He had too much information on her—the elusive Ebony Wick. It wasn't fair that he should have to pay for her reputation. Hicks needed her, but she could do nothing. Not without help. He probably hated her now—probably thought she had selfishly saved her own skin and left him to face the consequences. Images filled her mind of what the Snatchers could be doing to him to get information.

She had to get out. She spent hours contemplating the various ways she could escape the camp and hide from the Bounty Hunters forever. Hunter would probably double the guards this time; she had escaped too easily before. A few of her plans involved injuring her uncle—injuring, but not killing. If he was left alive and she had disappeared, he would go mad with worry. He deserved to worry. He deserved to stew in guilt and fear. After all, that was how he had left her feeling when he'd refused to rescue Hicks. Could she call on the fairies again and have the Bounty Hunters face their wrath? No. She couldn't risk it. Besides, would they believe her when she had only just turned down their help?

Hunter returned with food later that day. Ebony hadn't left her tent all day, choosing to stew in silence instead. As Hunter appeared, she he didn't move from her hammock, pretending to ignore the rich smell of cooked beef, but they could both hear her stomach rumbling.

"Forcing me to stay in the camp isn't going to help anything, you know. Boredom makes me reckless," she warned him. "Can't I even go hunting?"

"No. Not yet."

"When then?"

"When it's safe."

"And when will that be?"

"When our family stops being murdered," Hunter snapped.

"If it's safer in the camp, then why are you allowed out? Why aren't you watching Myla every second like you watch me?" She glared at Hunter. "Do you think Myla can look after herself better than I can? Are you really cocky enough to think you can protect us both against the …" She took a deep breath, unable to voice the word 'Shadow'. "Against the fires?"

"Myla is dying, Ebony." He turned on his heel and left her to eat. Her chest felt cold and hollow and the food was tasteless. Her cousin was dying in this very camp and she wasn't allowed to even glimpse her. She dropped her empty plate onto the ground underneath her hammock and stared at the ceiling.

6

It was still dark when Ebony heard voices calling from the other side of the camp.

"We've got him!" a voice called.

"Good work, lads!" Hunter called back.

"Let go of me!" a man seethed.

Ebony knew that voice. She shivered as her blood ran cold. Samuel Sanker. There was a clinking sound and a jangle of keys. They were surely locking him in that awful wooden cage. *He deserves it.* The last time she had seen him, he had left her tied up in a burning barn. She was quite sure Sam had planned for Hunter to die that night. And why hadn't the Foryx retaliated yet? Hunter was sure he had started a war with them when he'd burnt down their camp, yet there had been no sign of the gang all winter.

The camp steadily grew quieter as its inhabitants

turned in for the night, but she could feel his presence. Sam was in the same camp as her. Sam, who had captured her attention, who had managed to break through her wall of distrust, who had tied her to a pole and let her waste away. Just the thought of him made her heart twist. It was like there were two sides to him. One of them was warm and loyal. The other was cruel and conniving. But he had known so much about Hunter. Did he know about Myla, too? Maybe he could tell her more about her family?

Ebony took a deep breath and quietly stepped outside her tent. The camp was utterly still. With silent footsteps, she crept across the clearing, passed the embers of the campfire and a slumbering man nearby, who was supposed to be guarding Sam, and tiptoed towards a cage at the edge of the clearing. The creature inside it was shivering and bent over. He could hardly fit inside, his arms squished against the bars, and his face was blackened and swollen. Her stomach twisted. *No one deserves this*. Sam had treated her badly, but he hadn't locked her in a cage.

"Ebony Wick. Friend of Demons." Sam's eyes looked haunted, tired. What had he been doing over the winter? He smiled at her, but his expression was sad. "I'm sorry. I couldn't stop it. I didn't want to."

"What are you talking about?" she whispered.

Sam gave her a long look as if trying to work out how to explain something, but then gave up, gazing at his feet. "Why are you here?" he asked.

"I live here."

His eyebrows rose and he chuckled darkly. "I meant why are you here, talking to me?"

"Nice to see you in captivity for once."

"I told you, I couldn't stop it!" he blurted out, and Ebony thought she saw his eyes turn glassy in the moonlight. He sighed deeply. "It's too late now. You hate me already."

Did she hate him? Could she hate such a sorrowful creature? He looked half mad, starved of rest and proper nourishment. He couldn't even sit upright in that cage.

"You left me to die in a burning barn."

He almost sobbed, moaning, "It wouldn't let me. It wouldn't let me."

"Who wouldn't let you do what?"

He gazed at her yellow eyes, mesmerised. "You're not the Demon in the woods. Your eyes aren't always red."

She ignored him and began her interrogation. "How did you find Hunter's birth certificate? How did you know so much about him?"

"Easy," he replied with a grin.

"How?"

"When you know the right people …" His voice trailed off as if he had lost his train of thought.

"Where … where do I find that kind of information?"

"Come with me," he whispered, with a glint in his eye. "I can show you."

"You're in a cage, Sam. You're not going anywhere."

He frowned and seemed to remember where he was.

"How did you do it, Sam?" she whispered.

"Do what?"

"How did you kill Bates?"

"I didn't kill Bates. *It* did."

Ebony shivered. She had an odd feeling she knew what *it* he was referring to. "But ... but his house didn't burn down."

"Didn't need to."

"Why didn't the Foryx take revenge on us? We set your camp on fire."

"You can't be harmed. Not yet."

She didn't know whether she should feel relieved or scared. Not yet? What did that mean? Had he gone mad over winter? It seemed he could only talk in riddles.

"Hey!" a voice shouted from behind her. Ebony jumped and spun on her heel as Sam's guard nearly collided with her. "Get away from him," the guard snarled. She did as she was told.

Hunter came to visit her the next morning.

"I heard you locked him in a cage," Ebony said the moment Hunter walked into her tent. She was lying on her hammock, inspecting the arrows she had whittled the year before. They were a bit damaged, having sat in a crate for so many months. Maybe she could use some of the camp's shafts and make better arrows for herself? Darrel had taught her so much about whittling.

"Heard or saw? I know you visited him last night."

"Are you going to stop me leaving my tent now?"

"No. You can't get far at night."

Ebony scoffed. "And you say I'm not a prisoner!" Hunter didn't reply. Ebony sat up and stared at him with a grimace. "You beat him and then locked him in a tiny cage," she said quietly, slowly shaking her head.

"It's what he deserves," Hunter replied.

"He can hardly move."

"Why do you care? He left you for dead."

"You're stooping to his level—no, worse. He didn't lock *me* in a tiny cage."

"Ebony, he tried to kill you!" Hunter looked at her like she was mad.

Maybe she *was* mad. Why was she defending Samuel Sanker? He was the only person to have successfully hurt her so much she had cried. She had cried herself to sleep for nights after returning to the Bounty Hunters' camp. Had she been mourning her old way of life? Or was it pain because she had allowed herself to trust? She'd felt like such an idiot, trusting a Human.

"We promised we'd get revenge on him," Hunter continued. "We have found evidence that he killed Bates … Well, I helped it along a bit."

"You mean you framed him. Getting good at that, aren't you?"

"I didn't *frame* him. I just sped up the process. He *did* kill Alastor Bates. You said you only injured him."

Ebony changed the topic, an odd twisting in her gut distracting her thoughts. Was it fair for him to take the blame for Bates' death when all he had done was rescue her from her own stupid actions?

"When will you let me see Myla?"

"Ebony ... she died last night."

She looked up at him, her jaw slack. Hunter was her last living relative. "How? Why? I thought Daya was ..."

"Daya did all she could, but the girl couldn't breathe. I'm really sorry."

She sighed. "I'm all you've got left. You'll never let me leave this camp." She wondered what was happening to Hicks right now. Was he even still alive or was his body hanging in the Common Market? Hunter wasn't going to help her rescue Hicks, and she had to give up hope that he might.

"I expect you'll find a way out sooner or later. Run away with your fairies again. They caused quite a stir last time."

"I won't use the fairies again." She had begrudgingly made a decision about that. "They're not safe entering this camp in small numbers."

"I will never understand why you protect them. They're dangerous and nasty little pests."

Ebony frowned at his words and shrugged. "They protect me. And if they were all here at once, they could take down the entire camp." She hoped that thought would scare him. Maybe the Fae would come without her asking? Maybe they would protect her as they had done before? She smiled at the thought, then remembered the carnage they had caused last time. Did she really want to unleash that on the Bounty Hunters?

"I'll get you some food," Hunter said, stalking out of the tent.

She visited Sam again that night when his guard inevitably fell asleep. She'd spent the day helping out in the kitchens and whittling arrows by the fire to distract herself, but Sam's presence had tugged at her mind all day, pulling at her gaze. Every so often, she'd watched as Hunter and his men dragged Sam from his cage and interrogated him. She expected they wanted information on the Foryx, but she couldn't get close enough to hear anything. And it didn't seem like Sam was saying much, anyway. They'd then lock him up again, bruised and bloody, only to return a few hours later. Sam may have trapped her in a burning barn, but what Hunter was doing was worse.

As night descended, she stalked up to Sam and sat down beside his cage, gazing at the wounds on his face. Darkness swirled in his eyes and his face looked haunted. They didn't speak. They just sat together, staring into the black night. All day, her mind had been swirling with a thousand thoughts—too many thoughts. Only with him would her mind fall silent.

She wasn't even sure he was still awake until he spoke.

"Thank you," he said.

"For what?" she replied without looking at him.

"For the company."

Her heart twisted. "You may have hurt me, but you

don't deserve to be in a cage."

"I hurt you?"

"You betrayed my trust."

He sighed, and she felt his breath on her hair. "I'm sorry. I couldn't—it wouldn't … I tried …" He seemed to be struggling to speak.

"You didn't have a choice?" Ebony finished for him.

"I didn't have a choice," he repeated, as if analysing the words. "You could leave this place right now and never look back, but instead you're sitting with me, your sworn enemy."

"Hunter won't let me leave." And she wouldn't be able to live with herself if she just abandoned Hicks to the Snatchers. She needed the Bounty Hunters to help her save him … unless Sam could help.

After a long period of silence, he said, "You should sleep."

"So should you."

"I can't."

"Right. Because … the cage." She grimaced.

"No. I haven't been able to sleep properly since I lost you."

She turned to look at him. His expression was so … earnest.

"Hunter has lost me too, now," she said, admitting the truth out loud for the first time. "Let's hope he goes mad with lack of sleep, too."

Sam laughed quietly. "I'm glad."

"Glad about what?"

"That he lost you. He never deserved you." His eyes glistened.

She looked away from him. Why did she feel so calm next to him? Was it *because* of the cage? Did she feel safe knowing that he couldn't hurt her? She yawned.

"Go get some sleep."

She nodded and clambered to her feet. "I'll come back tomorrow night."

"You don't have to." His eyes looked calmer.

"I know."

It began on the small bridge above a river, houses crumbling to dust around her. The castle loomed before her, but she ignored it. She knew where to go now. She had to get to the end of that corridor of archways. Did it ever end? She would never find out if she didn't walk the whole thing. The silhouette of Henry danced before her, flitting about like he was chasing cats. One more step and she would see the end of the hallway. Just one more step, and another, and another. The child cackled, the sound echoing on the marble arches.

She heard a splash and stopped walking. To her right, she could see out across a river, over the rooftops of burnt buildings, over to a harbour, where boats were burning and crashing into the sea.

"Ebony Wick," a voice rasped. It was all around her, inside her. The voice entered her mind and left again, echoing through her thoughts. "Ebony Wick," it whispered again.

The world went dark. Two red flames glared before her. No, not flames. Eyes. They grew bigger, getting closer. A figure came with them—a shadowy, flickering figure.

She woke, screaming into her pillow. Daya wasn't there. Where was she? Ebony's heart raced, her fists clutching her blanket as images of blackened cities and glowing orbs floated through her mind. How long had she been asleep? How long had it been since she had sat with Sam? It was still dark outside.

She clambered out of her hammock and crossed the clearing to Sam's cage.

"Back already?"

"I see it in my dreams," she spluttered, standing before him. "My dreams are dark and full of ash. Endless corridors and tall towers. What does it mean?"

"I don't know. Ask a dream specialist."

"But I see *it*."

"Lots of people do after seeing it for the first time."

Sam knew more about those eyes than anyone else, she was sure of it.

"Do you ... do you know a dream specialist?"

Sam laughed. "Is there such a thing?"

She scowled. "Please, Sam. How do I stop the dreams?"

"You can't stop them. But you *can* change them. Let me out and I could help you."

She froze and narrowed her eyes. She wouldn't be fooled by him again.

"I can't do that."

"But you want to."

He was right. She hated seeing him in that cage. But she couldn't let him out even if she wanted to. Hunter would be so angry. She turned around and stalked back to her tent, the first light dawning in the sky.

7

Every day, the camp felt smaller. She lay in her hammock, staring at the ceiling. Had she made a mistake, walking away from the Fae? No. She couldn't have the fairies help her rescue Hicks. They'd think she had chosen to join them ... or whatever it was they wanted her to do.

Hicks was likely being tortured for information. Had he given in yet? Was he even alive anymore? Her heart began to race and her hands felt clammy. She closed her eyes and tried to imagine the stars; the open sky, rolling hills. Freedom. But it didn't work. The tent grew smaller by the second and the night grew steadily darker around her. In the corner of the room, a shadow formed ... No. No, it wasn't real. It was just her imagination.

Ebony leapt to her feet. She couldn't do this anymore. She would drive herself mad. She began a rigorous training exercise to distract her mind; star jumps, crunches, sit ups, lunges. When her breath had left her, she lay on the dirty floor before searching through the storage boxes left in her tent. A few old pots and pans, a cracked vase, one brown boot with no laces, a pair of breeches with moth holes in them, and a small wooden bow. Beneath it was an old leather quiver. She smiled to herself. The bow wasn't her weapon of choice, and she'd never been particularly good with it, but she would start training herself tomorrow morning. And she wouldn't visit Sam tonight. She didn't want to look upon that tortured soul again and feel such guilt. It was her uncle treating his fellow man like a wild beast to be tamed, but what was she doing to stop it? Warring with her inner demons. *He deserves it. No one deserves that! He tried to kill me. Well, he left you in a barn to die. There's a difference.* Should a man have to suffer because she couldn't get her act together? Should she even care?

As soon as the sun woke her the next day, she climbed out of her hammock and stretched her muscles. She slung the quiver over her shoulder and marched out of the tent towards a row of targets. Hunter hadn't let her use them at all over the winter. She pulled at the bowstring, holding her arm in place, aware that people were watching. Her hands felt slippery and her heart began to thud. She hated being watched. With a huff, she let loose and an arrow thudded into the edge of the target. Hearing snickers from somewhere behind her, she grunted and trudged back into her tent, placing the bow and quiver under her hammock. She would try again tomorrow when there were fewer people around.

Star jumps, crunches, sit ups, lunges, weights—her regime filled the rest of the day. If anything, it kept the worst thoughts at bay. But it didn't keep the nightmares away. That night, the dream came again, more vivid than ever.

A bridge stretched before her—a blackened, decaying bridge, soot crumbling into the dark river below. It was a moat, leading to a black, looming castle, dead ivy hanging from its walls. Beneath her feet was a forest floor—a sea of dead bluebells—while above her the sky rained ash. It caught in her dark hair like falling snowflakes. The world was silent. Eerie.

Her right leg picked itself up and moved her forward. Then the left. Was she in control of her limbs or was somebody pushing her towards that bridge? She couldn't stop her foot taking the next step; it was like a force was keeping her moving. Her feet touched solid ground as she reached the bridge and made her way across, and an odd feeling of recognition crossed her mind. She knew this dead place. She crossed the river as a boy came into view. He had been hiding behind a blackened brick wall.

"Henry?" she called.

The child's shrill laugh echoed as he scampered away into the shadows.

Ebony stumbled forward—she couldn't stop herself. Was it her stumbling forward or that strange force? It was as if her legs were not in control. The silhouette of the child stood in a long corridor of archways that stretched as far as the eye could see. She had to know what was at the end. With one last look at the bridge behind her, she turned around. The archways stretched ahead of her, the bridge forgotten.

One step, then another. She would reach the end of the hallway of arches. She began to run. The world flew past as the final archway came within reach. She held her arm out, desperate to reach the light beyond the hall. But where had the child gone?

The hallway abruptly ended, and she stopped short at the edge of a cliff, looking down onto a blackened, empty city. No, not empty. She could see shadows moving about, slithering through doorways, hovering over the river.

"Ebony!" a voice called. She looked behind her but couldn't find its source.

The city was one step away— just one step more. All her answers lay before her. She didn't know how or why, or even which answers she was looking for, but she knew that was where she would find them.

The force was gone. The next step would be hers to take.

"Ebony!" the voice called again.

The world fell into darkness. All she could see were two red eyes staring at her.

It blinked.

Daya wasn't there when she woke up, sweaty and shaking. Her own scream had woken her. She couldn't bear the dreams anymore. Every time she woke up, she felt like she had been pulled away from something, torn out of her mind.

Sam had been in that cage for more than a week, and the thought of it made her feel sick. No person should be treated like that. But how was she any better than those who had put him in there? How was she any better than those who walked past him every day and ignored his suffering? She had to do something about it.

When the morning dawned, she left her tent through the back, shimmying under the fabric walls and creeping into the trees. She needed to find out where

Hunter had hidden the keys to Sam's cage. *They must be somewhere inside his tent.* She tried to sneak in around the back, but Rynn approached her, sneering.

"Caught you breaking into our leader's tent, have I?"

"Am I not allowed a stroll?"

"What do you want from Hunter that he hasn't already given you? Ungrateful," Rynn said, shaking his head sarcastically. "I'd suggest you get back to your own tent right now or I'll tell the boss you were trying to escape."

Ebony scowled at him and stalked her way to the fire. Minutes later, Hunter appeared, his face red and his fists clenched. She stood up and turned to face him, her eyebrows raised.

"Rynn tells me you tried to leave."

"I didn't!"

"Then what were you doing lurking behind my tent?"

She couldn't tell him the truth. "I just want a bit of freedom."

"I am only trying to keep you safe!"

Ebony chuckled darkly. "I think you just like trapping people in cages."

"This camp is *hardly* a cage."

"You're right. It's nothing like the cage you've locked Samuel Sanker in," Ebony spat with a grimace.

"He deserves to be treated like that after what he did to you."

"*Nobody* deserves that! I am a prisoner here because you fear for my safety. He is a prisoner because you fear that he is stronger than you. Why is he still here, anyway? Aren't you trading him for money?"

"Why are you defending him?" Ebony tried to reply but no words would come. "He's a Human, Eb. He can't be trusted." Hunter spied one of the bigger Hunters sheepishly walking by. "Davis, your job is to guard Ebony, day and night. Don't let her leave."

At once, the Hunter strode over and pinned her arms to her sides, then marched her to her tent. He stood by the entrance, not saying a word.

8

Ebony's blood boiled as she lay in her hammock. The bad thoughts wouldn't leave her today. It had been almost two weeks since Tusting had been captured by the Snatchers. Who knew what they were capable of in that time? She lay stewing for most of the day, half-heartedly practising with her bow before throwing it across the small space.

The night was calm, but not yet quiet. Ebony could hear some of the men and women by the lake, swimming under the stars, and felt a pang of jealousy. Would she be able to swim at night without being caught?

A patter of rain began on the roof of the tent. Ebony had always found the sound calming. The rain slowly grew harder, punching at the canvas sheet above her.

Through the calm came a woman's scream. Probably just one of the girls at the lake. But then she heard another scream, and another. Were they just having fun or … what was going on? Ebony sat upright in her tent. Had the Foryx come to rescue Sam and take revenge? Just the thought of the camp on fire had her catching her breath. She clutched at her chest, waiting for the smell of smoke. But it didn't come, and the night was still dark. She shook her head. It was *raining*. There couldn't be fire in the rain. At that moment, the rain seemed to respond to her thoughts. It hammered onto the tent's roof.

And then she heard another scream. A blood-curdling noise that set her heart racing.

"Halsey, with me!" Hunter's voice bellowed somewhere nearby.

What was going on outside? She could hear the thud of men's boots running past her tent as the screams increased—men's screams now.

"Help!" a distant voice yelled with a strangled cry.

Ebony tiptoed to the door of her tent. "What's going on?" she asked the guard outside.

"Nothing that concerns you," the guard barked in

reply, but Ebony could hear a hint of worry in his voice.

A flash lit up the night. It had come from the far side of the lake. "What was that?" The guard didn't respond. Another flash, then another.

With a knot of dread in her stomach, Ebony knew what it meant. The Fae had come. But why were they here? Had they come to rescue her? She hadn't sent them a message.

"Let me out," she said, stepping through the entrance of the tent. But the guard roughly pushed her back in. "You don't understand! I could help!"

"Hunter said to keep you inside at all costs."

"I don't care. Let me out or the Fae could wipe out the entire camp."

The man shuddered but puffed up his chest. "You're not going anywhere."

Ebony froze when an odd smell reached her nose. It wasn't smoke or ash, but *something* was burning. She heard a deep cry of pain and a heavy thud.

"What do you see out there?" Ebony asked. "What's going on?"

Her guard didn't reply. "Please tell me what's going on." Nothing.

Was he ignoring her or was he … She tentatively stepped out of the tent, expecting him to push her back inside again. A large shape lay before her, curled into a tight ball, smoke rising from his singed clothes despite the wet ground.

The camp was pitch black. The fire had been put out. And in the distance, the screams and shouts began to grow louder and more frantic. The lake plunged into darkness, then flashed and gleamed as bolts of lightning lit up the night. The rain was falling in sheets, Ebony's hair already plastered to her head and dripping down her back. She had to stop this before it got out of hand. She *could* stop it—all she had to do was find the king and queen and speak to them—explain to them that she was safe and these people weren't the true enemy.

"King Alvaro?" she said quietly. "Queen Coralia? I'm okay. I'm free now," she whispered into the night.

The camp was slowly waking up around her, distantly aware that something had happened—was still happening. Ebony gazed out at the shimmering glow of the FaeFolk, slowly making its way across the lake, spelling their impending doom.

What did she have in her tent that could help? Her bow and arrows were useless against the Fae. She had a dagger in her boot and—where was her blue ring? She frantically searched her clothes and her heart calmed as she found the ring deep in a trouser pocket beside her lock picks. Another flash tore through the night, and her heart began to race. She had seen the Fae in action before. But she could stop this—she was sure she could. She didn't have long. She had to find the king and queen before the Fae reached the innocents. Gene, the cook. Sarah, Darrel's latest fancy. Daya …

Ebony almost tripped over her feet as she ran

towards the oncoming blanket of light, slipping and sliding through the mud. A silent lightning storm surrounded the lake, the rain pelting into the water and causing ripples in the reflection. Her hands and legs shaking, she ran full-pelt into the sea of wings, which was advancing on her by the second.

"King Alvero!" she called. "Queen Coralia! Stop! I'm here! I'm okay!" she shouted, but none of the Fae turned her way. Perhaps they couldn't hear her through the rain? It dawned on her that maybe they hadn't come to rescue her. They had come for revenge. After all, the Hunters had disrespected them for years.

She shielded her face and plunged into the bright light, the buzzing of fairies filling her ears. As her vision adjusted to the glare, she saw piles of twitching bodies on the ground. The awful burning smell made her gag. Her heart rose into her throat, and she spun around, rubbing rainwater from her blurry eyes, taking in the chaos around her. Each and every fairy held a small staff, lightning dancing on the stone at its tip. She shuddered as she realised what their staffs were made of. Bone. Possibly the bones she had donated them over the years. She had never questioned their need for them.

Where was Hunter? Where were Darrel and Halsey?

"King Alvaro!" she bellowed. "Queen Coralia!" Her voice caught in her throat and her cries turned to growls of anger. How could the peaceful Fae cause such carnage? Ebony stifled a scream as the lights began to swarm through the trees, heading straight for the camp. She began to shiver, already soaked to the skin.

How could the Bounty Hunters possibly counter this attack? Hunter had said they had it covered, but he'd always underestimated the power of the Fae.

A voice bellowed somewhere nearby. "Daya!" Hunter was hurtling past the tents. Should she follow? There was no stopping them now. The Fae were at the edge of the camp. Ebony didn't know if she was scared or angry—or a mixture of both. Her heart stopped as she tripped over something in the dark and realised what it was—or rather *who* it was. A body, covered in burn marks. Halsey lay spasming on the ground. He gave a jolt as another lightning strike hit his chest.

"King Alvero!" Ebony cried, her voice choking. Would she ever be able to forgive them? An impenetrable swarm of fairies surrounded Ebony, their faces angular, their skin a mottled grey. Their eyes spoke of their battle fury, their long claws fighting for their rights. The Bounty Hunters had used their forest for their own gains for too long.

She was shrouded in light—a ball of electricity and heat. "Stop!" she cried. She didn't want them protecting her if this was the punishment they dealt. She tried to swat them away, but they easily avoided her touch. She leaned down beside Halsey, her chest filling with anger. He was lying on wet grass, stained with blood, taking rasping breaths, his legs splayed out underneath him. Ebony wanted to cry. Why did Hunter never listen to her? She swallowed her tears and touched her friend's pained face.

Daya. Where was Daya? She could help him. Ebony leapt to her feet and sprinted through the trees, the Fae still shrouding her, an impenetrable shield. She raced back to the camp, which was now blanketed with angry Fae, praying that she would be able to find her way back to Halsey. But she feared she was already too late.

"Run!" someone was yelling. There, at the far edge of the camp, were Darrel and Hunter, fear written across their features.

Lightning shook the air. The clearing lit up so brilliantly, Ebony closed her eyes tight. Her shield was attacking her friends. She could hear bodies falling all around her.

"Queen Coralia!" Ebony shouted. "This is not the right way!"

"Run!" Hunter bellowed and then launched himself into the trees.

"Help me!" a voice cried. Her shield of fairies

began to hum as one, the sound so loud she could hardly hear herself think. Ebony turned to see Sam rattling at the bars of his cage, his eyes wide with fear. "Ebony!"

An instant later, her shield dissipated, a stream of light speeding towards the centre of the camp, and she was left in the darkness of the trees, shivering as the rain froze her to the core. The Fae were slowly gathering in the centre of the camp. She couldn't leave Sam in that cage. She ran over to him, skidding in the mud, and wrestled at the door, but the large padlock wouldn't budge.

"Let me out and I'll tell you everything." Sam was talking so fast, she could hardly understand him through the downpour. "I'll teach you how to control your dreams. I'll tell you what it is and why it's killing—" He took a sharp intake of breath as if he was struggling to get the words out. She stared into his haunted eyes. Did he know more about the connection between the shadow and her family?

She reached for her lock picks, but the night was

so dark, they were useless. She needed the key.

Turning on her heel, she ignored his cry for her to come back and dived into Hunter's tent. She stopped short, noticing a figure huddling in a dark corner, a blanket over her face.

"Daya?" Ebony tiptoed forward and tugged at the blanket. Daya's face was white as the Fae's lightning, her eyes like glowing orbs. She was shaking uncontrollably.

"H—Hunter," she managed to splutter. "Where is he?"

"You need to get out of here! You need to run!" Ebony pulled at her friend's arm, but she wouldn't budge.

"Are we going to die?"

Ebony hesitated. "You will if you don't run. But Daya, I need the keys to Sam's cage."

Daya gazed up at her. "Why?"

"It isn't fair to leave him trapped in a cage, when the Fae are …"

Daya nodded and pointed to a box in the corner of

the room. Ebony rifled through it until she found a large keyring with about thirty different keys on it.

"Which one is it?" she snapped, the keys jangling in her hands. "Tell me, Daya."

Daya gave a jittery sigh. "The rustiest one."

It didn't take long to find it. Ebony paused before reaching towards Daya and pulling her into a tight hug.

"I won't be coming back," Ebony said. She'd made up her mind as soon as she had found the right key. If Hunter was running, then so would she.

When Ebony emerged from the tent, the clearing was bathed in light, but Sam was still in the dark. The Fae left a wide berth around him, but she could feel them watching. They didn't want him escaping any more than the Bounty Hunters did. Ebony crept up to his cage and gestured for him to be as quiet as possible. She silently put the key in the padlock and slowly turned ut, aware of every sound in the night. Even her heartbeat was too loud. With a clunk, the padlock fell to the floor. She wrenched the iron door open and reached for Samuel Sanker.

Sam gripped her arm and grimaced as he unfolded himself from the wooden cage. He stumbled and struggled to stand up straight, but she grasped his hand tight and launched them both into the trees. When darkness had swallowed them, they turned to watch the Fairy Gathering. The FaeFolk had claimed the Bounty Hunters' camp.

9

Ebony pulled her dagger from her boot, the only protection she had, and pushed its tip into Sam's stomach.

"If you come anywhere near me …" she growled.

"If you want me dead, why didn't you leave me in that cage?" he whispered.

"You have answers I need." It all seemed so logical, but Ebony knew the truth. She had felt sorry for him. She couldn't see another person die at the hands of the Fae.

Sam accepted her answer with a nod. "Come on, we need to get out of here," he said, taking a step away from her blade.

She took one last glance through the trees, watching the Fae destroy her uncle's home.

"We need to go." Sam grabbed her hand, but she shook it away, giving him a piercing glare. The rain had stopped, and the light from the fairies gave her a clear view. His eyes were still and his face was calm. Despite his bruises, he was nothing like the Sam in that cage. Had he been faking it?

"I'll explain later," he said, almost as if he could read her mind. "If we stay here, we could die. Follow me," he whispered. She faltered. Should she follow him? He might be leading her to a trap. She glanced back. Did she have a choice? He gestured again for her to follow, and hobbling as fast as he could, he led her through the forest, towards the South. She had never ventured this far, and soon the trees became unrecognisable.

"Where are we going?" she asked, panting.

"Home. It's safe there." He was leading her to his new camp.

"How far is it?"

"We'll have to sleep outside tonight."

They didn't talk much for the next few hours, they just concentrated on putting as much distance between them and the Bounty Hunters' camp as possible. Though, she supposed, it wasn't really their camp anymore. Where would Hunter and his people go? Maybe they would find a way to claim it back? She tried to ignore the tightness in her chest as she strode through the trees alongside her sworn enemy. She had escaped her tent, left Halsey for dead, and freed Hunter's prisoner. She doubted she would ever be welcomed back to the Bounty Hunters. Though maybe Hunter would never know what she had done? If Daya hadn't managed to escape … She scolded herself. That was a *horrible* thought. She hoped Daya *had* escaped and found safety, but she doubted she would be able to keep her silence.

She stopped walking. What was she doing? Following this madman to who knew where? It took a moment for Sam to notice her staring into the trees. He turned back for her.

"I think I know what's going through your mind right now," he said and tried to catch her gaze. "Please, give me a chance to prove that you can trust me."

She looked up at him as tears fell down her cheeks,

then turned away, wiping away all traces of vulnerability.

"I'll look after you, Ebony."

"I don't need looking after," she said quietly.

"I know you don't. What I meant was ... I will never keep any secrets from you. I will never stop you doing what you want. I know ..." It seemed like he was struggling for words. "I know I don't really have the best track record, but please, let me try."

"Why?" She stared at him defiantly.

"I guess I want to redeem myself."

It wasn't much of an answer, but it was good enough for now. She shrugged and continued walking. She had no camp of her own, she had betrayed Hunter, and the Fae had destroyed her home. She had nowhere else to go. And Sam knew something about her family's deaths, she was sure of it. If Hunter was determined to keep her in the dark, then she would have to find the answers herself.

They rested under a large oak tree that night, the

ground surprisingly dry given the rainstorm earlier. Ebony wondered if the Fae had brought the rain with them. Had it only affected the camp?

"What are you doing?" Ebony snapped as Sam came to lie down next to her. She edged away from him and gripped her dagger in her hand.

"We need to share our body heat to stay warm."

The pair had no blankets, and the spring nights were still quite cold. Begrudgingly, Ebony lay as close to him as she dared. She clutched her dagger and glared at him until her eyes began to droop.

The bridge stretched before her, crumbling into the ash-littered river below. Above her the sky rained cinders. Her right leg moved forward, then the left. Her feet touched solid ground as she reached the bridge and made her way across. She knew this dead place. She had been here before. The boy came into view and beckoned her across the river.

"Henry?" she called.

The child's shrill laugh echoed around her, and she ran after him, knowing exactly where he was leading her. The silhouette of the child stood in the long corridor of archways. She knew what was at the end now. The abyss. The city of shadows. The archways stretched behind her, the bridge forgotten. She had to know what would happen if she took that step. What was in that haunted place below?

The hallway abruptly ended at the edge of a cliff, and she could see the child—Henry—dancing amongst the shadows with glee.

The city was one step away—just one step. All her answers lay before her.

The world fell into darkness, and the red eyes grew larger against the dark.

"Ebony! Eb! Wake up!"

Ebony lurched upright, dagger in hand, her heart racing, her mind spinning. Her hands were clammy with sweat. Sam had his arms round her shoulders, holding her upright.

"What—where am I?" she asked, shrugging him off and brandishing her blade at him. Just now, she had been at the edge of the cliff, about to take that step ...

"You're in the forest ... with me."

She looked up at Sam and her eyes widened as images of the night before flashed through her mind. Halsey twitching on the ground ... Sam in that cage ... the Fae Gathering. She lowered her hand and let the dagger fall from her grip. What could Sam do to her that hadn't already been done? She stared into the unfamiliar trees surrounding them, the forest floor blanketed with bluebells. Had her friends survived? Where had they gone? Would she ever see them again? Had the Fae tried to warn her? They had practically begged her to leave the camp only a few nights before.

He reached for her hand and played with the blue ring on her finger. "Nice ring," he said.

"It was my mother's," she mumbled, pulling her

hand away.

He looked intrigued but changed the subject. "Are you okay? You were shaking and shouting a name."

Ebony looked up at him. "What name?"

"Henry."

Ebony's heart twisted and she felt faint. She hardly knew how to respond. It had been so real ... and she had seen it before. Her nightmares had returned. But this one had been different. She had been more ... present. She looked down at her hands, her eyes wide and grey as the ash in her dreams.

"A decaying bridge? A hallway of endless archways?"

She snapped her head up to look at Sam, her eyes turning a rich, wary brown. He shuffled away from her, propping himself up with his arms.

"How did you know?"

"I've been there myself."

"Wh—but ... but it's just a dream. *My* dream."

"No it isn't. It's the Shadowlands."

"The what?"

"It's this world but dead. There's nothing there—only your own fears and darkest memories. It isn't really a dream. It's an experience."

Ebony couldn't tear her eyes from him. "I felt like someone was ... pushing me forward."

"It's an alluring place. It sucks you in, tells you it holds all of your answers. And it probably does."

"I don't want to go there again," Ebony said emphatically.

"I don't think you have a choice, I'm afraid."

"Why? Why do I always dream of that place?"

"You have many questions, and it wants to answer them for you. It won't leave you alone until you get your answers. You can't stop yourself going there, but you can control what you do there."

"How?"

"You will be given small moments of control, and you can't ignore them. You need to assert your dominance;

then you can explore freely until you wake."

"How do you know all this?" she asked.

"Trial and error, I guess. I dreamed of the Shadowlands for a long time. I still go there sometimes."

"Do you see the eyes?"

"Every time."

"They're the eyes of the Shadow, aren't they?"

Sam nodded, and the pair fell silent. The day was just dawning and a particularly noisy bird was chirruping somewhere close to her head. With a groan, she sat up and leaned against the large trunk behind her, rubbing at her bleary eyes.

"Returning to our world can take a minute."

"You really think it's a different world?"

"I'm sure of it. Do you feel rested?" he asked. Ebony thought for a moment, then slowly shook her head. "That's because you weren't dreaming. You were really there."

Ebony fell silent, her mind reeling. Too much had happened too quickly. She gasped as realisation hit her.

She may be alone in the forest with an enemy, but she was free. Free from Hunter's grasp. Free to do as she pleased. Free to rescue her closest friend. If Hicks was still alive, she had to find a way to get him out from under the Snatchers' grasp. With or without Sam's help.

"Sam … I can't go to your camp with you."

"Why not? It's not like you've got anywhere else to go." He raised his eyebrows.

"A friend of mine was captured by the Snatchers. I have to find him."

"Tusting Hicks?"

Ebony's jaw dropped. "How did you know?"

"I was a Bounty Hunter not that long ago, remember? Hunter was always talking about your friendship with Hicks. He's a useful connection."

Ebony frowned. "Hunter didn't care about him when he got caught."

"Too much effort for not much reward."

Ebony scowled at him. "How can you say that?

Tusting is a good man—"

Sam held his hand out to stop her and said, "I know, I know. I'm only guessing at what Hunter might say. I happen to think very highly of Hicks."

"So will you help me rescue him, then? Though I don't know where they're keeping him …"

"One step ahead of you," Sam smiled. "My men have been searching the city for him all week. When we get to the camp, they'll fill us in on any new intel."

Ebony looked up at him, her eyes brown with disbelief. Could she trust him? If he could help her rescue Hicks, did trust matter?

"How do you know what your men have been doing all week? You've been in a cage."

Sam raised one eyebrow. "I asked them to find out everything they could while I was gone. Maybe they haven't done a thing, but they all have their own reasons for finding him."

Ebony didn't reply. If the Foryx Clan had known

about his capture, why hadn't they tried to rescue him? She narrowed her eyes. Sam was a tricky man to read. She felt oddly comfortable around him—he was the easiest person to trust. Yet her suspicious mind couldn't give in that easily.

"If he means that much to you, we'll make a move as soon as we know more. But we need to get to camp first."

"He *does* mean a lot to me," she said, hiding her dagger in her boot.

"Well then, we'd better get going."

Ebony couldn't help but feel grateful as Sam hauled himself to his feet and held his hand out to her. He may be untrustworthy, but he was going to help her get Tusting back. She ignored his hand and heaved herself to her feet.

"We'll find him, Ebony. I promise."

It was another few hours of walking before The Foryx camp appeared in the distance. Ebony gasped. She was looking upon what appeared to be an abandoned village, every building made of wooden logs. Some were larger than others, some only small huts, but many had smoke rising from their chimneys. The walkways were cobblestone paths, green with moss and overgrown with weeds.

"We lost a lot of men in that fire," Sam explained as they approached. "Only recently managed to regroup here … with a few new recruits." He stopped walking and turned to face her.

"What is it?" she asked.

Sam chewed his bottom lip apprehensively and took a deep breath. "I know you don't trust me, and you probably won't trust any of my friends, either. But we can help you. So if you want our help … please don't draw your dagger on my friends. You can be rather deadly when you want to be."

Ebony raised her eyebrows. "What if they attack me first?"

"They won't."

"Why should I believe you? This could be a trap, for all I know."

Sam raised his palms and gave her a pleading look. "Just ... please try to be civil. We all need to get along if we're going to rescue Hicks."

"Fine. But if there's one sign of trouble ..."

"There won't be."

Ebony scoffed as he took a deep breath and reluctantly gestured for her to follow.

Sam walked confidently into the wooden village, and men began to cheer as the pair of them appeared. A tall woman with plaited blonde hair and sparkling blue eyes ran up to Sam and beamed. "Knew you'd make it out," she said with a voice like thick honey.

Sam laughed. "I didn't! It's all down to Ebony here." The woman frowned at Ebony, who stared at her defiantly. "Her eyes change colour. Get over it," Sam snapped.

The woman raised an eyebrow. "Welcome, Ebony

Wick," she said. Ebony smiled politely. "Thanks for releasing him."

"I didn't really have a choice. The Fae—"

"We'll explain later," Sam cut in as a shadow of worry crossed the woman's face. "Ebony, this is Anna. She's our best swordswoman."

"You have more than one?" Ebony asked. In the Bounty Hunters' camp, she had been the only female to be considered anything close to a Bounty Hunter.

"We're not as old-fashioned as Hunter Sparrow," Sam said with a chuckle as he led her into their camp. "You can sleep under the stars if you want. Make your own den in the forest. Whatever makes you feel comfortable," Sam said.

"I won't be staying," Ebony clarified. "I'm only here to rescue Hicks ... and for some answers."

"Well, you'll need somewhere to stay tonight."

Ebony's stomach twisted uncomfortably. Could she risk sleeping in the enemy camp? *Yes, Hicks is worth it.*

And it's only one night.

While leading her towards what looked like a garden shed, Sam whispered, "Our Healer isn't quite as good as Daya, but we make do." He strode through the shed door, which creaked as it opened, Ebony at his heels. "Jaymes! Good to see you."

"You made it out alive, then?" Jaymes looked up at them, a curtain of brown hair falling across his face.

"Did indeed. But we might be in need of a little patch up. I had to sit in a cage for more than a week."

"Ouch. And who's your friend here?"

"Ebony Wick."

The Healer froze. "*The* Ebony Wick?" Ebony stared at him defiantly. "I used to be a Snatcher," Jaymes explained. "You're famous." Ebony chuckled lightly at his words. "They all say your eyes are bright red … but they look a kind of greeny-blue to me."

"They change colour."

Jaymes looked at her in wonderment. "Can I see?"

"I can't control it."

The Healer smiled and nodded, but she could tell he wasn't done with her just yet. Ebony watched as he sat Sam on a wooden chair and rubbed balm on his bruises, then covered welts of burned skin with gauze. "What happened?"

"The Fae," Sam replied.

Jaymes sighed. "Say no more." He turned to Ebony. "You're a bit muddy and tired, but otherwise you look fine. Maybe just a warm mug of chicolate will do for you."

"What's chicolate?"

The Healer gave her a bewildered expression. "Oh, my dear." He looked genuinely aggrieved. "You poor thing. Those orphanages …"

"The Clink, you mean?"

"Is that what you urchins call it? I'm not surprised. I'll get a mug ready for you in just a jiffy. You're gonna love it." He bustled out of the shed, leaving Sam and Ebony in silence.

"He talks very fast," Ebony noted.

Sam laughed. "He gave me my first mug of chicolate, too. We don't have it in … where I grew up."

Ebony's gut twisted. She would have to get over her prejudice of Humans if she was going to be spending more time with one. At least it would only be while they rescued Hicks—after that … well, she didn't really know what she'd do with herself, but she couldn't think about that now.

"How did you meet Jaymes?"

"He was rejected from the Snatchers and had to leave town. He and his boyfriend, Galen, heard about The Foryx through the grapevine. They've been members of this Clan for years. After the fire, Galen was the one who found this place for us."

"And you trust them?"

"About as much as I can trust anybody."

"What did Jaymes do to make the Snatchers hate him so much?"

"He started rescuing urchins instead of imprisoning them."

Jaymes opened the shed door, balancing a large tankard in one hand, and gestured for Ebony to follow him out. She looked back at Sam, who encouraged her to follow him.

"Can't have your first chicolate in a medical hut! The setting has to be just right." He led her into another barn, which was lined with comfortable-looking chairs surrounding a large hearth with a roaring fire. "Welcome to the common room!" The room was empty as he led Ebony over to a sofa and they sank into it. Ebony didn't think she had ever felt so comfortable—that was until she had her first taste of chicolate.

"Excuse the tankard—we don't really have the appropriate crockery here …"

Ebony closed her eyes and took a deep breath. It was one of the most delicious drinks she had ever tasted. Almost better than whisky. In fact, whisky might perfect it. It was warm and rich, but a little sweet for her liking.

"Good, isn't it?" Jaymes beamed.

"Amazing. But a bit of whisky might improve it."

"Ah, yes. Sam likes that too." He raised his eyebrows, clearly hoping she would reveal something about her and Sam.

"He trapped me in a burning barn," she blurted out.

"Yes … I heard about that. I'm sure he had his reasons."

Laughter filled her chest and bubbled out, taking her by surprise. She looked at Jaymes and laughed again, and he laughed nervously in return. She sighed. "Yes, I'm sure he did have his reasons for trying to kill me. And I rewarded him by saving his life." She shook her head. What was she doing here? So far, Sam's friends weren't anything like she had imagined.

"I'm sure you had your reasons for that, too. It takes an unusual person to save the life of an enemy."

Ebony frowned. "Hunter had him in a cage, and the Fae were everywhere …" Her voice trailed off. She didn't want to tell her tale now.

"Ebony?" Sam called from the doorway. "We know where he is."

Ebony leapt to her feet, almost spilling her hot drink all over her trousers.

"Off already?" Jaymes said.

"We're getting ready for a rescue mission." Sam grinned.

10

Ebony carefully placed her tankard on a nearby table and headed towards Sam, who was unnervingly brimming with excitement.

"You're coming too, Jaymes," he said and gestured for the Healer to follow them.

The three of them filed through the wooden village. Ebony and Jaymes followed Sam through narrow alleyways between buildings, past a small yard of men and women training with swords, the clang of steel echoing through the trees. They made their way up a flight of wooden stairs and onto a walkway overlooking the yard before entering a battered wooden door that creaked on its hinges to find Anna in the middle of what must have been a very good joke. The three men sat at the table with her were doubled up with laughter, Anna beaming from ear to ear.

Sam chuckled and patted one of the men on the

back. "Don't forget to breathe."

Ebony quietly sat down next to him, Anna on her other side, and Jaymes gave her a reassuring smile from the seat opposite.

"Harris, tell us everything you found out," Sam said to a large, hairy beast of a man.

"The bastards took him to the prison," Harris replied, flicking his shaggy brown hair out of his eyes.

Sam sucked in a sharp breath.

"What? Which prison?" Ebony's gut twisted and she sat upright in her chair, glaring at Sam.

"Everyone, meet Ebony Wick, the Demon in the woods."

"I'm not the Demon—"

"We know. He's just kidding. I'm Harris, by the way." Harris held his hand out across the table; Ebony had to stretch to reach him. "And this is Kai."

A lean, shrewd-looking man, with hair so short he was almost bald, leaned forward, then gripped her hand firmly and looked her square in the eyes. He didn't flinch once when they changed from orange to yellow. Nor did the others. "We know who you are, and we are well aware of the real Demon," he said.

They have seen scarier things than colour-changing eyes, she reasoned. Ebony shivered as Kai let her go and ran his hand over his short hair.

"I'm Owen," the third man said with a shy smile, then leaned back in his chair. He looked even younger than Ebony.

Sam coughed and the attention turned back to him.

"The Dwelling Prison is where they take people for life," Sam explained. Ebony's heart twisted and her chest felt hollow. "We have to hope they haven't given up on him yet. If he's a clever man, he will be drip-feeding them information. Once they're done with him—"

"So what are we waiting for?" Ebony blurted out, her hand balled into a fist on the tabletop. She had waited long enough.

"We'll leave first thing tomorrow morning," Anna said.

"Why not right now?" Ebony retorted.

"We need to prepare," Sam explained. Ebony huffed, but if doing it their way was the *only* way, then she would have to be patient.

"If we're unlucky, we might be drawn into the mountains, so we'll need to bring provisions," Anna said.

"And lots of weapons," Harris added. "How are you with a sword, Ebony?"

"Not great, but I can use a dagger, and I'm okay with a bow."

"I didn't know that," Sam replied, a look of curiosity on his face.

"You don't know everything about me."

"Clearly," Sam laughed.

"How do you think I survived in the woods alone for so many years?" Ebony said defiantly.

Sam raised his eyebrows. "Have we got a spare bow?"

"We, umm—they were lost …" Harris spluttered, avoiding Ebony's gaze. "Most of them were burnt."

Burnt in the fire that Hunter caused.

"Pretty sure Galen has a spare," Jaymes pitched in.

Ebony nodded her appreciation then sat back in her chair as the others hatched a plan.

"Our only problem now is actually getting in without being seen," Anna said.

The group fell silent and seemed to take a collective sigh. Ebony shot a curious look at Sam, who quietly explained, "Mace was our expert lock pick. We lost him in the fire." Ebony recalled the name—was he the one who couldn't speak? Her stomach twisted. The fire that Hunter had set to rescue her had torn its way through these peoples' lives.

"I'm no expert, but I can pick locks," Ebony offered.

"You still have your picks?" Sam asked.

"Always have them on me."

Sam smiled as Anna began giving her friends various jobs to prepare for the following morning, but Ebony couldn't keep it in any longer; a question had been running through her mind ever since Sam had agreed to this mission.

"Why do you care about rescuing Hicks?" she said loudly to the entire room. They all paused and turned to stare at her.

"I told you, we each have our reasons," Sam said.

"And what are they?" Ebony's eyebrows raised. She certainly wasn't about to put herself and Hicks in danger when she didn't know the Foryx Clan's motives.

"Hicks gives us information … the kind that we can cash in on. He tells us what is being bought and sold and by whom," Kai explained. "We deal in secrets, much like your beloved Bounty Hunters. Without him, Harris, Owen, and I don't have an income stream."

"I don't love the Bounty Hunters," Ebony snapped.

"Hicks looks after my elderly mother," Anna said, stopping Kai's retort. "I've been wanted by the authorities since I was a kid."

"Why?" Ebony asked.

"Had to make a living somehow … they just didn't agree with my way of doing it."

"No, why does Hicks look after your mother?"

"She lives near him, and I pay him to do it."

Hicks had helped other people? Had Ebony been stupid to think he only helped her? Something inside her began to ache. She thought she had known him better than anyone … but it seemed like she hardly knew him at all.

Ebony eyed Jaymes, who jumped when he realised it was his turn to speak. "Oh, umm, Hicks is my cousin."

"And you, Sam? Why do you want to save Hicks?"

Sam looked her square in the eyes. "Because he matters to people, and he matters to you. And he's a great contact to have."

"Why do you want to save him, Ebony Wick?" Kai asked, his eyes full of suspicion.

"Tusting has been my best friend—my only friend—since I left the city. He is loyal and good. And it's my fault that he's in that prison."

The group nodded and fell silent. They may not trust each other, but they all had the same goal, though Ebony chose not to remind them of one fact that might change their minds. Once they'd rescued Hicks, it was unlikely he'd be able to return to his old way of life. He wouldn't be able to look after Anna's mother anymore or feed the Foryx information. He'd be high on the Snatcher's hit list forever more. The meeting broke up, everyone agreeing to meet in the training yard at the break of dawn.

"So who's the leader here?" Ebony asked as she and Sam headed to Galen's hut to find her a bow.

"We don't really have a leader," Sam shrugged.

"Is there not like … a hierarchy?"

"We're not Bounty Hunters, just good old-fashioned outlaws. We're more of a village than a task force."

"So you're all just ... friends?"

"Some of us get on better than others."

"How do you make money? How do you get food?"

"Odd jobs in town—some of us work there and live here. Pretty exhausting walk, though, now that we're so far South. And we grow our own food in a large plot by the river. Some of us used to sell our crops in town. We were pretty self-sufficient until it was all burnt down. We'll get back there eventually."

They reached a little stone cabin, smoke rising from its chimney. Sam knocked and smiled politely as a weather-warn man answered, his long grey-brown hair brushing over his shoulders. In his hand he held a stick, which he waved before his legs, sharply jabbing Sam in the knees.

"Good day to you too, Galen."

"Come in, nice and warm in here," Galen grumbled.

The small hut contained a fireplace, one armchair, one bed, and a small kitchen unit. Jaymes and Galen may have been partners, but they clearly didn't live together.

"I've brought a friend with me," Sam said.

"We're not friends," Ebony snapped.

"Galen, meet Ebony Wick."

Galen laughed—a harsh cackle. "Caught her at last! I remember when that was Jaymes' sole mission. Then he saw what she was capable of and the coward scarpered—left the Custodians for good."

"I think there was more to it than that," Sam said, gesturing at Ebony to follow him into the stiflingly hot hut.

Galen ignored him. "I don't blame him. I would have done the same. I've heard all sorts about you, girl. Demon in the woods … it's all a load of claptrap. Can't a girl just be good with a dagger?" Galen didn't seem to require a reply as he sat down in a rickety wooden chair with a grumble. "Come here, girl. Let me get the measure of you."

Ebony cautiously approached and knelt before Galen as Sam suggested, and Galen grasped her face between his rough fingers.

"Ah, yes. You have felt hunger many a time. You need a good night's sleep, girl. You have bags under your eyes. Which colour are they now?"

Ebony tried to turn to Sam for reassurance, but Galen held her head fast.

"I can't tell what colour they are—but they're probably brown."

"Oh, how dull. I thought they'd be something interesting—yellow or orange or something."

Ebony frowned. "Give me a thwack with that cane and they might turn red." Galen cackled and let go of her face. "How do you know about my eyes?"

"They all said you had bright red eyes, but they only ever saw you fighting. I know who you are. I knew your mother." Ebony leapt to her feet. She stumbled and grabbed onto Sam for support. "Sorry," she mumbled to him as her cheeks warmed, and she stepped away from him.

"How did you know her?"

"Your parents ran a haberdashery shop in the East that I frequented."

"A haber-what?"

Sam answered her question. "Stuff for sewing and knitting."

Hunter said he'd told Ebony everything he knew about her parents. He'd either lied to her, which was very possible, or he'd hardly known her parents at all. He said he was looking for information on them ... was he so blind with hatred for the Foryx Clan that he'd overlooked them? He didn't dare touch the hornet's nest, even if it got him the answers he needed. *Coward*.

"How did my parents die?" Ebony asked.

"House fire," Galen replied with a frown. "Now then," he continued. "You didn't come to me to talk about death. What do you want?"

"Jaymes said you might have a bow we can use," Sam said.

"I do indeed. Quiver and all. Though it's a bit long in the tooth. Who is it for?"

"Me," Ebony replied.

"Dagger *and* bow? Quite a warrior you're becoming."

"I had to survive on my own somehow."

"Yes, we did wonder where you'd got to. Years on the streets with the Black Jade gang, then one day, you just disappeared."

How did this man know so much about her? It was a bit unnerving, though Ebony felt drawn to him somehow—perhaps it was simply because he'd known her parents.

"Sam, the bow is in the broom cupboard at the back somewhere. If you find it, you can keep it. Not like I can use it anymore."

It didn't take long to find the bow and quiver. It

was a little small for Ebony's liking, but it was better than nothing.

"I expect Jaymes will be gone for a few days," Sam said. "As will we."

"Where are you going?"

"To rescue Tusting Hicks."

"Ah, good man, good man. Third door on the left."

"Excuse me?" Ebony asked.

"That's where they torture for information."

How Galen knew that, Ebony didn't want to find out.

"Thanks," she said lamely before stepping out of the cabin before Sam.

Sam handed Ebony the bow and quiver, and she flung both of them over her shoulder.

"Why is Jaymes coming with us? He's not much of a fighter."

"Always good to bring a Healer along. You never know when he might be needed." She fell silent, following

Sam through the village, hardly knowing where he was taking her next. "How did Galen find this place if he can't ..."

"If he's blind? He knew about it already. Apparently, it was a small settlement at the base of the Rundlewood Mountains. Then a plague came."

"He knows a lot."

"That he does. Here we are."

Sam had led them to a large pile of branches piled up in a woodshed.

"You want me to chop wood?"

"No. I want you to build a bivouac. We have enough furs and blankets to keep you warm."

Ebony didn't know what to say. For months, she'd been forced to sleep in dizzying hammocks and stuffy tents, not allowed to even entertain thoughts of her old den.

"Build your den nearby and we'll make sure you're safe. If you want your own camp, that's completely fine. You could even pretend we don't exist if you want." Her gaze held almost every question in her mind. Why did she feel like she could trust him when he had treated her so badly? Why was he being so ... kind? Only the day before, he had been so haunted, so broken. How had he bounced back to health so quickly? Sam touched her shoulder gently. "Let's get Tusting back to safety, then we'll talk." Ebony nodded. "For now, let's make you a den."

"I can do it on my own."

Sam rolled his eyes. "See you later then."

She spent the rest of the day building a new camp for herself. She had chosen a spot in the woods that was quiet and beside a river, but she could just about see the settlement through the trees. She had to cross a small wooden bridge to get to her camp, which made it feel secluded and safe.

Ebony hadn't slept so well for a long time. She was home at last.

11

The birds were only just beginning to wake when the seven of them met in the training yard. They had packed as light as possible. Ebony had her bow slung over her shoulder, alongside her quiver. The others carried medical supplies, weapons, and food. They quietly traipsed through the forest, the edge of the West Dwellings within sight through the trees. The day started to brighten, a light spring breeze rustling the leaves. Soon, they were surrounded by a carpet of bluebells, stretching as far as the eye could see. They trod through the undergrowth until they came upon a blackened clearing, on the edge of which was a crumbling barn.

Ebony shivered. She knew where they were. That was where she had seen it the first time. The Shadow.

Sam approached her from behind. "I promise we'll talk when we're back at camp. When we're safe."

Ebony nodded. This Sam standing before her was

so utterly different from the Sam who had left her tied to a wooden pole in a burning barn. Could she trust him? Should she? But right now she didn't have a choice. She had to trust him if she wanted to see Tusting alive again.

Walking past the barn like it meant nothing to her, she strode on, and the others followed. They were close to the bridge into the Commons. From there, Ebony didn't know how Sam expected to get them all to the prison unnoticed. But he clearly had a plan up his sleeve. She paused as they reached the edge of the trees.

"Everything okay?" Harris asked, coming to stand beside her.

Ebony glanced at Sam, who had a surprisingly confident look on his face. "I'm kind of number one on the Snatcher hit list," she explained. "We're not exactly subtle—a group of outlaws marching through the Commons."

Harris smiled knowingly. "You're not the only one with good connections." He continued walking.

"What do you mean?" Ebony had to almost jog to keep up with his long strides.

"Sam has been working with some of the gangs." Ebony's stomach twisted. "He's got most of them on board, but the Black Jade are proving particularly difficult to work with."

"On board with what?"

"I'm sure Sam will explain when he's got a minute."

Harris fell silent and Ebony didn't press him any further. Somehow, she trusted that Sam actually *would* tell her. They had a lot of catching up to do.

"Sam," she called. He stopped walking and looked over his shoulder at her. "Please tell me where we're going. You can't expect us to just wander straight through town and not raise suspicion."

"You'll see," he said with a grin. She narrowed her amber eyes at him.

They reached the bridge into The Commons, which was swarming with people. Jaymes sidled up to

Ebony and whispered in her ear, "Most of these people are gang members here to escort us across."

Ebony raised her eyebrows. The Foryx had that much power over them? How did they organise this? The bridge had become the most dangerous route in and out of the Commons since Alastor Bates' death. The Snatchers seemed to watch it day and night. Ebony was glad they had extra bodyguards to get them across. They crossed the bridge with ease, blending into the crowd, and headed down a row of dilapidated houses.

After many confusing alleyways, they entered a small, dingy building. The floorboards were covered with dirty, brown, moth-eaten carpets that used to be a shade of green. The place had a thick, musty smell and was coated in a layer of dust. As they climbed spiralling stairs, a landing emerged from the gloom. Directly in front of them hung a beautiful painting of a picnic by a lake that stood out like a rose among thorns. In the small space was a wooden desk with a broken chair, a cracked vase, and a locked chest. There was one door, which led to a small bedroom—more like a broom cupboard – with a dirty, unmade bed and a mirror made from tin.

What were they doing here? Was this a meeting place for a gang? Sam reached the painting—framed with gold and painted with expensive oils—and carefully took it off the wall, revealing an empty attic room, at the end of which was a small door.

"Where does it lead to?" Ebony asked.

"A secret passageway to a network of tunnels. It should take us beyond the Clink," Jaymes explained. Ebony's jaw dropped. How had she never known about this?

Sam gestured for her to follow him before climbing up and through the hole in the wall. "Ready?" Sam called.

"Ready," they all mumbled in turn.

The attic's wooden floor creaked as they padded toward the door at the far end. Sam swung the door open and led them through a series of storage rooms, some piled high with dusty furniture and old carpets. They eventually reached a similar landing to the one they'd started in. To their right was a thin spiral staircase that seemed to descend forever. It was so steep, Ebony had to grab onto the metal bannisters to keep her balance.

Eventually, they found themselves in a dark cellar, and watched her companions crawl backwards one by one through a hole in a wall. It was a tight fit. They climbed down a rusty ladder until utter darkness ruled their sight. Her feet finally met solid ground and she felt a hand on her shoulder, urging her forwards.

They hurried along through the darkness. Ebony could feel rats running over her feet and had to touch the slimy, rotting walls around her to keep herself upright. She couldn't see her hand inches before her face. They crept along a low passageway, which was dripping with old sewage water. Tree roots hung from the domed ceiling, catching the knots in Ebony's hair.

At last, they reached steps that had been chiselled

into a stone wall. Up they went until they came to a large wooden door, which took them into another cellar and up a ladder through a trapdoor. They emerged in a small weather-worn shack and covered up the trapdoor with an old rug. Ebony glanced out of one of the windows as her eyes widened.

Before her was blue. Only blue.

"We're in the North Commons," Jaymes said to Ebony, who couldn't seem to move.

"It's—" Words had failed her.

"You've never seen the sea before?" Anna asked, her eyebrows raised.

Ebony slowly shook her head. "I have … but not *this*." It just went on—it was never ending. The water and sky were one and the same. Where did it end? Or maybe it never did?

"Come on," Anna said, linking her arm through Ebony's, who instinctively pulled away. Anna looked affronted at first and glanced at Sam nervously. Ebony bit the inside of her lower lip and took a deep breath. Anna had done nothing wrong. Was Ebony so incapable of trust? She reluctantly accepted Anna's arm and her a soft, reassuring smile. "Wait till you see the beach."

Leaving their bags and weapons in the hut, they stepped through the door to the shack, which creaked as it swung open. Ebony giggled as her shoes sunk into the soft yellow sand beneath her feet. Anna leaned against the wooden wall of the hut and began pulling off her boots.

"What are you doing?" Ebony asked, bewildered.

"Sand is always better without shoes on. Trust me." Anna gestured for Ebony to do the same. They tugged off their boots and leaned them against the wall before padding their way onto the large stretch of beach, grins lighting up their faces.

"You like it now, but try getting the sand off your feet!" Jaymes called from behind them. He turned to Sam, who was watching the two girls giggling as they reached the water. "I hate the stuff. Gets everywhere," Jaymes grumbled.

"We need to get going," Kai said, standing rigidly beside Sam and Harris, who sat comfortably on old rocking chairs inside the beach hut.

"Give them a minute," Sam said, entranced, watching through the window as the girls paddled in the water, their laughter carrying on the wind. Anna and Ebony slowly made their way up the beach, their cheeks rosy. Sam had never seen golden eyes before.

"We're coming back here," Ebony said to Sam, who smiled. "Once Tusting is safe."

"We?" Sam raised his eyebrows.

"Me—I mean, I am," Ebony stumbled. "Though I guess I won't be able to stop anyone else tagging along."

They piled back into the beach hut and found places to sit, Anna and Ebony drying their feet on the threadbare rugs that had been draped over the old chairs. *Who looks after this place?* Ebony wondered.

 "So, are we all clear on the plan?" Kai asked.

"Jaymes and I will hide near the entrance while Anna and Ebony break in and find Hicks," Harris said.

"And Kai and I will create some sort of distraction," Sam added.

"What kind of distraction?" Ebony asked.

"Leave that to us," Sam said, a mischievous look in his eye.

12

Bordering the beach was a woodland of tall pine trees growing in perfect rows. The Dwellings Prison was hidden in the trees, nestled at the base of what was known as the Fool's Crag, a steep incline blanketed with gorse bushes and scree. The cliff edge overlooked the expanse of sea, no other landmark in sight.

The prison was a grey fortress, solid and intimidating. The six of them hid behind bushes and thick tree trunks, watching the guards come and go.

"See you later," Kai grunted as he and Sam disappeared into the trees and headed for the other side of the prison. Minutes later, Ebony heard a yell, then a scream. What were Sam and Kai doing? The guards jumped into action and began racing to the other side of the compound, clearing a path to an entrance.

"That's our cue," Anna said, and she and Ebony looked at each other, a silent plan forming between them.

"Good luck," Jaymes said.

"See you soon," Harris added for reassurance.

Anna nodded at Ebony and the pair of them leapt to their feet and sprinted to the entrance of the prison. Within seconds, Ebony had her lockpicks at the ready while Anna kept watch for any returning guards. The prison door swung open and the two girls disappeared into its dark corridors.

Third door on the left, Ebony repeated to herself. That's what Galen had suggested. The corridor was long and dark, and it took them almost a minute to find the right door. It was locked. Ebony cursed under her breath and got to work. She tried the latch again and the heavy door swung open. It slammed shut behind them, leaving them in near darkness. The only light they had came from flaming torches held in brackets on the walls, but they were few and far between. The silence was deafening.

"Hey!" a voice yelled from somewhere ahead.

Ebony swore as three guards came charging down

the hallway. She reached for her bow as Anna unsheathed her sword. In the semi-darkness, Ebony let loose, but her arrow only skimmed one of the guards' shoulders. Anna sliced down one man, then another as Ebony's second arrow found the guard's leg. He dropped to the floor with a yell and Anna finished the job. The hallway fell silent.

"Now what?" Ebony whispered.

"We check every cell until we find him."

They tiptoed down the hallway, peering through the small windows in the cell doors.

"Tusting?" Ebony called quietly. No reply. She tried again. "Tusting?" she said a little louder. A grunt came from a few cells away. Her step quickened as she called out his name and the responses grew louder. She peered through a window and gasped. A pale, sickly version of Tusting Hicks sat slumped in the corner of a bare cell, his lip swollen and bleeding and his eyes purple and bruised.

"Keep watch," she said to Anna and got to work on the door. She pushed it open and her heart began to race as Tusting looked at her, pain and anger and hurt marring his features.

"Can you stand?" she asked.

"No—Ebony. You shouldn't be here," Hicks mumbled through a split lip. "You have to go. Leave me here."

"Anna, help me get him up," Ebony said, ignoring him.

The two girls heaved Tusting to his feet, but his knees buckled.

Anna huffed and shook her head. "We'll have to drag him out of here."

Together, they manoeuvred him into the hallway, his weight straining Ebony's back. They reached the door and turned right. Hicks raised his arm to cover his eyes as the late morning sun shone down the corridor.

"SAM!" Harris bellowed from outside.

Ebony and Anna looked at each other with wide eyes as they heard a stampede approaching through the trees.

"It's a trap, Ebony," Hicks mumbled. "They knew you'd come for me eventually."

Ebony's heart twisted. *Eventually*. Had he started to question whether she would come for him at all?

Through their small window to the outside world, Ebony could see Snatchers storming through the trees. No truncheons this time. They had swords and arrows and intent on their faces. They were here for her.

A large figure blocked the entrance and began striding towards them. Ebony swung her bow into her hands and nocked an arrow.

"It's me, Ebony," Kai barked. "Where's Sam? We need him."

"I thought he was with you?" Anna replied.

"He said just one isn't enough and stormed in here. He wants to free them all. But that was before the entire force showed up."

"He hasn't got any lock picks. How will he get

anyone out?"

Kai shrugged and Anna and Ebony looked at each other with incredulity. Without a distraction, the guards would soon be swarming the place. Ebony huffed with exasperation. "Get him out and keep him hidden." She nodded to Hicks. "I'm gonna go find that idiot."

"I'm going with you," Anna said, handing Hicks over to Kai. Ebony glanced over her shoulder as Kai dragged her friend out of the prison, praying to the Mother that he would keep him safe.

Ebony and Anna turned, glaring down into the long corridor that got steadily darker. "Sam?" they called.

"Over here!"

The girls found an abashed Sam hovering by another door much further down the corridor.

"Didn't think they'd lock *every* door," Sam said.

"What are you doing?" Ebony snapped. "We need to go!" She could hear the clashing of swords outside.

"There are so many innocent people in here. We

can't just save one."

"Your friends are outside! You need to help *them*!"

"They can take care of themselves."

Ebony huffed. "How can you tell the innocent from the guilty? How do we know who to save?"

"Does it matter?" Sam said.

Ebony shook her head and huffed with exasperation. "Fine. But you're carrying them out." She unlocked the door to the corridor and quickly began unlocking the first cell.

"Why would we need to carry them?" Sam asked.

"Tusting can't walk," Anna explained.

Sam swore. "That's going to make things more difficult," he said.

Sam pushed open the first unlocked door as Ebony got to work on the second.

"You're free to leave," Ebony said to each of the inmates as she broke open their cell doors and continued onto the next. The padlocks holding them in were almost primitive; easy for her to pick. She just wished she wasn't the only one capable of picking locks; having a helper would speed up the process somewhat.

"It's freedom day!" Sam yelled. "Let yourselves out!"

Ebony could hear anticipation rustling behind each door as she worked. At last, she reached the last door in the corridor and left Sam to convince the inmates that they were free.

"More, Ebony! Free another hallway!" Sam's voice sounded desperate.

A few hobbling inmates followed behind Anna and Ebony as they made their way back to the entrance of the long corridor.

Anna peered through a crack in the door. "Ebony … they're blocking our way out. The guards."

"Get ready for a fight, then."

Ebony pocketed her lock picks and swung her bow round into her hands as they approached the corridor's entrance and counted to three. They burst through and charged towards the guards, all wearing red just like the Snatchers.

Ebony counted six of them. Now five. Her arrow lodged itself in a forehead. Sam appeared from a doorway and charged forward, Anna beside him, while Ebony fought her way to the exit, dragging as many inmates with her as she could. There were more guards outside, swarming from every angle. Ebony stood just beyond the entrance, loosing arrow after arrow at oncoming guards with swords and truncheons. Kai appeared around a corner, revealing a belt of daggers hidden under his shirt. He weaved his way through enemy lines, stabbing, throwing, retrieving. Anna appeared beside Ebony, a few dishevelled prisoners at her side.

"Run!" Anna cried at the three prisoners, who were cowering in the sunlight. She pushed them towards the trees. "Run! Find the Foryx Clan."

The prisoners tripped their way into the forest as

Anna entered the fray, her sword swinging wildly before her. More prisoners swarmed out of the prison, narrowly avoiding the Snatchers.

Where was Tusting? Where was Owen? Ebony fired off another arrow, which hit her target, and saw Owen and Jaymes dragging a body through the woods. More guards appeared—too many for them to handle.

She was sweating so much, her hands became slippery and she struggled to keep hold of the bow. She flung it over her shoulder and grabbed the dagger hidden in her boot. She began weaving through the sea of red, striking at everything and anything in their way. They were hugely outnumbered.

Out of nowhere came a fist and her nose crunched painfully. She yelled and dropped her dagger, then stumbled backwards, tripping over a dead body. It was one of the inmates who had tried to escape. She cradled her bleeding face. A Snatcher stood before her with an ugly grin, sword poised. His eyes grew wide as a sword was thrust through him from behind. Blood gurgled from his mouth and he dropped to the ground. Sam withdrew his blade and lunged for Ebony's fallen dagger. He then launched himself at her and grabbed her wrist.

"Come with me!" he yelled. She hardly had a choice. She staggered behind him, her wrist held fast in his tight grip. Ebony shook off his hand, but he pushed her back through the door into the prison and pelted inside after her.

"Last door in the corridor will get you to a back entrance," Sam whispered. "RUN!"

Ebony didn't think twice. Almost tripping over her legs, she ran headfirst into the corridor, which grew darker and darker by the second. She could hear the pounding of boots as Snatchers filled the corridor. Would Sam make it out alive?

At long last, she could see a wall looming before her. The last door had been left ajar, and she flung herself through it into an identical corridor. Racing through the grey darkness, she tried to ignore the yells and screams surrounding the compound; tried not to look back in case the Snatchers had got past Sam. In the distance, she saw see a light. The back door. With fear pounding in her heart, reaching it felt like an eternity. Her lungs burned as she let herself out of the prison. All around her, the ground was littered with dead Snatchers. How had Sam and Kai managed it? Maybe she didn't want to know.

As she gasped for breath, she smelt smoke and dread filled her whole body. What had Sam done?

She turned and saw the roof of the prison cave in, already a heaving mass of flames, as if a living, breathing monster had claimed it as its home. Sam appeared at the back door, running out of the fire, his face black with soot.

"Run!" he yelled. He turned left and began running flat out, Ebony in tow.

"You burned down the prison?" she yelled at him.

"It wasn't me. The fire just ... appeared!"

The Shadow is here. Panic started to fill her mind

as she ran. She could see Owen up ahead, dragging Hicks through the trees. They ran the perimeter of the building, almost skidding as they got to the corner. Ebony paused to fire off an arrow at an incoming Snatcher, but Sam grabbed her arm and pulled her along.

"Get to the crag!" Sam called over his shoulder. The Fool's Crag. A cliff edge made of scree.

Ebony's heart thudded and her throat grew tight. The steep climb appeared before them, and Ebony spied Tusting halfway up it. He seemed to have worked out what was going on. He scrambled up the rock face on all fours. Owen was at the bottom, helping the others up. With a cry, he fell to the ground and twitched.

"NO!" Sam bolted towards him, but he was too late. Owen lay lifeless on the ground.

"You have to leave him!" Harris yelled, already at the top of the Crag.

Without a second thought, Ebony launched herself up the scree and almost slid onto her stomach. Sam caught her just in time and pushed her up the steep incline. Four guards had almost reached the bottom of the crag and attempted to follow them up, but their shiny black boots had little grip. Climbing up moving rock was harder than it seemed, and more than once, Ebony almost fell right into their waiting arms.

Ebony found her footing and let loose an arrow. It struck one of the guards just as Kai's dagger hit another. Both guards tripped and stumbled into the other two, giving Ebony and Kai a chance to keep climbing.

Sam and Anna lay flat on the grass at the top, their hands stretched out to pull their team members up. Ebony grasped onto Sam's hand, who pulled her with all his might. They collided at the top and lay panting on the ground, backpacks strewn across the grass around them. They had made it. It was unlikely the guards would attempt the Fool's Crag now that they had the high ground, but they might find another way up. Sam peered over the edge of the drop and, sure enough, most of the guards had already run back to deal with the carnage they'd left behind.

"Where's Hicks?" Ebony sat upright to see her friend leaning on Jaymes.

"What happened to Owen?" Jaymes asked. "He was right behind me."

Sam shook his head and frowned as he stood gazing at the burning prison below. "They got him, Jaymes." The group fell silent, though Ebony had the distinct feeling that none of them had known him very well. "He was a new recruit. We shouldn't have brought him along."

"We were doing fine until you decided to go in and free everyone," Ebony snapped. "Owen might still be alive, and we could be on our way back by now!"

"It *was* pretty reckless," Anna chimed in, clambering to her feet.

"You helped me do it, so don't point all the blame at me," Sam snarled. "You could have stopped me."

"No, we couldn't," Anna retorted.

"We had a chance to free everyone from that hellish place. I had to try."

"They'll probably die of starvation anyway," Ebony added.

Sam scowled. "Excuse me for trying to help others and doing what needed to be done."

"The Snatchers will never leave us alone now," Ebony said. "We'll be hunted. We won't be able to step into the Dwellings ever again. They already know my face."

"Isn't this what you want?" Sam added. "It's the beginning."

"The beginning…"

"Of taking down the Snatchers."

Ebony froze. Did he hate them as much as she did? Sam got to his feet and stalked off towards Jaymes.

However aggravating it was to admit, Sam was right. He'd given those poor souls another chance and risked his own life doing it. She'd said something similar to Hunter about Hicks. But Sam had risked his friends' lives as well, without their consent. The Snatchers weren't just chasing urchins anymore.

"Come on, we need to find shelter," Harris said, gesturing towards the dark clouds rolling in.

Forcing themselves to their feet once again, Kai, Ebony, Sam, and Harris ran ahead to find somewhere to set up camp.

"I know a place," Sam said and led them to a large cave hidden behind a waterfall of greenery.

Ebony went to direct the others to the cave and helped settle Hicks down against the cave wall.

"What hurts?" Jaymes asked.

"Everything," Hicks grumbled.

Ebony stared at her friend, glad to see him alive. But she hadn't anticipated this bit. She'd have to explain why his rescue had been delayed. But now was not the time. She sloped away and watched from afar as Jaymes poked and prodded at Hicks, offering him all kinds of lotions and potions from his backpack. Kai had already got a fire going and Sam was searching through their packs to find the meat they had brought with them.

Anna came to sit beside Ebony, who couldn't take her eyes off her injured friend.

"He'll be okay," Anna said as the rain began to pour outside.

13

Ebony could hear Kai and Sam whispering at the back of the cave. Were they whispering to avoid waking up their friends or because they didn't want to be overheard? She strained to hear what they were saying, but only caught a few words.

"We can't … I don't believe that she…"

"Keep your voice down," Sam hissed.

"I don't trust her," Kai snapped.

She knew what they were talking about. Ebony carefully stood up and silently trod to the back of the cave. The two men stopped speaking and looked up at her, Sam with worry in his eyes and Kai with a look of scorn on his face.

"You really should have kept your voice down," Ebony said.

Sam held his arm out as if to keep her at bay. "Ebony, he's just—"

"You don't trust me," she said, looking Kai up and down. "Is it because of my eyes?" she said, aware that they would be a shining orange in the darkness.

"What? I don't care about your eyes. I've seen scarier things than you, Ebony Wick," Kai spat.

"So what's your problem then?"

"Why should I trust you? How do I know you're not going to sell us out to the Snatchers to clear your name?" Kai said, not bothering to keep quiet anymore.

"Kai ..." Sam looked warily between the two of them.

"You could do the same to me," Ebony noted. "Why should *I* trust *you*? Didn't you see me killing Snatchers back there? I hate them more than anyone."

"Just because you hate them, doesn't mean you won't try to save yourself."

"So what are you gonna do? Whisper behind my back? The Snatchers want me more than any of you," she said, gesturing around the cave. Everyone had woken up now, listening to Kai and Ebony with bated breath. "I've been on their hit list for years. Most of you only just made it there."

"If I catch you doing anything suspicious—"

"You won't. I need you more than you need me."

With that, she trudged to the front of the cave, ignoring the stares that followed her, and sat down to watch the rain fall outside.

Hicks slept most of the day, refusing to talk to anyone but Ebony or Jaymes. Harris cooked them all a meat stew over the small fire and they huddled together for warmth, sharing stories of their experiences living in the wild, though Kai kept shooting Ebony looks of contempt. Jaymes hadn't been an outlaw for long and missed the comforts of a house in the city. But Sam had been an outlaw far longer than the rest.

"I fled Shalo County when a good friend was killed. I wasn't safe there anymore without him."

"Why?" Ebony asked.

"I was part of the rebellion."

"What were you rebelling against?" Anna asked before helping herself to another bowl of stew.

"You Dwellers really know nothing about Shalo, do you?"

"We know you're all Humans," Ebony replied, watching to see his response. The group fell silent. Even Hicks had turned his attention to them, his wary eyes glancing between Sam and Ebony.

"Every race has a mixture of good and bad people. Humans made mistakes in the past, but we're not all like that." He turned to Anna. "We were rebelling against the system. You think being a Commoner in the Dwellings is hard? We were known as Underlings; controlled, undermined, enslaved. The rebellion died with Bastion, and our identities were revealed. So I had to leave. I wear his ring in honour of him and everything he did for the Underlings in Shalo." He lifted up his hand to show them all the large ring on his finger.

"Where did you go?" Jaymes asked.

"Into Savolley forest. I headed to Westria at first, just beyond the Peregrine Plains. I wanted to get to the edge of the map, so I followed the river past Henley and found myself in Rundlewood Forest. Took me almost a year to get to The Dwellings."

The group nodded as if they could picture his journey in their heads, but Ebony frowned. She'd never heard of most of those places. She'd never seen a map that stretched beyond The Dwellings.

"How did you meet Hunter?" Ebony asked.

"I fell in with one of the street gangs—this must have been a few years ago now. Hunter was helping us on a job and offered me more than the gangs ever could." He shrugged. "Living in the woods felt safer than the city."

Ebony was sure he wasn't telling the full tale. What had made him decide to betray Hunter? But he'd said he would explain more when they got back to the wooden village. She would just have to be patient.

Harris turned to Ebony and raised his eyebrows. "So what's your life story?"

Ebony chuckled. "Not much to tell, really."

"Bet there is," Anna responded.

Ebony paused. How much should she tell them? "Grew up in an orphanage with …" She stopped short and took a deep breath. "With a boy called Henry." She looked to her feet. "A few years ago, there was a fire and …" Her dreams flashed through her mind; Henry's melting face, flames licking up the walls, a lingering feeling of panic coursing through her. She took another deep breath. "Well, anyway, I joined a gang for a few years, but that didn't work out. So I moved into the forest on my own."

"What happened to Henry?" Kai asked. Anna shot him a warning look, but he returned it with puzzled brows.

"He died in the fire," Ebony stated. The cave fell silent. Jaymes turned to Sam, realisation in his eyes. Sam had trapped Ebony in a burning barn. Hunter Sparrow must have really angered her if she'd chosen Sam over him. "Hunter took me in last autumn and promised me … all sorts. He said he'd help me find out more about my family. He didn't deliver, so here I am."

"Fair enough," Harris replied.

The light from the fire danced up the cave walls as Sam went to wash out their bowls in the pouring rain outside. Anna, Kai, and Harris sat by the fire playing a game of cards while Jaymes and Ebony went to check on Hicks. She sat down next to him, shoulder to shoulder, the cave wall cold against her back. Jaymes offered him a warm brew before joining the others by the fire.

"I'm sorry," Ebony said quietly.

"About what?" he replied without looking at her.

"That I didn't get you out sooner."

Hicks shrugged. "I didn't expect you to get me out at all."

"You were right, you know," she said, and he turned his head to look at her, though she wondered how he could see through such swollen eyes. "The Bounty Hunters ... they're not good. They locked Sam in a tiny cage and wouldn't let me leave the camp. Hunter said he was just trying to keep me safe, but then the Fae came ..."

"The Fae?"

"They attacked the camp. I don't know how many they killed. Halsey ..." Ebony looked away as her eyes began to sting. "I couldn't leave Sam in that cage. I needed help to rescue you, but Hunter refused. So I left the Bounty Hunters and joined Sam." She sighed. "I should have stopped the Snatchers from getting you. I should have fought for you ..."

Hicks turned his head to her, the glow of the fire on his face. "Ebony, *I* chose to follow you that day. I chose to go into that burning building. I should have run with you. The fact that you came back for me at all ..." He paused. "I thought I was going to die in there ... in the prison I mean."

Ebony gazed into his swollen eyes. "I was worried

I was too late."

Hicks gave a weak smile, wincing as his split lip began bleeding again. "I'm made of stronger stuff than you think," he said, dabbing a square of material on his mouth.

Ebony smiled, but something in his face had changed. He looked at her differently—without worry or laughter or fondness. His eyes were hard, like they had seen things they couldn't forget.

"I tried to warn you that it was a trap," Hicks said. "I was only there to lure you in. Well, they also wanted information about you …"

"And what did you tell them?"

"You have to understand Ebony … to stay alive I had to tell them *something*."

She looked away from him, hiding the anger in her eyes. It was her fault that he had been forced to betray his closest friend. "I know. What did you tell them?" Tusting gave her a hesitant look. "I need to know what they know about me, Hicks."

He huffed. "I told them you are a Bounty Hunter. I gave them some names ... Hunter Sparrow ..." He paused.

"Anything else?"

"I told them about the girl that Hunter rescued from that burning building."

"She died," Ebony stated. "Lung damage from the fire."

Hicks looked at his feet. "I guess most of the information I gave is irrelevant now." He looked up at her. "Please forgive me. I'm not strong like you are."

"There's nothing to forgive." Tusting gave her a weak smile that didn't reach his eyes. "What will you do now?" Ebony asked. "I don't expect the Snatchers will leave you alone anymore." He frowned in response. "You could join me and the Foryx Clan."

"So that's this gang's name, is it?"

"It isn't a gang. It's more like a small village. You'll be safe there."

"I don't know ..."

"Where else can you go?" He opened his mouth, but then closed it again and looked away. "That's what I thought. Come stay with us."

"Us already, is it?"

"I didn't have anywhere to go, either. I trust these people. Some of them, anyway," she said, looking across the cave at Anna and Jaymes. "Don't know why, I just do." She had hardly realised it herself until she said it out loud. She actually *trusted* them. Did she trust Sam, too? They'd welcomed her with open arms and rescued her closest friend. What could Hicks do for them now that he'd lost his job?

"You don't trust the others?"

"I don't know. Kai seems suspicious of me, and I don't really know Harris. But they're better than Hunter."

"I'll come with you to their camp," Hicks said. "But I'm not promising anything."

Ebony beamed. "We'll train you up with a sword and—"

"No. I'm not like you. I don't do that stuff."

"But you would be able to protect yourself."

"If I need protection, then I'm in the wrong place."

Ebony raised her eyebrows. What had happened to him in that prison? "Fine. We can find you something else to do…"

Hicks nodded. "When will we leave this damp cave?"

"When you're better, I guess."

"So I'm the one holding us all up?"

"You're not holding us up. We care about you, and we're not going to force you to make the journey back when you can't walk."

"I'm hoping you'll be okay by tomorrow," Jaymes said, standing over them both. "I need to re-dress your wounds for tonight."

Ebony stood up and mumbled something about feeling cold. She fetched a blanket from one of the bags and lay down near the fire, staring out of the cave's entrance. The rain hadn't stopped all day.

She was halfway across the bridge already, and she felt it again. It was like a hand was pushing her forward, urging her on. She took a step—but she hadn't chosen to. She took another, propelled towards the long corridor of archways that she had come to recognise. Was she in a dream or was this reality? The world around her was dark ... it was raining, but from her hair she pulled flakes of ash. She entered the hall of archways and followed it to the very end.

Where was the boy she always followed?

Before her was the edge of a cliff, and below was a bustling city of shadows. She could hear the patter of rain on its cobbled streets. The air was ripe with the dewy petrichor of rainfall.

Ebony!" a voice called. It had come from the city below. It was calling her. It was only one step away—just one step. Somehow, she knew that all the answers she was seeking lay in that shadowy city world. Why did she have colour-changing eyes? Why were her parents killed? Why did the Fae fear the Shadow? This city would give her everything she needed. But she had to make the decision to follow the voice.

"Ebony!" it called again.

With a sharp intake of breath she realised that this was her moment. What had Sam said? Assert your dominance. Take control. *With a deep breath, she stepped over the cliff edge.*

The sky soared past her and her senses screamed. Had she made the wrong choice? The wind pulled at her hair, and her heart was thumping in her throat. She would hit the pavement below and cease to be, she was sure of it. Not daring to look down, she concentrated on the pull of the wind and soared.

Then she landed. Not with a crash as she had expected, but almost as if she had been flying. She alighted on the pavement and gazed open-mouthed at the fortress before her. Tall, pointed turrets reaching high into the sky. A figure walked out of the great black gates that swung open without a sound. It was a boy.

"Welcome, Ebony," Henry said and smiled, his eyes red.

The world around her fell into darkness like a candle had

been blown out, and all that remained was Henry's red eyes.

"Ebony, wake up," a voice said, shaking her shoulder. Ebony grasped Sam's hand as her eyes shot open. They were a dark red, riddled with the colour of fear. "Shh, Ebony, you're waking everyone up."

"I—I took control," she stammered, her heart racing.

"And? Did it work?"

"I made my own choice."

"Good. You'll have control over your nightmares now."

Ebony smiled, but she wasn't quite ready to wake up. His hand on her back was comforting somehow, and her sleepy mind felt calm with him next to her.

Ebony woke with a start. The cave was silent … almost too silent. She could hear snuffling and rustling sounds to her right. She slowly turned her head. There was something in the entrance of the cave, blocking her view of the night sky. A dark shape sniffed at the stony ground, a low rumble echoing through the cave. Without moving, Ebony tried to look around at the others. Hicks was asleep next to a snoring Jaymes.

"Jaymes," Sam whispered from behind her. Jaymes mumbled and rolled over in his sleep. "Jaymes," Sam whispered again.

He groaned and gradually opened his tired eyes. In a flash, he sat upright and froze.

"Where are the others?" Sam whispered. Anna, Kai, and Harris were nowhere to be seen.

"They went hunting," Jaymes whispered.

Sam's foot lightly nudged Ebony's back.

"I'm awake," Ebony said as softly as she could. The wolf had smelled them, its eyes gleaming in the darkness. It growled, the sound rumbling through the cave, louder this time. Hicks jerked awake, his eyes instantly wide with fear. He looked to Ebony, then Jaymes.

"What do we do?" Jaymes whispered.

"My sword won't help much …" Sam replied. "I'd have to get too close."

"Pass me my bow," Ebony breathed.

"Where is it?" Sam asked.

"Propped up against the wall somewhere."

"I see it," Hicks replied, his voice weak. As quietly as he could, he reached over to the bow, then delivered it to Jaymes. He then reached for the quiver, which was less quiet. The bow and arrows slowly made their way around the group as the wolf prowled ever closer, bearing its teeth. Ebony's heart raced as Sam hooked the quiver over her shoulders and placed the bow in her hands. She sat up and tentatively nocked an arrow. A growl so deep it almost shook the cave reverberated through her ears, and the beast lunged. Ebony leapt to her feet and loosed an arrow, barely taking a second to think before loosing another. The wolf whined as it fell to the ground, but it was soon back on its feet.

Jaymes dragged Hicks to the back of the cave as Ebony loosed another arrow, which missed. It was close now—too close. She leapt over the embers of the fire as she unsheathed another arrow and turned on her heel. The beast careered after her, its jaws gnashing, teeth baring. She had one shot left. If she missed, she'd be dead—the others, too. She let loose and the arrow embedded itself in the creature's back leg. It hardly seemed to notice as it raced at her, claws at the ready.

"Ebony!" Hicks cried out.

She whipped a dagger from her boot as the wolf crashed into her, barrelling her towards the hard stone wall. She tripped and fell back, her head colliding with the wall, and a resounding crack echoed through the cave. Arms against the wolf's broad chest, she wrestled its snapping jaws away from her, its stinking breath hot against her face. Just as she thought she was winning, the wolf grew heavier, pinned against her. Sam grabbed its thick neck with one arm and stabbed at its side, over and over. Eventually, its snapping stopped, but the dead weight didn't lift. She gasped for air as Anna appeared beside her, pushing at the beast. Air rushed into Ebony's lungs, and she coughed as she sat upright.

Jaymes rushed up to her, pale as a sheet. "Are you hurt?"

"No," she coughed. "Just winded."

"We need to get out of here," Sam said, blood coating his hands and dagger. "There are probably more nearby."

"There are," Kai said. "We saw them." He and Harris were already putting out the fire and packing their bags. When had they got back?

"You're not gonna take its fur?" Ebony suggested.

"Don't have time. We need to go."

Ebony eyed the wolf beside her. It was a beautiful creature, still breathing shallowly. She reached over to its head and it growled weakly.

"What are you doing?" Kai snapped.

"Giving it a peaceful send off," Ebony replied. Using her forefinger, she traced a circle on the beast's forehead and repeated the Fae words of Death until the wolf's spirit faded away. "Mother, Sister, Daughter of the Forest. We thank you for the circle of life. Take this soul to the second land."

Ebony sighed as the light died in the creature's eyes, and she turned back to her friends. "We can go now."

"You believe in the Fae religion?" Anna asked.

Ebony shrugged. "Nothing else to believe in."

"Will you teach me?"

Ebony looked up at Anna with surprise. She had always been scorned for her choice of faith.

"Yeah, of course." Ebony smiled and held out her hand, which Sam grabbed. He helped her up and embraced her.

"You just saved our lives," he whispered into her ear.

14

Jaymes helped Hicks onto his feet as Ebony and the others prepared to leave the cave. The darkness pressed in from all angles as their eyes grew accustomed to the night. It was the perfect time to slip past the prison undetected, though it would have been easier if Hicks could walk on his own.

"I know another route down to the beach," Harris said and led the group to a steep incline of gorse bushes.

They pushed their way through the prickly hedges and slid down the scree before reaching the larger rocks leading to the sand. The tide was so far out, Ebony could only just see the glistening reflection of the moon on the water. Their feet sank into the sand that stretched before them as they began the walk back to the little wooden hut.

Anna approached Ebony and smiled. "So, explain the Fae religion to me. What exactly do you believe?"

Ebony thought for a moment as she walked,

relishing the feeling of her shoes sinking in the wet sand. "We worship the Mother, the Sister, and the Daughter. The Three. They made the Fae and protected them like children."

"They don't anymore?"

"Well, we believe their spirits can be found in the woods, in nature. We protect ourselves from dark spirits and we thank good spirits for keeping us alive and well."

"So the symbols you draw …"

"They're to invite in the good or protect against the dark. There are so many symbols, even I don't know them all."

"The Fae attacked you and your friends," Kai said, drawing up next to Anna and Ebony. "Why do you still worship their religion?"

"The Three didn't do that. The religion didn't make them do it. A religion and its followers are not one and the same."

"Whatever you say," Kai said. "Either way, we have

to be quiet now." He gave Anna a pointed look. "We can't talk in the tunnels or we'll be overheard and discovered."

"Nice to see you're still your charming self, Kai," Anna snapped and smiled sarcastically.

They reached the wooden hut and, one by one, descended through the trapdoor and padded down the stone steps, along the low passageway, up the rusty ladder, through the hole in the wall, and into the dark cellar. All the while, Anna quizzed Ebony on various aspects of the Fae religion, even asking her to say to Fae words of Grace and Peace.

Jaymes was practically dragging Hicks by this point. They rested for a few minutes in cellar before heading up the steep spiral stairs and continuing back through the attic rooms. They eventually found themselves in the Common Dwellings.

"Do we cross the bridge or take the long way round?" Harris asked. Jaymes sat Hicks down against the wall of a house and collapsed next to him. Dragging a full-grown man through secret passageways was hard work.

"Quickest route possible please," Jaymes said. "Unless Harris could—"

"No." Hicks replied. He was refusing to let any of the others come near him.

"I could help Hicks," Ebony offered.

"No, we need you to be ready with your bow in case anything happens," Sam replied. "We'll have to risk the bridge."

There were no crowds to protect them now. It was likely the Snatchers would be guarding it, but how many? Could they battle their way across? With trepidation, they reached the bridge, hiding in the shadows.

"All together. We run across," Anna suggested. "On the count of three."

Sam counted and they ran, Jaymes dragging Hicks behind them.

"Look out!" Jaymes yelled. Snatchers appeared from the Shadows—Ebony couldn't count how many.

They'd been tipped off, on high alert after their prison had been burnt down. She loosed an arrow and took one down, but another took their place. Swords were drawn, and Kai lifted his daggers, ready to let fly, but there were too many. They were almost surrounded—the only way left to turn was back.

"Sam?" Ebony called. He had defeated this many before and had left unscathed.

"Retreat!" Sam yelled.

Ebony let loose another arrow, then turned on her heel and fled alongside the others. Hicks seemed to have found his legs. With a limp, he ran down the street they had just come from, and they all followed him toward the trees at the end of the road, including a group of Snatchers.

"Keep going!" Ebony shouted and turned to face the oncoming danger.

Sam stopped running and launched himself at the Snatchers, Anna beside him. Ebony let loose arrow after arrow, but in the darkness she could hardly tell if she had hit her mark. With a thunk, Ebony's arrow shot down the last man standing.

"Run! There will be more coming!" They had caused such a ruckus, almost all of the Common Custodians would soon be headed their way. They needed to make themselves scarce. Sam grabbed Anna's arm and pelted into the trees, Ebony in his wake. It didn't take long for them to find the others. Jaymes and Hicks rested against the trunk of a large oak tree, breathing hard, and Harris and Kai were glaring into the darkness, their swords drawn.

"It's just us," Anna said, and the two men stood down, seeing Ebony's bright red eyes lighting up the night. "We should be safe now. Snatchers never come into the woods."

"Guess we're taking the long way round then," Harris said.

Jaymes groaned and scrambled to his feet before offering Hicks a hand. Something whistled past his ear and, with a twang, he looked up to see an arrow embedded in the tree trunk before him.

The Snatchers had entered Rundlewood Forest. The group stared at each other in disbelief.

"Run," Ebony said. "Don't lead them to the wooden village."

"Aren't we near Lake Ava?" Anna asked.

"Bounty Hunter territory," Harris confirmed.

"Maybe the Fae could help us?" Kai said, looking to Ebony with expectation.

"Let's hope it doesn't come to that," Sam replied.

"Meet at the north bridge over the River Ava," Anna said.

Figures began to appear through the trees, running towards them. Ebony nocked an arrow and fired at an approaching Snatcher, who fell with a thud.

"Run. Now!" Harris called, and the group fled.

Ebony fired off as many arrows as she could before Sam grabbed her wrist and ran beside her, sprinting towards Lake Ava. They did their best to put as much distance between themselves and the Bounty Hunters' camp as possible. Who knew what state it was in? The Fae might still be there, claiming their territory.

The trees whipped past them as they rounded the lake and followed the cart tracks through the trees. Ebony doubted the Snatchers would venture so far into the forest—they didn't know it well enough to find their way back. They didn't know the Fae, the lake, the rivers, the bridges. But now that they had crossed the tree line, they would only push further, bit by bit.

Eventually, the wooden bridge came into sight. The others had got there before Sam and Ebony, sitting on the mossy wooden planks and catching their breath.

"I think … we lost them," Anna panted.

Kai sidled up to Ebony. "I might have judged you too soon," he said.

"You think?"

"Today you saved us all from a wolf and you helped

keep the Snatchers away from our village."

"Kai, if I was going to hand you all over to them, I would have done it just now."

"But you didn't," Kai acknowledged.

"No, I didn't. But just so you know, this goes both ways. Now it's your turn to earn *my* trust."

She strode away from him and went to relieve Jaymes of his burden. They made their way over the bridge and set off towards the wooden village. Eventually, Hicks grew too tired to continue and the group agreed to spend the night in the forest, taking it in turns to keep watch.

"I've been here before," Hicks said to Ebony as they watched Harris struggle to light a campfire. They sat on the forest floor, leaning their tired backs against two large tree trunks.

"This is near our rendezvous point, where we used to meet after a loot," Ebony explained.

"Ah yeah," Tusting smiled, but it quickly faded into a frown. "Can't do that anymore."

"I'm sorry, Hicks. I'm sorry you had to get involved at all."

Hicks shrugged. "I knew what you were about. I should have guessed it would reach me in the end."

Ebony's heart twisted painfully. "Get some sleep."

Hicks nodded and rested his head against the hard bark. The night was chilly without the blankets Ebony had grown used to over the winter. She stood up and shook out her arms and legs to stay warm.

"I'm going on a walk," she announced and trudged away before anyone could follow her.

She crossed the little wooden bridge over the River Ava and traipsed towards the lake. An image of the Bounty Hunters' camp wouldn't leave her alone and she needed to set it straight. Smoke, ash, and decay—that was the scene coming to mind. She was too cold to sleep, anyway.

The trees were quiet as she waded through the bluebells. But then she heard it. Laughter. She paused, straining to hear it again. Maybe she had imagined it? A yell and more laughter. She carefully crept towards the sound but soon stopped dead in her tracks. Darrel sat at a campfire, Daya on one side of him and Hunter on the other. Daya looked up and jumped, noticing Ebony's eyes shining through the darkness. Ebony put a finger to her lips.

"What's the matter?" Hunter asked.

Daya tore her gaze away from Ebony. "Nothing, I'm just really sleepy. I'm calling it a night."

Daya stood, then looked straight at Ebony and nodded her head to the left. Ebony circled the camp to find Daya scrambling out from underneath their one tent. She silently led Ebony further into the forest before launching into a hug.

"You're alive!" Daya gasped.

Ebony's jaw dropped. "You don't hate me for setting Sam free?"

Daya scoffed. "Losing Bates' killer pales in comparison to what the Fae did to us. But where have you been?"

Ebony looked at her feet. "You're not gonna like it."

"You've been with Sam," Daya stated.

"How did you know?"

"I watched you go to him every night." Ebony's eyes turned a stormy grey. She thought she had been so discrete. "Nothing slips by me." Daya smiled.

"And Hunter? What's his take on things?"

Daya's smile slipped. "Hunter isn't happy with you."

"He hates me."

"I wouldn't go so far as hate."

"I freed his enemy and then disappeared."

"Well, yeah … to be honest, he's not sure you're still alive. I think it helps him to think you died—it hurts him too much thinking you switched sides …"

"What did he expect?" Ebony snapped, and Daya had to warn her to keep her voice down. "He trapped me in a tent again. He locked Sam in a cage …" Ebony gazed into the dark trees. "I couldn't leave him in there."

"I know. I don't blame you for leaving. But Hunter … he's different now. More paranoid. He won't let us out of his sight."

"How many of you are there?"

"Well, he wouldn't let anyone go on any missions … so a lot of people left. But at the camp there's just Hunter, Darrel, and me. About fourteen of us survived." Ebony could hardly believe the massacre the Fae had caused. "Everyone scattered that night, so it's hard to tell what actually happened. They might just be in hiding." Daya paused. "We tried to go back to camp but the Fae still have it. But Ebony … we found Halsey."

"I know. I saw it happen."

The pair fell silent.

"I'm just so glad to see you alive. But be careful with the Foryx."

"They helped me rescue Hicks."

"Ah. I see."

"Hunter refused."

"Well, I hope Hicks is worth it."

"You should join us. They're good people—"

"I will *never* join the Foryx," Daya spat.

"Sam isn't what you think. He isn't evil."

Daya raised her eyebrows. "We will have to agree to disagree."

"What will you tell Hunter?"

"Nothing. He doesn't need to worry about you, too."

"There's nothing to worry about."

Daya pursed her lips but didn't reply.

"I should get back," Ebony said.

"So should I."

"See you around," Ebony said lamely.

Daya frowned then turned back to her camp. Ebony watched her leave before turning back herself. She'd never be welcomed back as a Bounty Hunter—not while Hunter was in charge. But did she want to be? She could only hope she'd made the right decision.

The wooden village finally came within sight later

the next day. Tusting was given a bed in Jaymes' medical hut as Ebony found her way back to her new den, Sam at her heels.

"How are you feeling?" Sam asked as he got to work on Ebony's campfire.

"Exhausted."

He sat back and admired his work. The fire was crackling merrily and warming their fingertips. Sam took a deep breath. "I expect you have a lot of questions for me." He paused and looked at his feet. "I've got some explaining to do."

Ebony stared into the flames—red hot tongues licking up the side of a barn, the heat, the ash raining from the sky. She didn't want to bring it all up again, but she needed answers. Why was he being so good to her now when only four months ago he had kidnapped her and tied her up in a burning barn? There were two sides to this man.

"I do have a lot of questions," she said with a nod.

"Just ... let me tell my story first. Then you can ask them, okay?" Ebony nodded, and Sam turned his attention to the flames. "When I arrived in the Dwellings, I had nowhere to go," Sam began. He had clearly been planning this conversation for a while. "I joined one of the street gangs—I don't think it exists anymore. Hunter was known amongst the gangs, but the man they feared the most was Everret Anders. They said he'd risen from the dead."

Ebony listened to Sam, not daring to interrupt. At last, she was getting something close to the truth.

"Hunter and Everret were fighting for the same mission, as was my gang. You know, I don't even remember what the mission was now ... but there was so much pressure on me to win it from the Foryx and Bounty Hunters. I managed it ... but not on my own.

"I had to enter a burning building to retrieve a weapon that had been left at a murder scene. The gang wanted to pin the murder on someone else. The fire was so hot I couldn't breathe. I remember falling, wooden beams crashing around me. I crouched in a corner, terrified. But then ... Ebony, I haven't ever told anyone this. You have to promise me you won't say a word."

Ebony looked up at him. "Of course. Thank you for trusting me." Was she actually grateful or did she just want him to keep talking? She shook the thought from her head.

"I have to tell you this so you will understand. I was dying, Ebony. But a hand pulled me up—a hand wreathed in shadow." Ebony shivered but let him continue. "It held the weapon I needed and said I could have it if I joined the Bounty Hunters. I thought I was dreaming or already dead. I shook its hand, striking the deal, and suddenly I was outside the building, the murder weapon in my grasp.

"I handed it in to my gang. Of course, Everret and Hunter soon found out. Everret was angry, but Hunter was so impressed that I'd done it single-handedly that he offered me a place in the Bounty Hunters. I couldn't tell him what had actually happened. He'd think I was mad!" Sam laughed darkly. "I didn't tell a soul. A month later, the Shadow appeared to me when I was on night watch by Lake Ava." He paused and grimaced. "Eyes more red than fire, its figure a swirling mass of shadow. Ebony, it doesn't have a face." He looked at her, fear marring his features.

"I know, I've seen it," she replied.

"Not like I have." He paused and took a deep breath. "When I shook its hand, it ... it attached itself to me somehow. It won't leave me alone." His eyes now had a haunted look in them. "When the Shadow discovered you, when you joined the Bounty Hunters ... I felt its joy. But the feeling was dark and twisted." He gave Ebony an earnest look. "If you're to ever to trust me, you have to know that all it wants is to keep you safe. I don't know why, but the Shadow cares about you."

"It was there when my parents died ... and in the fire that tried to kill my cousin."

"It's been going after your family for years, Ebony.

I've been trying to find out why, but it only ever talks when it wants to. I think Hunter is searching for answers, too."

"It talks?"

"Yeah. A raspy, cold voice … But Ebony, it has looked after me … well, it looks after me when you're around."

"It helped you kill all of Bates' men, didn't it?"

"You've never seen anything move so fast."

"If it's part of you, how do I know it isn't speaking to me now, through you?"

"Oh, you'll know. It was speaking through me when I tied you up in that barn. It *claimed* my mind. I felt that joy again when it discovered your bloodline. It forced me to break into government offices to get that birth certificate, but I'm sure there's more information somewhere. I know it sounds like an excuse and it's really hard to believe … but it wasn't me tying you up in that barn. It wasn't me who left you in the fire." He gave her a pleading look, desperate for her to believe him.

"If it cares about me and wants me safe, why beat me and leave me to die?"

Guilt riddled his features. "I don't know. It never tells me its motives ..." Sam looked at his feet. "It had a plan, but it went wrong. After the fire, when Hunter rescued you, it was so angry. It gave me back my mind but haunted me with twisted images of a burning world. It didn't let me rest until I got you back. I got myself caught by the Hunters to try to get closer to you. Kai knew what was going on—he knows I'm haunted by the Shadow, but he doesn't know why or the full extent of it. He knew I didn't want any Foryx rescuing me." He paused, his eyes filled with the nightmares of the last few months. "The cage didn't help my peace of mind, but the dreams have stopped.

"I'm better at fighting it now. But when I worked with Hunter, the Shadow led my every move. It knew what it wanted from me. It wanted me to spy on Hunter, so I did. It wanted me to help you kill Bates, so I helped. It wanted

Anders dead, so I killed him. He didn't rise from the dead that time." He grimaced. "The Shadow threatened me if I didn't do as it wished. It told me it would harm you. And when I tried to leave you and the Bounty Hunters alone … Suddenly, you're tied up in a barn with a black eye." He shook his head and sighed. "I'm so sorry."

"Why do you care what you—it—did to me?"

"I always cared. From the moment I met you. A feisty girl with colour-changing eyes. How could I *not* care?"

Ebony's cheeks grew hot, and she looked away from him.

"It doesn't have a bargaining chip when you're around, and I've learned how to keep it out of my head."

"And when I'm not around? You can't keep me by your side every second of the day."

"My next challenge is finding a way to get rid of it for good. I don't care how useful it can be. I don't want the darkness whispering in my ear anymore."

The pair fell into an eerie silence, which Ebony finally broke.

"What is it though?" she asked.

"I honestly don't know. It doesn't come from this world."

Ebony didn't reply. She didn't know what to say. The silence that fell between them was eerie and dark; full of questions. They were both in the same boat now. Both just as scared and confused. But why did she feel that she could trust Sam despite knowing that he was *connected* to the Shadow? The darkest, most terrifying nightmare she had ever encountered. She'd hardly let herself think about what she'd seen ... those red eyes, the dark figure ...

She knew he was telling the truth—all of it. She just ... trusted him somehow. But maybe she should run— live alone again? She had managed it before. That would surely be the sensible thing to do. But she had burnt too many bridges already. Could she really live alone forever? Did she want to? Hicks' absence had already left a gaping hole in her life. And if Sam was telling the truth, then the Shadow would torture him for losing her again, and it would be her fault.

"You're wondering whether you should leave, aren't you?" Sam said.

Ebony bit her lower lip and took a deep breath.

"Please don't go, Ebony. I only want to keep you safe. And I can't handle the Shadow's wrath again."

It took her a few moments to answer, a thought forming in her mind.

"I can't live how I would like to live as long as the Snatchers are around," she explained.

"How would you like to live?"

"I want to walk through town without being attacked. Even when I come of age, the Snatchers will never leave me alone. I'm stuck in Rundlewood Forest." Hicks had been right. She was lying to herself if she thought she had freedom. She had *more* freedom without Hunter breathing down her neck, but she wasn't truly free. Not yet. "I'll make a deal with you," she said.

Sam raised his eyebrows. "Go on. I'm listening."

"I'll stay here if you promise to help me take down the Snatchers. For good this time."

"You sure? You didn't seem happy about me burning down the prison."

"They tortured Hicks. I lost him because of them." She looked him square in the eye. "I won't ever be free until the Snatchers are gone."

Sam nodded slowly and pursed his lips. "I could help you. But we'd do it my way."

"What's your way?"

"With a little help from some friends."

"You mean the Shadow?"

"Yes—and no. The Shadow would be a last resort. But I have connections with the gangs in the Common Dwellings. If we worked at it, we could cause an uprising—a mutiny."

"Harris said you had the gangs 'on board'. With

what?"

"Well … I've kind of been planning this rebellion for a while … I was hoping you'd be in on it."

"So you really think we could manage it?"

"It would take a lot more planning, and we'd likely have to forget our morals every so often."

Ebony nodded. "I can do that."

"And we'd need to train you up."

"What? I can fight. I've killed loads of Snatchers."

"You'd need more than just daggers to pull this off. You'd need to practice your swordplay, your bow technique."

"Okay."

"Okay? That's it?"

"I will do whatever it takes to fight for my freedom."

Sam smiled. "Let's start tomorrow, then."

Ebony held out her hand and he shook it. "I'll stick around and train if you help me take down the Snatchers for good."

"It's a deal."

Ebony smiled, ignoring her thudding heart. All she could do was trust her gut that she was making the right decision.

"I need to get back," Sam said and stood up. He gave her a smile before heading back into the trees.

15

Ebony split the next few days between Jaymes' medical hut and setting up her camp. Hicks could walk fine now, but it would be a while still before he was fully back to health. Her gut twisted. It was her fault that he had been hurt in the first place.

Ebony made a spit over her fire and begged for some spare pots from one of the cooks in the village. She cooked stew and made nettle tea. She whittled arrows like Darrel had taught her and set traps in the nearby trees; stake pits, tripwires, feather spear traps. Her new camp very quickly began to feel like a home.

One afternoon, Sam found her sitting by the fire, whittling arrows.

"Are you okay? You've been hiding out here for days," Sam asked as he approached.

"I'm used to living alone."

"Hicks wants to speak to you."

"Why? I only saw him yesterday."

"He wouldn't say. He'll only talk to you or Jaymes."

"Can you blame him? He's a bit out of his depth ... He was framed for murder and tortured for information because of his association with people like us."

"I know. It could take him a while to trust us."

Ebony returned to the wooden village with Sam, who delivered her to the medical hut.

"How are you doing?" Ebony asked Hicks as Jaymes opened the door and let her in. Tusting was sitting upright in his bed. Jaymes nodded at her and smiled as he left the hut, heading home to find Galen.

"I'm okay, physically. I can walk again."

"And mentally?"

Hicks sighed as Ebony perched on the end of the bed.

"Look, it's not that I'm ungrateful for you rescuing me ... I just ... I don't belong here, Ebony."

She could tell he'd been practising that line for a

while. He turned his head away from her, unable to look her in the eye.

"Where else do you have to go? You can't go back to your old job."

"I know."

"So stay with us."

"There's nothing here for me."

"There could be. *I'm* here." She tried to look in his eyes. "We could build a life here. You and me."

Hicks looked at her and smiled sadly. "I can't risk the Snatchers finding me. I can't go through that again," he said, slowly shaking his head.

"You won't have to. You'll be safe in this village. The Snatchers don't know the forest. They won't find us here."

"So we're stuck here?"

Ebony shrugged. "For the time being … But I'm sure the Snatchers will forget you soon enough."

"They know I'm involved with Ebony Wick. I'm

now on their hit list. They're never going to leave us alone."

Ebony looked at her feet. "The Bounty Hunters hate me, and I don't know who to trust … I need you here." Ebony's blue eyes filled with tears.

Hicks reached for her hand and squeezed. "*You're* safe here. *You* could build a life here. Jaymes tells me his partner Galen knew your parents." He paused. "But you and I … we both know it will only ever be one-sided."

"I can change. Just … just give me some time." She gazed at him with pleading eyes.

"I love you, Ebony Wick. But I will never force you to love me back."

"You won't have to force me! I can learn to love you." A tear dropped down her cheek. "You're the only person I trust. Isn't that enough?"

Hicks' took a few deep breaths. "I have to leave this place, Ebony."

"And go where?"

"I've got a cousin somewhere on the Peregrine

Plains. If I could send a letter to him …"

Ebony's chest tightened and she let out a sob. "Please don't go."

"I have to."

Ebony turned away from him and glared at the door. He was the closest she'd ever had to friendship, to family, since Henry had died. She had always taken him for granted. But she knew he was right. What would he do here, really? He would be safer away from the Dwellings, where he could start a new life.

"With the Foryx Clan's help, you could continue being a highwaywoman, you know."

"How? You're my only connection to the port."

"I'm going to tell you something—but you have to keep this information to yourself, okay?" Ebony turned to face him, her brows furrowed. "The Port Master is in charge of all the carts that come in and out of the port," he continued. "I used to get my information from him before giving it to you. He is the man you need to know. Tobias

Riley is his name."

"I can't just waltz up to him and ask him to give me the cart lists."

"I know that. But Riley has a secret. If you know it, you have power over him."

"What kind of secret?"

"I can't say here," Hicks whispered, "In case anyone overhears. Find the safe in my Nan's house—it's behind the painting of a dog—the papers are all there," he said, placing two small keys into Ebony's palm. "The bigger key opens the house."

"Tusting …"

"Once you've read the papers … *then* you could waltz up to him."

Ebony's face grew hot, and she looked away from him. "I can't read."

"Oh. I didn't know. Fine. Take someone you trust who *can* read."

"So if I tell him that I know his secret, he'll just …

give in? He won't try to kill me?"

"You could mention that Tusting Hicks sent you," he replied with a grin.

"Why tell me this? I'm safe here—you said it yourself."

"With power over the Port Master, you could get your life back, earn some money, and get out of here. You were always better off living alone, anyway."

"No, I wasn't," Ebony admitted. "All I had was survival."

Tusting sighed. "I want you to be free of Snatchers and Bounty Hunters."

"So do I. But running from it all won't solve anything."

"Well. You know about the secret now. Do with it as you will."

"Thanks for always looking out for me."

"I've tried my best. But this time I've got to look out for myself."

Ebony nodded slowly and chewed on her lip. "I'll ask Sam if we can find a way to send a message to your cousin," she said.

"Thank you," he replied.

She stood up and opened the door without looking back. "I'll miss you more than you think."

With that, she closed the door and almost walked straight into Sam. He looked into her bloodshot eyes, but she turned away to hide her fresh tears.

"What's wrong?"

"He's leaving," Ebony said with the steeliest voice she could muster.

"Come with me," Sam said softly and led her to the common room and its large fire.

She stood in the entrance to the barn and gave the fire a stern gaze. "I'm fine, Sam. He's made his mind up. Nothing I can do about it now."

"Just sit down."

She reluctantly did as he said, refusing to look him

in the eye. She hated feeling so vulnerable. Weak.

Sam found a blanket and wrapped it around her shoulders. "Where will he go?"

"Peregrine Plains," Ebony mumbled.

"Maybe it's for the best? He'll be safer there."

"I know. I just … I thought after saving him I would get to see him more."

"Do you love him?"

Ebony gave a shaky sigh, and her eyes shone a brilliant turquoise. "No. But he loves me."

"He's hurting, Ebony. He needs to find a new life."

"I know. But he's my only friend."

"Aren't we friends?"

Ebony looked at him, his brown eyes warm and trusting. He hadn't shaved for a while, stubble lining his chiselled jaw. "I hardly know you."

"You don't have to know a person well to be friends with them. And you *will* know me soon enough if you stay here. Anna wants to be your friend. I know Harris isn't good at showing it, but he does too."

"And Kai?"

"He's a bit more suspicious of you."

"I spoke to Daya," Ebony blurted out.

"What? When?" Sam sat upright, his brows furrowed.

"That night in the woods ... I went on a walk and Daya saw me. Don't worry, she's not going to tell Hunter. He thinks I'm dead, by the way, though he knows I set you free. The Bounty Hunters have practically disbanded. There's only four of them left."

"The Fae still have their camp, then?"

"For now, yeah. I don't know if Hunter has a plan to get it back."

"Maybe we should keep an eye on him."

They fell silent as they stared into the fire.

"I'm really sorry, Sam."

"Sorry? About what?"

"You went to all those lengths to rescue Hicks, but

he won't be useful to you when he's gone. For you it was a wasted mission."

Sam leaned back and glared at her with confusion in his eyes. "Is that really what you think of me?"

"What do you mean?"

"You think I saved him for my own selfish gain?"

"I didn't mean it like that …"

"Ebony, the man needed saving, regardless of his usefulness. He's a good guy, and he's on our side, so he was worth saving. Simple as that."

"Well … thank you."

"You're welcome."

"Can you help him get to the Peregrine Plains? He needs to send a message to his cousin."

Sam smiled. "We happen to have a flock of carrier pigeons."

A message was sent to the small village of Henley on the Peregrine Plains, and it didn't take long for it to return with a reply. All too soon, Sam had acquired a horse for Tusting.

Ebony didn't sleep a wink the night before Hicks was to leave the Dwellings for good. She waited till the morning dawned, then persuaded one of the village cooks to help prepare some food for Tusting's journey. It would take a few days for him to reach Henley. Ebony and Marian, the short, stout, plump cook with wild ginger hair, baked a fresh loaf of bread and bottled some berry juice. They carefully wrapped it in some hessian, which they tied closed with rope.

With a heavy heart, Ebony approached the stables, where Hicks was tacking up his horse.

"I brought you something," she mumbled and handed him the small package. He breathed in the warm smell of freshly baked bread and smiled gratefully. "Don't forget me," she whispered, looking at the dusty floor.

Hicks tucked the bread and juice into a pannier that was draped across his horse and held Ebony in a tight embrace. "I couldn't forget you if I tried."

When he let her go, Sam was approaching. The two of them led Hicks and his horse out of the stables and into the trees.

"You know the way?" Sam asked.

"I've done the journey a hundred times."

"Right. Yeah. You're a carriage driver."

"*Was* a carriage driver."

Sam frowned. "Try to avoid the main road. Keep a low profile."

Hicks nodded and mounted his horse. Ebony's chest felt hollow, and she bit back a tear.

"I'll see you again," Hicks promised.

Ebony just nodded, Sam's reassuring hand on her back.

"Safe journey," Sam said.

And with that, Tusting Hicks rode into the trees and away from his birthplace.

Ebony sighed deeply. *Goodbye old friend*. She

turned to Sam.

"What now?" Sam asked.

"I'm going to my camp. I'd like to be alone for a while …"

He looked into her dark eyes—almost black—and frowned. He hated to see her mourning, but it would pass. "You'll be okay?" Sam asked. Ebony nodded. "See you tomorrow, then."

Ebony crossed through the village and over the wooden bridge, towards her camp. She sat staring into her campfire, reminiscing about the good old days with Hicks. The day slipped by, and she crawled into her new bivouac and curled up, listening to the spring wind through the trees. She just wanted to be alone, and she loved the fact that the Foryx all seemed to understand that.

Shadows slithered around her, but they hardly seemed to notice she was there. Where was she? In a town square— the Common Market. But every building and stall had been burnt—blackened and covered in a layer of ash.

Her heart began to race. No! No! I don't want to be here!

She looked up into the dark sky—where was that cliff she had jumped from? Where was the hall of archways? All she could see was sky, no cliffs, hills, or mountains in sight.

A shadow stopped as it passed her and turned to look at her. "Welcome," it said in a raspy whisper.

"No!" Ebony replied.

"No? But you belong here now. You chose to be here."

"No! No I didn't!" Get me out! *she screamed, but the words wouldn't come out of her mouth.* Mother, Daughter, Sister, get me out! Help me! *From across the square she saw a figure—not a dark and shadowy figure ... a solid form with golden hair.*

The scene around her began to drift away like a rug was being pulled from over her eyes. She was in darkness; never-ending darkness, and before her were the orbs, glowing like fire.

"No!" Ebony screamed.

Nobody was there to wake her this time. She had woken herself. The day was dawning and her mind was foggy, but she didn't dare let herself fall into that world again—the Shadowlands, as Sam called it. She had to face the day. She groaned as she climbed out of her bivouac and smiled, watching fairies eating berries by her fire. They had returned to her.

16

Ebony focused on her target, took a deep breath, and threw her dagger at the straw man before her. Straight into the heart. She smiled and went to fetch her weapon.

"You're good, but you're not as good as you think you are," a voice said from behind her. She turned as she retrieved her dagger. Kai held two wooden swords in his hands and offered one to her.

"I hit it where it matters, didn't I?"

"You took your sweet time about it! Can you hit a moving target?"

"I've done it before."

"Can you hit them where it matters?" Kai raised his eyebrows and held out the wooden sword again.

"Why do you want to help me train?"

"If you're going to be one of us—if I have to learn to trust you—then I at least want to know that you can hold your own in a fight."

"I can."

"You can only use arrows when you're at a distance, and daggers are best when you're only fighting one person at a time."

"A dagger is less cumbersome."

"What do you have against swords?"

Ebony huffed in defeat. "Nothing." She might as well learn how to use another weapon.

"Let's get started, then."

Ebony took her surprisingly heavy wooden sword from him and poised, ready to fight.

"Fighting with a sword is different to using a dagger. With a dagger, you need speed. With a sword you need agility. Don't try to strike at me from the front—with a sword and shield I'm too well protected and dangerous. Sidestep to get around my defence—keep nimble, keep fast. Take small steps—you don't want to lose your balance. Balance is key."

"I know all of that," she scowled.

"Fine. Prove it."

Left, right, left, right, their swords parried. She blocked a blow to the head and a stab at the heart, but eventually she had to pause, out of breath. She cried with rage as he hit her leg. "Give me a minute!"

"In a fight you may not have a minute."

She growled as she stood upright again, fighting to keep her sword held up before her. She lunged. With one strike, Kai had her disarmed and in a messy heap on the ground, gasping for breath, the feeling of his boot still prominent on her chest.

"You need to build up your strength. You're spending all your energy just holding up your weapon!" Kai chuckled before helping her back up onto her feet.

"It's bloody heavy," Ebony grumbled.

"This is only a wooden sword. Wait till you get to the real thing."

They sparred non-stop until Ebony refused to get up off the floor yet another time. She spent the rest of the day back at her camp, nursing her bruises with an ointment that Jaymes had given her.

The next day, Ebony and Kai were back in the training arena, working on some foot movements. Next, they moved on to her bow technique. Sam and Anna watched from the sidelines of the training ground as Ebony made light work of her targets.

"Okay, you're better at this than I expected," Kai said.

"A compliment?" Sam said with a smile.

"We need to get you on horseback, though." Kai suggested. "That way, you could work on hitting a moving target.

"Need to learn how to ride a horse first," Ebony replied.

Kai chuckled. "Yes, that would help. But for now, it's time to call it a day," he said, with a playful thump to Ebony's shoulder.

"Thank the Mother," she mumbled.

"We'll get you lifting weights tomorrow," Kai added before collecting Ebony's wooden sword, which she had gratefully discarded on the hard ground.

Ebony sloped towards Sam and Anna.

"Water?" Sam offered, holding out a large tankard.

Ebony grabbed it and tipped the contents over her throbbing head. Sam grinned and went to fetch some more.

"What are those markings on your wrist?" Anna asked as Ebony shook the water from her messy, dark plaits. She gazed down at her hands.

"Oh, um, Fae symbols."

"What are they for?"

"Strength," Ebony laughed. Perhaps she had drawn them wrong? Or maybe nothing could protect her from her own weakness.

"How did you mark your skin like that?"

"Berry juice and wet clay. It's not exactly what the Fae use, I don't think, but it's good enough. The symbols are the most important part."

Anna nodded as if this was already obvious to her, though her expression was curious.

"Why did you decide to practice the Fae religion, not the one you were brought up on?" Ebony looked at Anna with yellow eyes, frowning. "Sorry for all the questions. I'm just interested. I never thought a Dweller could take on the Fae religion."

"I wasn't really brought up with a religion. The Clink only cared about keeping us contained. And the Fae don't seem to mind."

"How do you know, though? They might find it offensive or something."

"I think they would have let me know by now. They've happily joined me saying grace before."

Anna's jaw dropped. "You've met a fairy?"

"Many."

"And they've ... spoken to you?"

"Occasionally." Ebony shrugged. "They're not the

most talkative creatures in the land. And they always speak in riddles …"

"Wow. Though they still attacked you at Lake Ava."

Sam approached with a fresh mug of water, and seeing Ebony's questioning gaze, he said, "I told her what happened."

Ebony nodded slowly. "They didn't actually attack me." She took a large gulp of deliciously cold water. "But they will attack anyone who disrespects them or the forest. They hate Hunter Sparrow."

"Can't have been too happy with you for joining him, then."

Ebony frowned. "The Fae are stuck in their own ways. They don't like changing their minds about things." She paused. "I need to speak to the King and Queen soon. They could have warned me about the attack."

"You don't seem very upset about it," Anna said. Sam gave her a warning look. He knew that Ebony had lost a friend that day. Halsey. She had also lost a home.

Ebony looked Anna square in the eye. "Hunter and his men deserved what they got. They disrespected the Fae religion, despite my warnings."

Anna raised her eyebrows. "Can you teach us how to respect them?"

"I can try." She drank the rest of the water in one gulp. "Any more?" she asked Sam.

"Come with me. See you later, Anna."

The two of them walked away, leaving Anna standing by the sparring grounds.

"Sorry about all her questions," Sam said as they walked.

"I'd rather she asked than stay ignorant. The best way to protect yourself from the wrath of the Fae is simply to respect them."

She followed Sam to the kitchens, where Ebony gulped down another mug of water.

"I want to show you something," Sam said, leading her to the smallest cabin in the village. He opened the door and gestured to her to follow him. Inside was one bed, an old wooden chair, and shelves stacked with books, clothes, and various weapons.

"Is this all yours?" Ebony asked.

He leaned down to get something from under his bed. "I wanted to give you this."

Ebony's heart skipped a beat. In Sam's hands was an intricately carved longbow and a leather quiver full of beautifully crafted arrows.

"Where did you get this?" Ebony whispered.

"I've had it for years, but a bow isn't really my weapon of choice." He handed it to her, and all she could do was gaze at it in awe. "It's yours now."

"But why?"

"Because I want you to have it."

"Why do I deserve this?"

"If today is anything to go by, you're clearly better with a bow than a sword. You deserve it. You saved our lives in the mountains."

"I didn't have a choice."

"You could have run."

Ebony looked up at him, her golden eyes glazed over. "I've never had a gift before."

Sam beamed. "Don't get used to it." He chuckled. "We'll train with it."

"I always wanted to learn how to shoot while on horseback."

"That can be done."

"But I'm kind of ... scared of horses." Her cheeks grew hot.

Sam laughed. "That dream might be tricky then!" He held her shoulders and gazed into her glittering, turquoise eyes. "You'll get better with horses when you know how to control them."

"Thank you," she said so quietly he almost missed it.

He smiled. "Come on, let's get something to eat. You can leave that here for now. We'll have a go with it later."

Ebony carefully placed the bow and quiver on his

bed and turned to leave as her stomach rumbled.

Next to the kitchens was a dining hall, similar to the one in the Bounty Hunters' camp, though this was in a wooden barn, not a large tent. It was warmer, and at the far end a large fire roared. Ebony spied Jaymes leading Galen to a table. She nudged Sam and made a beeline for them. It was time she got to know Galen better.

"Ebony Wick," Galen said. She stopped in her tracks. "I never forget the way someone walks. It is part of their identity."

Ebony slowly sat down beside him. "How are you?" she asked.

"As well as can be expected."

"I'm sorry Jaymes was away longer than anticipated."

"I can manage fine on my own. He's good company though." Ebony looked at Jaymes who shrugged and smiled. "Let's get straight to it, shall we? You're here to ask me about your parents."

Ebony shifted in her seat and the table fell silent. "Maybe I just want to get to know you?"

"An old blind man? I doubt it. It's okay. Go ahead. I'm ready for your questions."

Ebony hardly knew where to start. But she had to be careful. Jaymes and Sam were listening with bated breath like they'd never heard Galen tell a story before.

"Is it true that my mother's eyes also changed colour?"

"I wouldn't know. I'm blind."

"Right. Yes—sorry."

"Some people feared her. Her husband was very protective of her—almost too protective. Your father was a nervous man, always paranoid. Well, with Hunter for a brother, can you blame him?"

"You knew Hunter back then?"

By now, more people had joined their table, the lure of the blind old man and the red-eyed highwaywoman enough to distract them from their day.

"I knew *of* Hunter back then. He was a wayward boy, always with the wrong sort. He and Everret Anders were joined at the hip. After Everret's run-in with death, he changed. Became a better man."

Ebony didn't reply. She'd never met Anders.

"You may not have known Anders, but his legacy lives on." Ebony jumped—it was like Galen was reading her mind. "He formed The Foryx Clan."

"So … he *did* rise from the dead?"

"No. He almost died. His cousin, Alastor Bates, gave it a good try."

"Bates tried to kill him?" Ebony's jaw dropped as Galen nodded. "How do you know this?" she asked.

"I helped rescue Anders. Who do you think taught Jaymes how to heal people?"

Ebony caught Jaymes' eye, whose nod confirmed Galen's story.

"The other day, I didn't tell you something, and I suppose I should have," Galen said. "When Jaymes and I had to leave the city, your father tried to give us shelter, but the Snatchers would have come for him, too. We couldn't be the reason for them coming to his door."

"But the Snatchers only cared about urchins until a few months ago."

"Ah." He pointed his finger at Ebony. "The *Common Custodians* only care about urchins. The Snatchers were everywhere back then, and they didn't just snatch children. Alastor Bates changed that, though. It was about the only good thing he did."

"So where did you go?"

"I fled into the trees. It didn't take me long to stumble upon Everret's new gang. He gave me a home amongst the Foryx Clan."

"What were my parents like?"

"You father was a kind, soft man, but he could be paranoid. Your mother ..." Galen sighed. "The world lost something when she died. She was strong and loyal. She kept your father sane, that's for sure. She wasn't afraid to speak her mind."

Galen fell silent, and the room seemed to wake up. The whole canteen had been listening to his every word. Ebony gazed around at their audience, whose eyes darted from hers as they turned from yellow to hazel. They feared what they didn't know.

"Her eyes may change colour," Galen said to the whole room, "But she doesn't. She can be trusted if you treat her well." With that, Galen reached for his cane and stood up. Jaymes jumped to his feet and helped lead his partner back to their hut.

"You must have made an impression on him," Sam said with awe. "We've all been desperate for his stories, but he refused to say a thing about his past. You're the only person who has managed to get him to speak."

"Ebony Wick?" a voice asked.

Ebony looked over her shoulder to see a boy around her age with brown, floppy hair that needed a good wash. Something about him was oddly familiar.

She'd seen this boy before ... not that long ago.

"You don't remember me, do you?" the boy said. "I saw you last winter in The Cloak and Dagger."

A faint memory came to her mind. "Right, yeah. You were writing in a notebook ..." What did this boy want with her?

The boy smiled. "You still don't remember me."

"What? Yeah I do. In the pub ..."

"What about in The Clink?"

A look of confusion stretched across Ebony's face, and she turned herself around to face him fully.

"You were in The Clink with me?"

"West Bensley?" he said. "Ring a bell?"

Realisation dawned on her. He looked so different now, his hair so much longer. He had filled out and grown tall. She gaped and eventually found her legs. She strode towards him and pulled him in for a tight embrace. The last time she had seen this boy she had been so young and innocent.

"Where did you go after the fire?" she asked him.

"I might ask the same of you."

"How did you wind up here?" She expected he'd be asking the same question. "We have some catching up to do." She turned to Sam, who had been watching the whole interaction, and gave him a reassuring smile. "I'll see you later."

She led West to her camp and sat him down by the fire. As she brewed them steaming mugs of chamomile tea, he told her his story. One of the maids had rescued him from the fire and then taken him in to her own home and raised him as her son.

"You remember Hannah, don't you?" he added.

Ebony smiled. "She and Hilda taught me to cook."

"She essentially became my mother. We were never rich, but we survived."

"I can't believe she's still alive!" Ebony said, beaming. She would like to see that friendly face again.

West stared into the fire with a look of sadness.

"She isn't alive, Ebony. The pox took her."

"Oh." Ebony took a short, sharp breath. Yet another childhood memory taken from her. "I'm so sorry, West."

"That's how I got here. Without a legal guardian anymore, I was back to being an urchin. I'd heard about you on the grapevine, leaving the Dwellings and becoming an outlaw. I figured, if you could, why couldn't I?" He laughed. "I was taken by a gang before I even got to the woods. Lucky they were harbouring the Foryx Clan from the Bounty Hunters at the time!"

"So you've only recently joined them."

"Yep. And I'm happy here, working on the crops near the river. I get to write as much as I like! These people are so interesting ... full of rich stories for me to put in my books."

"You write books?"

"I'm going to be a famous writer one day," he said confidently.

Ebony raised her eyebrows. She couldn't think of

anything more boring and pointless.

"Anyway, how did you get here?" he asked. "I didn't know you'd joined us."

Ebony then told him her story—the bare bones of it. Lived on her own, joined the Bounty Hunters over winter, then betrayed them by rescuing Sam. And here she was, training to be a fighter for the Foryx Clan.

"It's good to see you, Eb," West said with a smile. "But it's getting dark, so I should head back."

"See you around, West."

17

Today was the day. Ebony's heart thumped in her chest and her arms shivered in the cold morning breeze. She took a deep breath and continued applying berry juice and clay to her arms, legs, chest, and forehead. Today, she would use every Fae protection symbol she knew.

Maybe she should back out now? She didn't *have* to do it. But she wanted to. She took a deep breath. She had done it before, so she could do it again.

"Okay. I'm ready," she said as she finished the last symbol, an arrowhead, to protect her from Wind Spirits.

Sam turned to look at her and burst into laughter. "It's only a horse! It's not going to kill you!"

Ebony's skin was covered in Fae protection charms.

"It could buck me off and trample me. I want the Mother, Sister, *and* Daughter to protect me. I'm not ready for this, Sam."

Sam took a step towards Ebony, who was sitting

by her campfire, and placed a hand on her shoulder. "You *are* ready for this. You're a quick learner. And you haven't been bucked off yet."

Ebony shrugged him off and grumbled as she reluctantly stood up. "But this is my first time with a bow."

They had been training her on horseback for weeks. She knew how to ride now and had even managed a canter once or twice, but it was time she learned to use a bow at the same time.

Sam placed a hand on her back and smiled at her, a twinkle in his eye. She didn't shrug him off this time. "I'll be there the whole time. The horse won't hurt you. And you're a very quick learner. I've never seen anyone take to it so quickly."

He drew her close to him and she let out a long breath. He was surprisingly warm and comforting. She wasn't used to such close contact … but she felt drawn to Sam, and this felt right somehow. "You're so brave," he said into her hair. "You've faced your fear of horses and embraced it." With his hands on her shoulders, he looked deep into her eyes. "Some people *never* face their fears."

Ebony looked to her feet as blood rushed to her cheeks. "Yeah, but have you faced your fear?"

"Which one?"

"Your fear of being slower than me."

She laughed and raced away from her camp. She could hear Sam racing to catch up with her as the trees flew by. She launched herself onto the wooden bridge to find Kai on the other side, waiting with two large brown steeds, the reigns held fast in his hands. His brows knitted together as Ebony approached, out of breath, Sam in tow.

"What are those marks on you?" Kai asked.

"Good morning to you, too," Ebony replied.

"But what are they?"

"Fae protection charms."

"Against what?"

"Against dark spirits." Pointing to each clay mark, she explained. "Wind, Earth, Water, Air, Heat, River, Tree—"

"And you think they'll work?" Kai interrupted.

"Well, the Fae seem to think so, and everyone else is scared of the Fae."

Kai shrugged before handing her the reigns to one of the horses. She gingerly accepted them and stood beside the fidgety creature.

Sam swung himself up onto his horse's back, but Ebony needed a leg-up from Kai. She heaved herself into the saddle and tried her best to look confident. She followed Sam into the trees, away from camp.

They spent the first few hours of the morning going over what she had learned already. How to slow down the horse, how to speed him up, how to hold herself, how to use her knees, how to hold the reigns, and how to raise herself in the saddle. This would be vital for aiming her bow, which was slung over her shoulder, along with the quiver.

Deep in the heart of Rundlewood Forest, the

sound of hooves thundered through the undergrowth. A leap, a bound, panting, pounding. With a whoosh, an arrow narrowly missed the horse's mane and thudded with a twang into a large oak tree. The horse careered to a stop, its rider swivelling in her saddle, searching the trees. All Ebony could see was an endless bed of bluebells, stretching through the forest. She lowered the bow in her hands.

Sam!" Ebony yelled. The horse pawed at the forest floor. "Sam," she growled. "You almost hit him!"

"But I didn't, did I?" a voice spoke from the trees.

"You almost hit *me*."

"You need to be able to dodge oncoming attacks," Sam said as his horse stepped into view.

"Let me know how to attack, first! How am I supposed to get any better if you ambush me every time I practice?" Ebony snapped.

Sam grinned. "Keeps you on your toes."

Ebony turned away from him and gazed into the

dappled spring sunlight.

"Keep going. I'll see if I can keep up."

"Fine. But don't … don't be annoying, okay?"

Sam grinned. "Would I?

Ebony raised her eyebrows, then kicked her horse into action. The trees raced towards her, thick and fast, and she was soon galloping again. She raised her bow and nocked an arrow from the quiver strapped to her back. The trees were a blur now, her horse leaping over roots, Ebony ducking under branches.

Ebony slowly stood up, her feet firmly in the stirrups. With a deep breath, she let loose her arrow, which burrowed itself in a tree trunk up ahead. The wrong tree trunk. She almost dropped her bow as she raced past, pulled the arrow loose, and readied herself to shoot again.

"Ebony, stop. Stop!" Sam called from behind her. "STOP!"

Ebony swung her horse around, her face beaming with exhilaration.

"We're about to reach the edge of the forest."

Ebony chuckled. "Oops. Didn't mean to go so far."

"I know you didn't. But you know we can't be seen in the city. Come on, let's go back—slowly."

Ebony's face fell.

"Your horse needs to rest," Sam said. "And so do you."

They trotted alongside each other, back towards the wooden village.

"We should continue with your swordplay," Sam said. "You need to practice your footwork."

Ebony smiled. "Sure."

When they'd returned and brushed down the horses, they sparred until the sky grew dark and their stomachs rumbled. Walking into the food hall, they spotted Anna, Kai, and Harris sitting together.

"Let's eat in peace today," Sam suggested and led Ebony to an empty table in a quiet corner. They were both thoroughly worn out.

"So what's the plan?" Ebony asked.

"What plan?"

"You know, to take down the Snatchers."

"There is no plan yet. You need to keep practising."

"And in the meantime?"

Sam rolled his eyes. "Patience, Ebony. I'll let you know when plans start to form."

"Will you, though?"

He sat back in his chair and stared at her with confusion. "We made a deal."

"I made a deal with Hunter, but he kept me in the dark."

"How many times do I have to tell you? I am not Hunter."

"But—"

"I am not Hunter," Sam reiterated. "I promise I won't ever keep anything from you. You know my darkest secrets."

"I just—"

"I know, you're impatient. We will get your

freedom back, I promise. But it will take time. Now eat up, your dinner is getting cold."

Ebony gazed at her sausage and mash as her stomach rumbled. They spent the next hour discussing their practice sessions and what Ebony could work on to improve.

"You're exhausted," Sam noted as Ebony yawned. "We should get some sleep."

"Walk me back to my camp?" Spring rains poured outside, and the forest floor was slippery with mud. Walking back in the dark over an old bridge didn't appeal.

"You could stay at mine tonight."

Ebony's cheeks grew hot, and she gazed at the far side of the hall, where Harris had just told Anna a particularly funny joke.

"I didn't mean it like that," Sam added. "I could sleep on the floor …"

"No. I'll sleep on the floor."

"No—"

"I sleep on the floor every night, and I have done for years. I can't sleep on bedding."

"Fair enough. So you'll stay at mine?"

She hesitated, grimacing at the thought of her damp and cold bivouac. "Fine. But only because it's raining."

Sam grinned. "Let's go, then."

They quietly left the food hall but paused as they reached the barn doors. The rain was so heavy, they could hardly see the huts before them.

"Ready?" Sam said. "One, two, three!" He grabbed Ebony's hand and launched them both into the driving rain. "Watch it!" Sam called as Ebony nearly landed head-first in a large puddle. Sam caught her and steadied her. "That was close!" He had to yell to be heard over the downpour.

"I'm freezing!" Ebony cried, but as she looked up at the deluge coming from the skies, she couldn't help the beaming smile that reached across her face. Laughter bubbled up from her chest as Sam held her.

They slipped their way to his small hut and barrelled in, slamming the door shut behind them, laughter in their eyes. Sam handed her an old towel to dry herself with, but the rain had soaked her to the skin.

"Here, we'll dry your clothes by the fire tonight," Sam said as he got to work on his wood burning stove.

They were soon huddled together by the warmth of the fire, their sodden clothes draped on the floor before them. Ebony was wearing one of Sam's shirts, which fell past her knees.

"Warmer?" Sam asked. Ebony nodded and smiled at him, her purple eyes shining in the light of Sam's oil lamp. "Your eyes are amazing, you know," Sam said.

"Shut up."

"They are. They're purple now."

"I think they change with my mood."

"I think so too. What mood is purple?"

Ebony thought for a moment. "Comfort." Yes, that

was it. She was comfortable in this small cabin with Sam, warm while the world stormed around them. When was the last time she had felt true comfort like this? They looked at each other, listening to the rain pounding on the roof. Ebony yawned.

"I've got a blanket you can use," Sam said and heaved himself to his feet. He rummaged in a cupboard and returned with a thick wolf-skin blanket that was big enough for the two of them. He draped it across her shoulders and sat down beside her again. She lay down on the floor and offered him half the blanket. It didn't take long for them both to fall asleep by the warmth of the fire.

18

She was in a courtyard—no, a town square. It was the Common Market, but at the same time, it wasn't. Every building and stall had been blackened, covered in a thick layer of ash, like a winter snowfall.

Shadows seemed to slither through her, but they hardly seemed to notice she was there. She was back. Back in the dark realm of the Shadowlands. She could either let the tide take her or do as Sam said—take control. She took one step forward, the motion so light she could be flying. Another step, and another. Before long, she was running through the blackened streets of the Commons, a smile on her face. This place felt like freedom!

She ran to the end of a long alleyway, and before her loomed a tall, dark tower. On the steps leading up to its large doors sat a young boy, feasting on burnt cookies.

"Henry?" she called. She had found the boy again! The only true friend she'd ever had. "Henry!"

He looked up and smiled at her darkly, his eyes a

burning red. Her heart began to race. That wasn't Henry. It was something else, enticing her into the realm of darkness.

I'm not supposed to be here. *The thought rang through her mind like a chime as the child got to his feet and approached.* Get me out! Get me out! *Her voice didn't seem to be working.* Mother, Sister, Daughter, get me out!

The scene around her began to drift away and she was in darkness; never-ending darkness. All that remained were the eyes, like balls of fire.

Ebony bolted upright, trying to catch her breath. She was in a barn surrounded by walls—wooden walls. The image of flames appeared in her mind, and she scrambled backwards, away from the body that lay next to her. She gazed around, her hands shaking. No. Wait. She was in a small room, swathed in a large fur blanket. Not a barn.

"Ebony?" a voice mumbled.

"Where am I?" she asked.

"You're in my hut," Sam replied. "You stayed here last night, remember?"

Ebony's world slowly came back to her, and she took a few deep, steadying breaths. "Right. Yeah. I remember."

She had pulled the blanket off Sam in her attempt to escape. She shuffled back over to him and returned his half to him.

He smiled appreciatively and asked, "You okay?"

"Bad dream," she mumbled.

"Ah. Shadowlands again?" Ebony nodded. "It takes a moment to come back, doesn't it?" She nodded again. "Here, drink some water. You'll feel better." Sam got to his feet and fetched her a glass of water from a barrel outside.

She went to take a sip, but all she could think about was Henry's red eyes. She choked and placed the mug on the floor.

"What did you dream about this time?" Sam asked. He perched on the edge of his bed.

"Henry."

"Who?"

Ebony gazed out of Sam's window, the sky now blue after the storm the night before. "When I was a child, living in The Clink, my best friend was a boy called Henry. We went everywhere together." She smiled ruefully. "But he died in a fire. Our orphanage burnt down … I tried to find him, but I couldn't. That was when I joined the gangs."

"So Henry is in the Shadowlands?"

"I don't know. He has always been in my darkest dreams."

"You saw too much, too young."

She looked at him with dark eyes and shrugged. "I grew up pretty fast, that's for sure."

Ebony shivered. She didn't want to think about it anymore. She turned away from him and went to inspect her clothes, which had mostly dried.

She pulled on her warm trousers and top as a sharp

rapping almost knocked down the door to the hut.

Sam wrenched the door open to find a short, stocky man on his doorstep, who Ebony didn't recognise.

"Harris was recognised in town," the man garbled in a hurry. "The Snatchers said he helped burn down the prison."

He noticed Ebony and raised his eyebrows, then turned back to Sam.

"Good morning, Cooper. Is Harris okay?" Sam asked calmly.

"Yeah, he got out, but it was a close call. He's never even been on their radar before. Why do they think he burnt down the prison?"

"Because he was there when I did it."

The man gaped incredulously. "You burned down the Dwellings Prison?"

"Yep. And I would do it again. The bastards have tortured too many. It was their turn to lose."

The man shook his head and rolled his eyes. "Right.

Well, Harris can't go into town now."

"Plans will have to start today, then."

"What plans?"

"Our plans to take down the Common Custodians. Meet Ebony Wick. She's going to help us."

Cooper's gaze drifted over to Ebony, whose yellow eyes shone out from the darkness of Sam's cabin. He gave her a tentative smile and she smiled sarcastically in return.

"Fetch Anna, Harris, Galen, and Kai. Oh, and Erin. This is a job for her. Tell them to meet us in the common room."

Cooper turned on his heel and Sam turned to Ebony. "You ready?"

"Who's Erin?"

"You'll see."

Together, they walked to the common room, to find Anna, Kai, and Harris already waiting for them in front of the large open fireplace. Galen sat close to the fire and turned his head as they entered.

"What's this about?" Harris asked.

"Wait till Erin gets here."

"We might be here a while," Anna said.

"Erin West? Why is she joining us?" Kai asked.

"Patience," Sam replied. He began pacing the room, waiting for the final member of their team to appear.

"Just tell us already," Anna snapped. "You can fill her in later."

Sam huffed. "Fine. We're going to take down the Common Custodians."

"Finally, a plan I actually agree with," Anna said, dropping down onto one of the sofas.

"I wouldn't have agreed to it before today," Harris added, sitting down beside Anna.

"I'm always up for a rebellion," Kai said, remaining standing.

"Galen, explain to us how the Snatchers organise themselves," Sam said, his expression expectant.

"The Common Custodians," Galen corrected him,

"are ranked according to their length of service," he said slowly, never taking his eyes off the fire. "The longer you work for them, the more authority you are given. The lowest rank are Fours, made up of those in training. Threes are in charge of Fours. Twos are in charge of Threes. The leader is the only One. The Custodians that you tend to encounter on the streets are Twos and Threes.

"So there's a hierarchy," Sam finished for him, as if this explained everything.

Anna, Harris, and Ebony looked nonplussed.

"If there's a hierarchy, they can be taken down," Kai explained.

"But how? There are so many of them … and if we kill their leader, he will just be replaced," Ebony said.

"You've been going about it all wrong," Sam said. "Leaders only have power then they have a task force. Knock out their lackeys and they won't have an army to fight for them."

"You want us to kill that many people?" Anna

gaped.

"We don't have to kill them. Just give them an incentive to disobey their superiors."

"So why am *I* here?" a voice said, making Ebony jump. A slight, skinny girl had appeared beside her. She couldn't have been much older than Ebony, her brown hair in tight cornrows against her head. How had nobody noticed her arrive? "And who's this?" she said, glaring at Ebony.

"This is Ebony Wick," Sam said.

"The Demon in the forest. Your name precedes you." Erin held out her hand, which Ebony shook.

"How do you know me?"

"Who doesn't? The Snatchers have been after you for years. Besides, Hicks never shut up about you."

"You knew Tusting?"

"He was a trusted friend. Shame about his death."

Ebony glanced at Sam, who shot her a warning look. Erin knew Ebony's name but didn't know that

Hicks was still alive? Perhaps he would be safer with fewer people knowing the truth.

"He was a good man," Sam said.

"You still haven't told me why I'm here, Sam," Erin said, tearing her eyes from Ebony and joining the others by the fire.

Sam and Ebony sat down on the remaining sofa. "We need a spy."

"To spy on who?"

"The Common Custodians."

Erin gazed at each member of the group. "Harris is too big and clumsy to be a spy, Kai is a terrible liar, Anna wouldn't have the patience, Galen is too old and blind, and Ebony is number one on the Snatcher hit list. Why can't you do the spying, Sam?"

The group bristled. Erin clearly wasn't a popular member of the Foryx Clan.

"I burnt down the Dwellings Prison. They know my face now."

"I see." Erin hardly seemed phased by this news. "I'll need payment."

"We can get you money."

"Can you? Harris has just lost his job, I hear. No more smithing for you," she said, eyeing the big man.

"Ebony is good at getting money," Sam said. Ebony wasn't sure that was a completely fair assessment, but she kept her mouth shut. "We need you to become a Common Custodian. Infiltrate them, give us inside knowledge. Spread discord amongst them and turn them against their superiors."

"And how am I supposed to do that?"

"Offer them a better alternative. Money, freedom. Get to know them and find out what they want."

"When do I start?"

"As soon as possible. Harris brought in good money to this camp. Ebony and I can't set foot in the Commons. We need the Dwellings back. We need more control or we might as well rejoin the gangs on the streets."

"I'll sign up tomorrow morning. Send Cooper to the docks every morning and I'll get him a message, if there's anything to tell." Erin stood up. "I doubt I'll be seeing any of you for a while. I sure hope not." With that, she slipped out of the barn.

Anna shivered. "I can't stand that girl."

"So what do we do while she becomes our mole?" Kai asked.

"We need money."

"Sam, I'm not *that* good at finding money," Ebony admitted. "That's one of the reasons why I joined the Bounty Hunters. They gave me bugger all in the end … I haven't earned a penny in *months*."

"We'll find a way. In the meantime, to help Erin, we need to find out who's who in the Snatchers so she can target the most influential of them. Galen?"

"Couldn't say, I'm afraid. Command changes so quickly, I expect everyone I knew is gone. Or dead. You need the list."

"What list?" Ebony asked.

"When you sign up, you are added to the list of Custodians and assigned your rank. The list will give you everyone's names and roles."

"How do we get the list?" Sam asked.

"You tell me. It's stored in the Government Headquarters in the South Dwellings. Alastor Bates used to keep it under lock and key in his office. Can't tell you where it's kept now, I'm afraid."

"So we have to break into the Government Headquarters?" Sam said as if it was that straightforward.

"Not so easy," Galen said. "Guards everywhere and complex locks. You'll need someone better than Ebony to get you in." Ebony looked affronted but didn't reply. "I'm sure you're a fine lock pick, my girl, but you need a professional."

The group felt silent. The task felt close to impossible.

"Erin will find the information on her own—just

give her some time," Kai said.

Sam nodded with a grimace. "She will have to do. Stealing the list … it's too risky."

"So we'll wait for news from Erin," Anna said with a shrug.

The group seemed to collectively sigh. None of them liked sitting around, waiting for answers, Ebony included.

Anna and Harris got to their feet. "We'll have a think about how to bring in money," Anna said, before heading out of the barn.

"Sam." Ebony tugged at his arm, stopping him from leaving the barn with the others.

"You alright?"

"I need to tell you something." He raised his eyebrows. "Somewhere private. Come to my camp."

Sam eyed her up and down, his brows furrowed. "Okay." He wandered out of the barn, Ebony on his heels. "We'll make plans later today," he said to the group before he and Ebony made their way over the small bridge, towards the seclusion of her camp.

"What is it?" he asked when they were sure they were out of earshot.

"I might have a way for us to earn some money."

He beamed. "Do tell."

"Before Tusting left, he told me something … a way to get the Port Master under our control. Tobias Riley is the man who gave Hicks all the information about carts and their cargo."

"I know Tobias. Not a nice man."

"He has a secret," Ebony blurted out. "Hicks used it to get information from him."

Sam's eyes widened. "A secret? So Riley *doesn't* have a perfectly clean slate. What is it? What is he hiding?"

"Well …" Ebony looked to her feet. "I don't know what the secret is, but Hicks said it's kept in his safe."

"And where is his safe?"

"In a house."

Sam gave Ebony an expectant look, waiting for her to give more information. "That isn't much to go on."

"I know where the house is," she added.

"That's a start. But how do we get into the safe?"

"Hicks gave me the key."

"He always was a good man," Sam said with a grin.

"He told me to keep the secret to myself. He wanted me to use it for … something else, not this." Ebony looked away from him, into the surrounding trees. What would Hicks say about their plan?

"The secret is yours now to do with as you please."

She turned to him with a look of defiance. "I don't want to tell the others. They don't need to know how we get our information, only that we're bringing in money."

"Agreed."

Ebony paused. "Erin thinks Hicks is dead."

"Best keep it that way."

19

Spring was growing warmer by the day. Ebony could smell summer in the air—the smell of change. Summer was her least favourite time of year. *Clammy and sweaty* she thought to herself with a grimace as she cooked over her campfire. She had promised Sam a bowl of her infamous stew. In the summer, she could never find enough clean water to drink. But this time it would be different. The wooden village had everything she needed, and its Foryx inhabitants actually treated her well. They respected her abilities, they helped her train, they gave her responsibilities. Summer would be much easier for her this year.

A figure appeared through the trees, making its way towards her.

"Good timing," she said as Sam approached. "Food is ready."

"Smells great," he said with a grin as she ladled it

into bowls that the kitchens had generously given her. "What's in it?"

"Potatoes, rabbit, various vegetables, and herbs I found growing nearby. Might want to wait a minute till it's cooled down a bit. You know, I used to live off stew when I was on my own. I haven't had it for ages."

"Do you miss it?" he asked before blowing at his bowl to cool it down.

"The stew?"

"No, living and working on your own."

"Yes and no. I did when I was living by Lake Ava. But back then, life was all about survival. I couldn't really think beyond that. You're helping me achieve other goals than just staying alive."

"About that. We've had a message come through from Erin," he said. "This stew is really good, by the way," he added.

"Thanks! It's my specialty," Ebony replied with a grin. "What did Erin say? It's been about a week since she joined up."

"Apparently she won't have to work very hard at sowing discord amongst the Snatchers. Ever since Bates' brother took over, their pay has been cut and their workload doubled. There are a lot of unhappy rumblings already."

"That's good, isn't it?"

"Well, it makes Erin's job easier, but she's suspicious. It shouldn't have been so easy …" Sam shrugged. "She said we'll win them to our side if we can offer them higher salaries. They could work for us instead."

"What are their salaries now?"

"I don't know. But that list would probably tell us …"

"It's too dangerous, Sam. Breaking into the prison is one thing … but the Government Headquarters is something else entirely. We don't want to catch the attention of the Southerners."

"I know. I agree. Too dangerous. We'll have to find another way."

"We need to know the secret that Hicks told me

about."

"Let's finish our lunch and then head into town."

"We need to be careful … we're public enemies numbers one and two."

"It's always busiest at this time of day. If we wear hoods, we can go unseen."

"We'll need weapons in case the Snatchers recognise us."

"Bring your dagger."

With a smile, Ebony waggled an ankle, the hilt of her dagger just showing over the top of her boot.

"Sometimes I forget how dangerous you are," Sam said.

"Because I'm a girl?"

"Because you're so young."

Ebony scoffed. "You're not much older than me. I don't actually know how old I am. We might be the same age."

They laughed and finished their bowls of broth.

Ebony ducked into her den to fetch her cloak, a few more daggers, and her new bow and arrow.

"Ready?" Sam asked, and she nodded. They stopped off at Sam's hut to fetch his own cloak and weapons. When they were kitted up, they started the trek towards the Dwellings, winding their way through the trees and listening to the birds sing happily in the canopy above. As the city came into sight, they avoided the bridge into the Commons and instead walked along the busy promenade beside Rundlewood River, which was lined with shops and eateries. As expected, on a sunny day like this, the riverside was teaming with people. They blended into the crowd so easily, they almost lost each other once or twice.

Ebony fought her way through the crowds, trying to keep up with Sam. They were heading for the bridge that led into the port. She couldn't see Sam's brown hood anywhere in the sea of heads. She spun around on tiptoes, but he had disappeared. *Keep going. I'll find him at the bridge*, she told herself. As she turned back, she walked straight into someone in a red cloak that covered most of her face. Ebony mumbled an apology and stepped out of the woman's path, but a hand shot out of the red sleeve and grabbed Ebony's wrist.

"Ebony Wick," a female voice said from under the hood. Ebony stared, her heart racing. Was it a Snatcher? She mentally prepared herself to grab the dagger from her boot. But the hand let go and the red robe disappeared into the crowd.

A hand touched Ebony's shoulder and she jumped. "Where have you been? I lost you," Sam said in her ear. Ebony heaved a sigh of relief.

"Come on, I need to get out of this crowd."

Ebony latched onto Sam's hand and almost dragged him through the sea of people. At last the bridge was in sight. Once across, they turned into a dark alleyway. Ebony leaned her back against a brick wall, her heart thumping erratically.

"What's the matter?"

"Nothing," Ebony replied. "I just thought … Doesn't matter. This way."

She led Sam down a series of alleyways. If she could find one specific alleyway, she would know the way. Each path looked almost identical to the last.

"Be careful," she said as they walked. "Some of the gangs live on these streets."

"I know. But it doesn't matter if they see us, right? We're not in their way."

"Well … The Jades don't like me much. I was supposed to give them Bounty Hunter secrets."

"And you didn't?"

"I avoided them all winter. Hunter never gave me any secrets to tell, anyway."

"Why didn't you tell them that then?"

"I tried. They didn't believe me."

"So we're avoiding the Jade Gang as well as the Snatchers. Great."

"Sorry. I told you I was public enemy number one."

She stopped in her tracks. There it was. She was sure of it. Quickening her pace, she led Sam down one last alleyway and stopped outside a door. Tusting's family home. She pulled the keys out of her pocket and approached the front door—but there was something wrong. The door was ajar.

"Someone broke in," she said, observing the broken lock. "They must have kicked the door open."

Sam put a finger to his lips and entered the house before her, his hand on the hilt of the sword sheathed in his belt. Ebony mentally checked where her weapons were hidden about her person, then stepped inside. The house was cold and very dusty. Other than that, it looked just like it had before. Untouched.

"Where's the safe?" Sam whispered.

"Behind a painting of a dog."

"Which room?"

Ebony gave him a dazed look and a sheepish smile. She had no clue. They crept from room to room, expecting to be ambushed at every turn. At last, Ebony spotted it—a little black dog sleeping on an armchair. The painting was amazingly lifelike. She fetched Sam from the next room, and they approached the painting together. She leaned forward and carefully took the painting off the wall, lying it on the floor beside her. There was a small door set into the wall, still locked. She produced the key and heard the lock click, and the little door swung open. Inside was a large envelope sealed with wax.

"Don't move," a voice growled. She'd heard it somewhere before.

"Ebony..." Sam said.

She slowly turned to see a dagger at Sam's throat, a hooded man behind him.

"Put your bow on the floor," the man said.

Ebony did as she was told. Whoever this was, he clearly didn't know her very well. Did he really think they were the only weapons she had on her?

He pushed Sam forward and instructed him to

fetch the envelope from the safe and hand it over. Ebony reached into her boot, and, in seconds, the dagger was at the man's throat. An elbow slammed into Ebony's stomach, and she staggered backwards, her dagger clattering to the ground.

"I should have known," the man said, turning around, the envelope in his hand and his dagger still at Sam's throat. "Ebony Wick always has a trick up her sleeve."

"How do you know who I am?"

"Don't you remember me?"

She remembered the voice …

"Hand over the envelope," she snapped.

"You know, I think we could make a deal."

Ebony raised her eyebrows but took a step back. The man pulled down his hood and she scowled. The last time she had seen him, he had purposefully destroyed a fairy ring.

"You brought the Fae to the camp, Rynn," she spat, saying his name like it was a swear word. "You caused the attack by disrespecting them. Halsey's blood is on your hands."

"You remember me now."

She scowled.

"We need those documents," Sam said.

"So do I. But there's something else I need more. If you get it for me, I'd be willing to trade."

"Do you even know what's in the envelope?" Ebony pointed at the files clutched in Rynn's hand.

Rynn shrugged. "Job's a job. But my other job will pay me more, and I'd much rather not do it myself."

Ebony glowered. "What's the other job?"

"I need something from the Government Headquarters."

"What is it?" Sam demanded.

Rynn pushed the dagger into Sam's throat, drawing a trickle of blood. "I need a piece of paper … it lists everyone working for the Common Custodians."

Ebony's heart sank and she glanced at Sam, whose

eyes betrayed his thoughts. Who else wanted that list? Who else knew that the Port Master had a secret? Hicks hadn't been as discrete as he had thought. Maybe Erin's suspicions were right ... something else was at play.

"I'll give you this envelope if you get me that list."

"Break into the Government Headquarters? Are you kidding me? That's a whole mission."

"I know where you're living, and I'm sure Hunter would love to find out, too."

How does he know so much? Or is he bluffing? He was a Bounty Hunter, after all. Information was their trade.

Ebony growled. "I've always hated you, Rynn."

"I know," he said, crossing his arms, a smug look on his face. "Meet here in three days—"

"You're only giving us three days?"

"It shouldn't take any longer, unless you get caught."

"Fine. But you can't open the envelope. I'll know if you did because the seal with be broken."

"Deal. Now then, I'm going to step out of the door …" he said, pulling Sam with him to the entrance. "And when I let Samuel Sanker go, you're not going to try to kill me, agreed? Otherwise, all deals are off. My friends know where you live, and they will attack if I don't return."

Who were his friends? Was he no longer a Bounty Hunter? Ebony gritted her teeth and nodded. She watched the envelope leave Hicks' house, her stomach in knots.

"Why does he want the list?" Sam asked as soon as Rynn had disappeared. "What use does Hunter have for it? He never wanted to take down the Custodians."

"I don't think Rynn is working for Hunter anymore."

"So who *is* he working for? And what do they want?"

"Only the Mother knows."

"I guess we're breaking into the Government Headquarters, then," Sam said with a frown.

With one eyebrow raised, Ebony said, "Let's try not

to burn down the entire building this time."

Sam grinned sheepishly. They left the house, pushing the door closed behind them. The key was useless now that the lock had been broken.

20

"Damn, damn, damn," Harris swore when they filled him in later that day, huddled around Ebony's lit campfire. Kai stared into the flames as Anna sharpened her sword with a whetstone. "This isn't going to be easy, Ebony."

"I know, but we really need that envelope."

"What's in it?" Anna asked.

Ebony sighed. "I don't know. But Hicks said it would help us."

"*How* will it help us?"

Ebony didn't reply, she just stared at her feet and kicked at a stone on the ground.

"It doesn't matter what's in it," Sam replied for her. "All that matters is that we need it if we're going to take down the Snatchers. It will help us get some money together."

"But to get it, we have to get that ruddy list for a Bounty Hunter," Harris clarified. "And we don't even know what *he* wants it for."

"We could waste so much time trying to guess the motives of someone as slippery as Rynn," Sam said. "Let's just focus on our plan."

"We could make a copy of the list," Ebony suggested. "That way we get both things."

Harris nodded. "As Galen said, we'll need a damn fine lock picker."

Sam sighed. "Jackson."

Kai nodded.

"I wouldn't trust Jackson as far as I could throw him," Harris said.

"I don't think we have a choice," Sam replied.

"Neither do I. I'll scout out the government building," Kai said.

"I'll find Jackson," Anna said. "He listens to me."

"I'll gather supplies," Harris said, and the three of them disappeared into the trees.

Ebony stared into the flames. "I've never been into

the South Dwellings."

They left the next night. Anna, Kai, Harris, Sam, and Ebony. They only had three days to get the list and a whole day had already gone. Ebony was wearing a newly made dark outfit that Sam had commissioned from a tailor in town. The material was thick and warm. The knees and elbows were padded with black leather, and there were so many secret pockets, she was worried she might actually lose her hidden daggers. Jackson hadn't turned up when they'd agreed to meet, but Anna assured them that he'd be able to catch up before they reached the South Dwellings, which wasn't even an hour's walk from the wooden village.

She was right. Standing at the edge of the tree line was the silhouette of a large figure, his hair billowing in the evening wind.

Anna rolled her eyes and whispered to Ebony, "He thinks he was birthed by the Mother."

Ebony smiled, appreciating Anna's attempt at referring to the Fae religion.

"Good evening, comrades," Jackson greeted them with a large grin.

"Look who decided to show up," Harris said, walking straight past the big man. Jackson and Harris were almost the same size.

"What devilry do we have planned today?"

"Shut up, Jackson. You know what the plan is; I filled you in yesterday," Anna snapped.

"And where is the Demon you promised me?" Anna looked at Ebony with an apologetic look. "Her eyes are yellow, not red. How disappointing."

"If you call me disappointing again, they might *turn* red."

"Aah. So the eyes change colour according to mood?"

Ebony shrugged. "You know as much about it as I do."

"Never thought to seek the truth about it?"

Of course I have, you moron. "I've had other things on my mind," Ebony replied.

"Like breaking into a government building and stealing secret documents?"

"Be quiet, Jackson," Anna snapped. "Let's go."

Jackson seemed unusually interested in Ebony and kept watching her as if waiting for her eyes to change colour. He almost jumped when they did; curious yellow to irritated orange. They entered the South Dwellings by following the coastline. There were few beaches at this end of the Dwellings, only cliff edges and shingle. The South was full of tall, red brick office buildings, designed for rich, important people to do expensive, important things. But the building they were heading for was designed to 'keep the city running'. In single file, they walked down a dark alleyway, flanked by imposingly tall walls, the ends of which opened out into a large courtyard, the floor decorated with a huge mosaic. In the darkness, Ebony couldn't make out what it was depicting, but she supposed it had been designed to be viewed by those working at the tops of the tall buildings, not those walking across it. In the middle of the square was a glistening, large, ornate fountain that looked as if it was made of pure gold, depicting some kind of sea monster embracing a human figure. Ebony grimaced. How could the Southerners have pure gold statues sitting around while the Commoners starved?

Before them stood the Government Headquarters. Ebony thought it looked like a palace lined with cloisters, the walls adorned with rich, green ivy. The main door was huge—the biggest Ebony had ever seen. It was unguarded, so Ebony figured it was rarely used. Kai had told them the best route in and out, which was through a much smaller door, currently manned by two guards dressed in silver armour and red cloaks.

Ebony knelt down, Kai behind her and the others in a long line behind him. She wielded her bow and nocked an arrow, aiming for one of the guards on the other side of the courtyard.

"Remember what I taught you," Kai said quietly into her ear. "Take a deep breath in and a breath out upon release. Take your time aiming, and aim for the gaps in their armour. You can do this, Ebony." He stood back and let her focus.

Seconds later, they heard a cry and thump from the other side of the courtyard, then another. Ebony had taken them both down. Her hands shook as she lowered her bow. She hated killing, but sometimes it was necessary.

"I'll see you in a bit," Kai said and flitted into the shadows along the edge of the courtyard. He was to stay on the outside to help them escape should anything go wrong. He and Sam were particularly adept at distractions.

The rest of the group sneaked towards the smaller door, which was open, and filed into the headquarters.

"So, we're in. Now what?" Anna whispered.

"Now Ebony and Jackson work their magic," Sam

explained. "We'll follow."

Ebony had been briefed on this part of the plan and held a map in her hand that Jaymes had drawn on parchment for her. It showed which door they needed and how to find it. "Stay close," she whispered to Jackson. Pulling a dagger out of a hidden pocket in her dark outfit, she stealthily slid round each corner. The Headquarters was made up of long, wide corridors, adorned with marble and stone statues. The floors were mosaics and the ceilings were decorated with gold leaf. Ebony did her best to ignore the sickening opulence of it all and continued tiptoeing round corners. There were surprisingly few guards inside, but there were some stationed in front of rounded, dark brown doors. Ebony spared as many as she could, knocking them out with the hilt of her blade, but some fought back. She had no choice but to slit their throats. She made light work of it, helped by her recent bouts of training with Kai.

Jackson followed in her wake and grinned when

she nodded at him, her eyes a burning red. At last, they had reached the right corridor, which had only one guard in red: a Snatcher. Ebony's lip curled. This was the door they needed Jackson to break into.

Ebony brazenly walked out into the corridor and smiled at the Snatcher. "Good evening," she said.

He gasped as he saw her red, glowing eyes and genuinely looked scared. She wouldn't kill this one. She wanted him to send a message. Before he had time to react, she had him in a choke hold.

"The Demon has come for you," she said before thwacking his head against the cold, stone wall. He dropped to the floor like a rag doll. She only hoped she hadn't accidentally killed him.

Jackson rushed up the hallway and instantly got to work on the door. The others appeared behind him, expressions of awe on their faces.

"Don't want to get on *your* bad side," Harris said to Ebony with a light chuckle.

Time dragged by as Jackson worked on the lock.

"How much longer?" Sam whispered.

"I don't know. Stop interrupting me," Jackson snapped. "It's a bloody complicated lock."

"Galen was right," Anna said.

"Just keep watching out for more guards and shut up," Jackson replied.

At last, Ebony heard the tell-tale *click*, and the wooden door swung open, revealing a mess of an office, papers piled high and strewn over every surface.

"Now what?" Anna asked.

"Now we look," Sam said and began rifling through a pile of papers.

"What does it look like?"

"I don't know. A list of names, I guess," Sam said.

They each chose a corner of the room, checking every piece of paper they could find. To Ebony, the papers only showed scribbled markings—instead, she busied herself with picking the locks of the desk. She pulled out a thick wad of paper from a desk drawer and put it on the floor beside her, searching for anything else that might be useful. A secret compartment perhaps?

"What've you got there?" Jackson asked, bending down to look at the papers by Ebony's feet. "Seems to be a list of Bounty Hunters. Oh, look ... Ebony Wick." He began rattling off names. "Samuel Sanker, Harris Baker, Darrel Smith, Huntington Sparrow Price ... well, isn't that a stupid name!"

"Wait, what?" Ebony grabbed the paper from him and stared at the odd marks on the page. "Sam ..."

Sam was busy rifling through a desk drawer but turned to her and stood, seeing confusion in her brown eyes. She handed the paper to him.

"Huntington Sparrow Price?" Sam read out loud. They looked at each other, a silent conversation passing between them. Hunter was a Wick. How had the Snatchers got that wrong? Or maybe Hunter had changed his name?

"Hey, you lot, I think this is it," Kai said, interrupting

Ebony's train of thought.

Sam tucked the list of Bounty Hunters into a pocket and the group gathered around the wad of paper in Kai's hands.

"Look at the top of the page," Sam said, pointing at something else Ebony couldn't decipher. They all nodded, but Ebony's brows furrowed. "This is it, Ebony," he said, looking at her. "It even lists their salaries." He took the papers from Kai and began looking through them. "Look, there's Erin," he said. "It says 'Four' by her name. Her rank, I guess."

"That doesn't say Erin," Jackson said.

"Rene Wist is her spy name," Sam explained.

"What are we waiting for, then?" Jackson said. "Let's get our asses out of here."

At that moment, Ebony heard shouting outside the room. Her eyes flashed between grey and red; Jackson could hardly take his gaze off her. "They must have heard us … or one of the guards woke up and got help."

"How many are there?" Ebony asked.

"Four, I think … five? Looks like we're going to have to fight our way out," Jackson said, peering through the door.

"That's what *we're* here for," Sam said, gesturing at himself, Anna, and Harris. He folded the papers and tucked them into a pocket. "Ready?"

The three of them nodded and charged out into the corridor.

Ebony looked to Jackson, who seemed only too ready to join the fray. "Ready, Demon?" he said with a grin.

"I'm not the Demon," she snapped, but she was too late. He was already out in the corridor, fighting with one of the guards.

Ebony took a deep breath and opened the door. She wielded her bow and aimed an arrow at a guard, but it was too difficult to shoot without hitting one of her teammates, who were steadily fighting their way to the other end of the corridor. She'd have to make a run for it to keep up with them. She pulled the dagger out of her boot and weaved her way through the melee, leaping, diving, somersaulting, slashing—before she knew it, she had fought through the throng and was running down the corridor with the others.

A sharp pain pierced behind her knees, and she yelled, skittering to the ground. Sam grabbed her hand and yanked her to her feet, almost dragging her down the corridors, leaving Jackson and Anna to keep the guards at bay. She chanced a brief glance behind her and felt dizzy when she saw a long arrow sticking out of her leg. The guards weren't far behind, but Sam whisked them round corner after corner. Ebony had her bow in her hands once more, shooting any guards she could see coming at them.

"Pull it out!" she yelled at Sam. "It hurts!"

"Pulling it out will do more damage," he said, dragging her down a short flight of steps.

"I can't walk with an arrow in my leg!"

"You have to!"

At last, they reached the door they had come in through. They barrelled out of it and legged it across the dark courtyard, where they found Kai waiting in the shadows. Sam launched Ebony towards him, who stumbled into Kai's arms.

"Now?" Kai asked.

"Not yet! Anna and Jackson are still in there." Sam turned on his heel and headed back in.

"What happened?" Kai asked Ebony.

"We found the list, but then the guards came. We almost escaped … then I was shot. Anna and Jackson stayed back while Sam dragged me out …"

Anna and Jackson emerged from the door, bloody and out of breath, and launched themselves across the courtyard. A cry echoed through the square and Ebony heard a thud.

"No!" Anna yelled. She doubled back and stooped down over Jackon's lifeless body as a guard came charging towards her.

Ebony drew her bow while leaning against Kai, who yelled, "Run, Anna! Leave him!"

The arrow left her bow and the guard collapsed beside Jackson as Anna hurtled towards Ebony, her blonde hair streaked with blood.

"He's dead," Anna panted. "Jackson's gone."

"Where's Sam?" Ebony's heart raced. He was supposed to come out with them.

"He'll be out in a minute," Kai reassured her.

Ebony closed her eyes—she wanted to sit, lie down, anything but stand. She wanted to sleep—her head was growing so heavy.

"You're losing a lot of blood, Ebony," Harris said.

"We need to get her to Jaymes," Anna added.

"No. Not until Sam is out," Ebony replied, praying to the Mother to see him emerge from that door.

Ebony felt a *whoosh* and a burst of heat. She opened her eyes to see a circular wall of flames. She yelled and tried to back away, but Kai held her still. The flames seemed to part before her, like flickering doors, and Sam walked through them, his face gaunt and pale.

"We need to go now," Kai said quietly and led her down the alleyway.

Her leg throbbed painfully, and she could feel the arrow digging deeper into her flesh. Any weight on her leg made her knees buckle. She gritted her teeth and tried her best not to yell. They'd got the list and Sam was safe. That was all that mattered.

"I want to see if Sam's okay," she said feebly.

"No, you don't. Not right now."

"Why not?"

"He isn't safe right now. How do you think he walked through that flame?" Ebony wasn't sure if she'd imagined what she'd seen—was it some kind of feverish side-effect of the wound? "He's channelling the Shadow, Ebony. He needs to take some time to come back to himself."

Ebony took a shaky breath. "Does that mean all

those guards …"

"They're probably dead, yes."

"—I tried my best not to kill them …"

"You needn't have bothered."

"But how did the flame … where did it come from?" The world began to swirl around her, and she started to wonder whether she was walking forwards or backwards; both hurt just as much.

"I lined the square with flammable oil," Kai's faded voice said from somewhere far away.

A gentle rocking woke Ebony. She was lying down, but she wasn't very comfortable. She was in someone's arms. She slowly opened her eyes and saw Kai's chin. He was saying something. Then he handed her over to a different pair of arms. Jaymes looked at her with an expression full of worry. He carried her somewhere, and then the world went soft. So soft. She lay on a cloud and could feel clouds on her fingers. But her lower half felt like someone had ripped into her flesh with claws. Jaymes pushed something into her mouth and then poured something cold down her throat. She choked, but slowly, the pain disappeared and the world fell away around her.

21

Everything was dark and blurry and there was pain—but where? Something was hurting. Ebony blinked, but her vision didn't get any clearer. Where was she? She heard footsteps outside, and a bright light blinded her, despite her arm covering her face.

"Ebony?"

She let out a long breath. She was safe. The bright light disappeared, and she was shrouded in darkness once more, but someone was beside her.

"How are you feeling?" Sam asked.

How was she feeling? She was alive and breathing. She was warm, under a thick fur blanket, and she was comfortable. But there was a dull ache in her right leg—her calf.

"Ebony? How are you?" he asked again.

"Um …" she croaked. "I'm okay."

"You had an arrow in your leg. You're *not* okay."

Memories came flooding back to her—the fire, the guards, the list, Jackson's lifeless body, and that searing pain.

"Oh, yeah."

Sam chuckled. "Jaymes said you'd be out of it for a while. He gave you something to dull the pain."

"How are you?" Ebony croaked.

"Me? I'm fine. It's you I'm worried about."

"But the fire—Kai said the Shadow …" What had Kai said? She shook her head. Her thoughts were so muddled and sentences wouldn't form in her mind.

"I've got something to show you. But maybe I should come back later?"

Ebony tried to tell him to stay, but the words wouldn't form on her lips as she slipped back into darkness. Her dreams were fitful—Henry running through blackened streets, Sam walking through fire, archways, long corridors, and the eyes that would never leave her, no matter how hard she tried to forget them.

When she woke again, Jaymes was next to her, rummaging through his cupboards. She grunted and he turned, then knelt down beside her. "How are you?"

"Where am I?" she asked.

"You're in my medical hut."

"Why is it so dark?"

"I covered the windows so the light wouldn't get in and wake you up. You needed sleep."

"How long have I been in here?"

"A few days."

Days? She had been sleeping for *days*?

But the list ... The Bounty Hunter ... They'd missed the deadline. She tried to sit up on her elbows, but Jaymes pushed her back down.

"Don't worry. Sam took care of it," he said. "I'll find him."

With that, he left her in the dark, alone once more. Her mind felt clearer now. The door opened again and Sam strode in. He perched on the end of her bed, careful not to touch her leg.

"How are you feeling?"

"You keep asking me that."

"I want to know that you're okay."

"My leg hurts, but otherwise I'm okay. But Sam, we were supposed to get the list back from Rynn."

"We did."

"What? When?"

"Kai made a copy of it as soon as we got back, then the next day I delivered the list to the Bounty Hunter."

"Did he give you the secret?"

"He did."

"And?"

"In the envelope was a wad of identification papers. The Port Master has a secret daughter stashed away in one of the orphanages." He paused. "The mother of the child isn't his wife."

"An illegitimate child?"

"The mother is a scullery maid for the Donahues.

If anyone finds out about this, Tobias Riley's reputation would go up in smoke, as would his marriage. And the child could be in danger."

"So he's just trying to protect his daughter?"

"And himself."

"Hicks threatened him with this information?"

"Must have."

"But ... Hicks is a good man. He wouldn't have used the child's safety against Riley."

"We all have to do things we don't agree with sometimes. You've killed people."

"To protect myself."

"Yes, that was *your* reason. We all think our own reasons are valid."

"So ... Hicks *did* threaten the girl's safety?"

"Likely, yes. And we're going to have to do the same."

"But—"

"This was what Hicks intended."

"Yes, but—"

"Do you want to take down the Snatchers or not?" Ebony fell silent. "It's not going to be an easy and clean process. We've also lost Jackson. We'll have to get some blood on our hands, so to speak …"

"Okay, I get it. We have to get our hands dirty to get what we want." Sam nodded. "So we need to speak with the Port Master."

"Yeah, Kai and I will go into town tomorrow."

"I'm coming with you."

"No, you're not. We need to get this sorted, and you need to get your strength back if you're going to start looting again."

Ebony huffed, but knew he was right. Her part would come later. At least they hadn't dropped her from the plan entirely. Hunter would have.

"There's something else, Ebony." Sam pulled out a rugged piece of paper from his pocket, then paused, a guilty look spreading across his face.

"What is it?"

"Well ... you know we found that list of Bounty Hunters?"

"Yeah?"

"We thought Hunter's name had been written down wrong. But ... Well ..."

"Spit it out, Sam."

He looked at her hesitantly. "Back when ... when *it* told me to find Hunter's birth certificate ... See, it was just me breaking into the government building. I didn't have any help. So I just grabbed a whole load of papers with his name on them and ran. This morning I went through them again and found something ... it just didn't occur to me last year that you knew so little about your family. I thought you knew everything, and so did the Shadow."

"Sam, what are you talking about?"

"I found Hunter's family tree." Ebony's brows furrowed and she impatiently gestured for him to continue. "Turns out the name on that list we found was right."

"What? But Hunter's a Wick like me."

"No, he's a Price."

"Are you telling me he's not my uncle?"

Sam leaned away from her and braced himself. "I'm telling you ... you're not a Wick. You're a Price."

Ebony felt dizzy. How could she have gone seventeen years not knowing her real name? None of it made any sense.

"But ... But his birth certificate ..."

"Forged? I don't know. He must have changed his name at some point."

"So where did Wick come from?"

Sam shrugged. "When he handed you into the orphanage, Hunter was already well known. His surname was already a target for the Snatchers ... and your parents, the Prices, had just died in a mysterious fire. Maybe he didn't tell the orphanage your surname in an attempt to protect you?"

"That still doesn't answer where Wick came from."

"Maybe the orphanage made it up? When Hunter discovered the name they'd given you, he must have adopted the same surname to escape the name 'Price.'"

She narrowed her eyes. It made sense ... sort of. But how could she know if the Shadow was speaking through Sam now and feeding her lies? But if it was ... why would it want her to know this? What would its motive be?

Sam leaned forward and showed her a piece of parchment with names and lines drawn all over it. "I know you can't read the names, so you'll just have to trust me, okay?" He pointed at various scribbles. "This is your father, Michael Price, Hunter's brother. This is your mother, Terra ... See, Ebony, this family tree doesn't just show Hunter's family. It shows your mother's family, too."

Ebony didn't say a word, just let him continue. She wanted to believe him ... but why hadn't Hunter told her any of this? She *had* suspected that he was keeping something from her. Was the name 'Price' so dangerous?

"Your mother was a Poulter. She had one sister, Mary, who married and became a Donahue …"

"What?" Ebony glared at him.

"What?" Sam looked genuinely confused and even a bit worried.

"Mary … Donahue?" She knew that name … the Bounty Hunters had mentioned the Donahues …

"Yeah, she was your mother's sister."

A memory came flooding back to her. One cart last autumn … she had tied a lord and lady to a tree. "If you're telling the truth, then she still *is* my mother's sister." The Lord had been a bit fat, but the Lady had brown, plaited hair, much like Ebony's. *We are Lord and Lady Donahue!* the man had said.

"You know her?"

"Sort of. I think I looted her cart last year."

"She's your aunt, Ebony. You said you joined the Bounty Hunters to get more information about your family, but Hunter didn't tell you anything. He just kept you hostage, paranoid that you'd be in the next fire. Understandable, but …" He paused, his mind whirring. "Maybe he didn't know about your mother's family?"

"Mary Donahue is my aunt?" Ebony mumbled.

"I bet she'd know loads about your family!"

"My blue ring …"

Sam gave her a look of bewilderment. "What about it?"

"It was my mother's. But I stole it from the Donahues. It was her sister's ring …" It made sense. Why else would the Donahues have had that ring?

Sam's eyes were full of excitement and wonder … the feelings that Ebony knew she should be having … But how could a Southern Lord and Lady be her aunt and uncle? She had been born in the East and raised in the Commons. She was the lowest of the low. She couldn't possibly be related to a Lady.

"If you don't believe me, maybe you should show this family tree to Mary Donahue? If I'm not telling the truth, or if I'm wrong, she'll turn you away pretty damn fast. But if I'm right …"

"I can't just wander up to her front door and expect to be welcomed in. I can't even set foot in town nowadays, let alone walk."

"When the Snatchers are gone, we'll have more freedom in town. We'll find a way to talk to her, okay?"

Ebony slowly shook her head and grimaced. "My uncle knew I was alive this whole time, yet he abandoned me. If she knows that I'm her niece … then how is she any better than Hunter?" She couldn't look at him. It was too awful to think that she might have yet another family member who had abandoned her. She had been searching for information about her family for half a year, but now that she finally had a strong lead … something was telling her to hold back. Finding Mary Donahue would be reckless—she could be seen by guards or Snatchers, or even the Black Jades. The Donahues could call in backup and get her arrested. Even if she managed to talk to Mary

Donahue, they might be wrong about Ebony's lineage, and she would look such a fool. And if they were right … could Ebony let herself get her hopes up again? Her mind reeled and she felt dizzy.

"Sam, nobody can know. If my family are being murdered, then the Donahues could be in danger too."

He gave a solemn nod in response. "Here, take this," he said, handing her the family tree.

"But I can't read it."

"You'll need it when you talk to Mary."

Would it ever come to that? Would she ever have the courage? "Put it in one of my pockets, will you?" She pointed at a pile of clothes on a chair against the wall.

Sam stood and tucked the parchment into her breeches. At that moment, Jaymes walked into the cabin and smiled to see Ebony so talkative.

"How's our patient?" he asked as he began removing the blankets covering the windows. Bright sunshine flooded into the wooden cabin, making Ebony shield her eyes. "I need to re-dress your wound," Jaymes said and reached for a roll of bandage material.

"I'll leave you to it," Sam said, standing up. "I'll keep you in the loop with tomorrow's mission, Eb. I promise."

Ebony nodded and he left, closing the door quietly behind him. She yearned to go with him ... to be out there doing something. She hated feeling left out.

"Why is it always me in the medical hut?" Ebony said with an exasperated groan.

"Get injured a lot, huh?"

Ebony nodded. "Last time it was because of a fire."

Jaymes pulled the blanket from her leg and slowly peeled the bandages off her skin.

"Want to see it?" he asked.

"Not particularly."

"It's not too bad, actually. You got really lucky."

"Good. I need my leg."

"It was a clean cut and didn't hit any bone. I had to pull it out—"

"Okay, okay, I don't need any more details. How long until I can walk on it?"

"Let's give it a go once I've re-dressed it."

After a few minutes of wincing, Ebony let Jaymes help her up onto her feet, then she let go of him and put weight on her right leg. Her knees buckled and Jaymes had to catch her before she collapsed onto the floor.

"As expected," he said. "But your leg straightens—that's good. We'll try again tomorrow."

"How long, Jaymes?"

"A week? We'll keep working on it. You might be limping for a while, but you'll be able to use it soon."

"What do I do in the meantime?"

"Rest."

"For a *week*?"

"You're safe, you're warm, and we'll keep you fed and watered. When was the last time you could put your feet up and do nothing?"

"Never."

"Precisely. Make the most of it while you can, I say."

"But there's so much to do … I can't just sit around all day."

"It's all about small steps. A castle is built brick by brick, not overnight."

Over the following week, Sam and Jaymes helped Ebony gain strength in her leg. They walked her out of the cabin a few times. Sam would often stay to keep her company, but he couldn't be there all the time. He was planning an uprising, after all.

Sam and Kai successfully persuaded the Port Master to give them trading information, and Ebony had a deadline. She had another week before her first loot would trundle by; two carts carrying gold and silver headed for the Peregrine Plains. Hicks had never told her about these carts, perhaps doubting that she could take them on alone. The carts would be heavily guarded, but she was sure she'd be able to handle them. They didn't know yet what they would do with their loot, but they would deal with that problem later. What would the village do with so many large bars of gold and silver? Without drawing suspicion, they'd somehow need to find someone in town who could turn it into coins, which would be a challenge in itself. But Ebony had to loot it all first.

22

At last, Ebony was allowed to leave the medical hut, but Jaymes didn't want her sleeping alone in her den. He'd practically demanded that she stay in the village, so Sam had set up a temporary bed for her on the floor of his hut.

Ebony was even allowed to practice with her bow again but couldn't quite manage swordplay or horse riding yet. Her leg was weak and painful, and she grew tired quickly.

"Bet you can't hit five bullseyes in a row," Kai crowed.

"Challenge accepted," Ebony replied with a grin. One bullseye ... two ... The third was further away, so she'd have to concentrate more. She took a deep breath and focused on the centre of the target.

Something moved in the trees, and she looked up. Had she imagined it? No. There was a figure walking towards them. Was it just a member of the clan returning from town? She heard a shout from behind her.

"Stay there," Kai said and drew his sword. Anna appeared in the yard, and they watched as the figure came nearer, striding into their camp with confidence. The intruder stopped upon reaching the boundary of the trees.

"I'm here to see Ebony," he called.

Ebony recognised that voice. She took a few steps forward—she couldn't quite see the man's face. Anna strode towards him, bow and arrow at the ready.

"I come in peace," the man said. Ebony drew in a sharp breath. She definitely knew that voice. Was it … could it be?

"Darrel?" Sam said from behind her.

"Samuel Sanker. Hunter's number one enemy," Darrel replied.

"Stand down," Sam said to Kai and Anna.

"But he's a Bounty Hunter," Anna replied.

"Let's hear what he has to say."

They approached Darrel and Ebony beamed. She

couldn't help herself. She was just happy to see him alive and healthy, unlike his best friend, Halsey. She launched into a hug and Darrel gave a surprised chuckle. She had to stand on tiptoes to reach his shoulders.

"Ebony Wick. I'm glad to see you're alive and well," he said, holding her shoulders and looking down into her yellow eyes.

"You knew I was or you wouldn't have come here."

"I wasn't sure if you'd come here willingly." Darrel turned to Sam. "If I hear you have hurt her in any way—"

"Darrel, it's okay," Ebony interrupted him. "It's hard to explain, but he isn't the man you think he is. He has looked after me, and he helped me rescue Hicks."

"I didn't quite believe Daya, so I had to see for myself. To be honest, I don't think she believed it, either."

"What are you doing here?" Sam asked.

"Can we speak in private?" Darrel asked Ebony, eyeing Sam, Kai, and Anna.

Ebony looked to Sam and nodded, reassuring him

that she would be fine.

"Call us if you need us," Kai said as Ebony walked through the yard, Darrel and Sam at her heels.

Sam led them to his hut then hesitantly shut the door, leaving them alone. It took a moment for either of them to speak.

"I thought ..." Darrel began.

"You thought they'd have me tied up in a barn. You thought they'd be torturing me for information about Hunter."

Darrel nodded. "Daya was acting so strangely ... like she was hiding something from us. Every time either of us mentioned you, she found an excuse to leave the conversation. I knew something was up. I followed her when she went looking in the trees for food and got the truth out of her. She's worried about you."

Ebony huffed. "I'm better here than I ever was under Hunter's command."

"So whose command are you under now? Sam's?"

"No one's. There *is* no command here. We're just ... outlaws. I'm free here—well, more free than I was before."

"He tied you up and left you in a burning barn."

Ebony looked to her feet. She wanted to explain, but it wasn't her secret to tell. "He's different now. He cares about me. We're friends." Her stomach fluttered, thinking about their race through the rain and sparring sessions in the yard.

"You can't trust him."

Ebony gave Darrel a critical look, her eyes a bright orange and her mouth set in a tight frown. "I *can* trust him. And *I* get to choose who I want to trust, not you."

Darrel took a step back. Was he still scared of her eyes?

"What are you doing here?" she asked.

He took a minute to formulate his next words. "Hunter is impossible to live with. He is paranoid and controlling."

"You don't say."

"I thought … I thought you, Daya, and I could join forces and make our own camp."

"Well, I'm sorry, but I'm staying here. And if you've left Hunter, I suggest you stay here too. He won't be happy when he discovers where you went." She sat down on Sam's bed.

He turned away from her, then took a few deep breaths. "I'm staying wherever you are. I know your family are being murdered—Hunter told me." He turned to her and placed a hand on her shoulder. "I'll look after you, Ebony. I'll keep you safe."

Ebony laughed as she shrugged off his hand and he raised his eyebrows. Had he ever heard her laugh so freely before?

"Thanks for the offer, but I can look after myself. My swordplay is getting better every day."

"They're teaching you to fight?" he asked.

"They're doing everything Hunter never let me do."

"I'll help."

"Kai is doing just fine."

"Please let me help. I know you're good with a dagger already, but I can teach you more tricks."

"Go on then," she said with a smile. She wouldn't pass on the opportunity.

"Why do you want to learn to fight, anyway? Looks like you've got everything you need here," Darrel said, gesturing towards Sam's furniture and the spare bed on the floor.

"Oh, I don't live in this hut. This is all Sam's. I'm only staying in here temporarily. I have my own camp over the bridge."

"Protected by the Fae, no doubt."

She ignored his remark. They had reappeared but she wasn't sure they were protecting her anymore. "I need to get better at fighting if I want to take down the Snatchers for good. Imagine a world without The Clink."

"You can't just … take them down. It will take months of careful planning—maybe even years."

"That's why we're starting now."

He raised his eyebrows. "I'll help in exchange for lodgings."

"You'll have to talk to Sam about that. But why do you want to help?"

"Hunter is a lost cause, but you're not. I want to fight for something I believe in … some*one*."

"You believe in me?"

"You're different. You've faced challenges that most of us can't even imagine, and you're only … how old are you?"

"I don't actually know. Sixteen? Seventeen?"

"You're destined for something big, I'm sure of it. And I want to be there when it happens."

"Well, you'd better learn to trust Sam, then. I do."

Darrel sighed. That would be a challenge. "Daya said you rescued Hicks."

"Yeah, we did."

"Where is he, then? I would have thought he'd be

right at your side."

"He left the Dwellings." Ebony looked out the window as a knot tied in her stomach. She had successfully avoided thinking about Tusting for many days now.

"Ah. Well, I guess he couldn't keep working in town. Where did he go?"

Ebony knew, but it wasn't her news to tell. It was better that he was forgotten by the Dwellers, left to his new life. "He didn't say," she replied.

"Well, I'll take his place by your side."

Ebony smiled. "You'd better meet everyone, then."

As they left Sam's hut, Ebony lead Darrel to the Common Room, where they found Jaymes with Galen, sitting close to the roaring fire.

"A new recruit?" Galen said as they approached.

"How did you know?"

"I don't recognise his walk."

Ebony gave Jaymes a bemused expression. "This is Darrel. He wants to join us," she said.

Jaymes jumped to his feet and pulled up chairs for the pair of them. "A friend of Ebony's is a friend of mine," he said, then began chattering away, debriefing Darrel on the ways of the Foryx. Jaymes had a knack for getting anyone to talk.

Just as Ebony sat down, a voice called her from the doors of the barn. Cooper stood, quietly gesturing at her to follow him.

"I'll see you in a bit, Darrel," she said, before following Cooper across the camp.

They crossed the training yard and headed up a flight of wooden steps into one of the meeting rooms. Inside, Sam, Kai, and Anna stood round a table, their attention on a young man in red, who sat at the table with ropes binding his hands.

"What's going on?" Ebony asked, and all heads turned in her direction. How had they managed to capture a Snatcher? And why?

"He walked straight into the village this morning,"

Cooper explained. "Claims he wants to be one of us."

Ebony looked at each face in turn. Kai's expression was rife with distrust, Sam looked apprehensive but willing to hear more, and Cooper looked confused as he left. Anna's expression was less readable—nervous, intrigued ... she looked to Ebony, as if waiting for her response.

Ebony pulled up a chair that creaked as it moved and sat down, opposite her enemy. "How did you know how to find us?" she snapped. The Snatcher was closer to a boy than a man. He had a wisp of a beard and messy mouse-brown hair.

"Got my own sources," he replied.

Ebony pursed her lips and glared at him. "Why do you want to join us?"

"Isn't safe in the Custodians anymore. They don't treat us good enough. Ain't the job I signed up for."

"And what was the job you signed up for?" Ebony snarled. "To beat and imprison children?"

Sam looked like he wanted to interrupt but

stopped himself. The group seemed happy to let Ebony lead this interrogation.

"Not all of us are like that. We clean up the streets. At least, that was what we used to do. Now …"

"Now what?"

"They want us to hurt 'em. Teaching us harsher punishments. Making us work more. Paying us less. I was told you'd offer me double and I wouldn't have to hurt anyone to get it." The boy's guilty eyes flitted around the group, then dropped to his hands on the table.

"How can we trust you? You might be a spy."

"Custodians don't work like that. We go in groups—don't work alone. There's power in numbers, they say."

"He's right about that," Kai said, and Ebony scowled at him. *Trust Kai to take the side of a Snatcher.*

Ebony looked to Sam, silently asking him what to do, but he gave her a look of bewilderment.

"Have we got anywhere we can keep him?"

"Yeah, there's a barn ..." Sam began, but stopped as he saw Ebony shiver and take a deep breath. "We can find somewhere else."

"No, a barn will do."

"I'll get Jackson," Anna suggested and almost fled from the room.

"Why Jackson?" Ebony asked.

"He's the best at interrogation," Kai replied, a spark of malice in his expression as he glared at the enemy before him.

Ebony motioned for Sam to speak with her privately outside.

"Back in a moment, Kai," Sam said as he followed her out on the platform looking over the yard.

Ebony rounded on him. "How did this happen? How have they found us? What do we do?"

"Hey, hey, calm down," he said and placed his hands on her shoulders. "We wanted this, remember? The Snatchers are jumping ship. Erin told us there was already discord amongst them."

"We have a Snatcher in the village," Ebony hissed.

"I know." Sam's face turned serious. "He can't be trusted until we know for sure that he isn't a spy. Jackson will get everything out of him."

The idea of interrogating someone in a barn, of all places, sent shivers up her spine. Ebony took a deep breath to calm her nerves. "Darrel wants to be one of us as well."

"Where is he? Where have you left him?"

"With Jaymes and Galen in the Common Room."

Sam chuckled. "Go and rescue him. I'll deal with this."

Ebony gave a relieved smile and turned on her heel.

23

Darrel fitted into the Foryx clan well, though many were wary of him. He was charming and, within days, had managed to make friends, especially with those in the kitchen. Food always had been the way to his heart. But no matter what Ebony said, he would always be wary of Sam, and she was worried that Sam would always be wary of Darrel.

"I just can't understand why you've decided to trust him," Darrel said to Ebony as she showed him her camp for the first time. She ducked into her bivouac and retrieved her dark outfit and dagger. He stood before her as she emerged. "He tied you up in a burning barn and left you to die."

She didn't know how to explain the truth behind Sam's actions, and she couldn't betray his trust. She had promised not to tell anyone.

"Turn around," she said.

"What?"

"I need to get changed. Could you turn around?"

Darrel spluttered and quickly swivelled to face the trees as Ebony pulled on her dark outfit.

"I didn't *decide* to trust him. I just do." She smiled and shook her head in disbelief. Had she really just said that out loud? She knew full well what Sam was capable of—whether it was him doing it or the Shadow. It seemed logical to distrust him, to be wary of him … but it was getting harder by the day. "Yeah, I trust him," she confirmed. "He has looked after me, given me freedom. He listens to me and respects my decisions. I'm not here because I have to be. I *chose* to live with the Foryx. I often came close to leaving the Bounty Hunters, but somehow, Hunter always dragged me back in. He wouldn't have let me leave even if I'd begged."

"And you think Sam would let you leave the Foryx?"

"Sam would, yes." She couldn't say the same for the Shadow, but Sam in his right mind? She knew he'd understand.

She sat down beside her unlit fire and Darrel sat on a log opposite her. "There are things about Sam that you don't know, and it isn't my place to tell you. But it seems you have a choice now, Darrel. Leave here and find a new life for yourself, just like Hicks did. I doubt Hunter will welcome you back when he discovers where you went when you left him. Or you can learn to trust Sam and the Foryx and build a life here, like I have."

Darrel stared into the ashes on the ground before him, and Ebony could almost imagine the flames reflected in his eyes.

"You're planning something," he said at last. "You and Sam."

"And Kai, Anna, Harris, and Erin."

"Who's Erin?"

"You haven't met her yet."

"Okay, so what are you planning?"

Ebony took a moment to think. "Will you stay

with the Foryx?"

Darrel paused for a moment. "I gave everything to the Bounty Hunters. My brother and best friend died for Hunter."

"Hunter is different now. You said so yourself. He treats the Bounty Hunters like his own private army. But against what? He's too cowardly to fight for anything. He just hides."

"Are you not hiding here?" Darrel replied, his eyebrows raised.

"From what?"

"The world. The city. Hunter. The Snatchers."

"I am *not* hiding," Ebony snapped. "I'm fighting back."

Darrel smiled, knowingly. "So that's what you're up to? You think you can take the place of the Snatchers?"

"No, I just want them gone."

"And what will happen when you've destroyed them? Who will take their place?"

"No one. I don't know. Anything is better than the Snatchers."

Darrel scoffed. "Be careful what you wish for," he said to his feet.

He gave her an earnest look, but she scowled. "Fine. Leave the city you grew up in. Leave all of us behind to fight our battles," she snapped.

Ebony stood and began to stride out of camp, but Darrel caught up with her. "I'll join your cause. But don't cry to me when the Snatchers' successors are worse. It was bad when they weren't in power. The streets were more lawless than they are now."

"I remember. I was young, but I remember. Henry and I used to steal food on the streets in broad daylight."

"Who's Henry?"

"He was my best friend until the Clink took him from me."

Darrel gave a solemn nod. "They have taken from us all." The pair fell silent as they crossed the little wooden bridge back into the camp. "So what's the plan?" Darrel asked. "How are you going to do it?"

Coming to a stop beside Sam's wooden cabin, Ebony turned to face him and said simply, "We're going to destroy them from the inside out. But we need money first."

"Why? How much money?"

"We're going to get them to jump ship by doubling their salaries."

"How do you know what their salaries are?"

"We … acquired some information that tells us." She decided not to tell him about their captive Snatcher. They were either making headway with their rebellion or the Snatchers knew what they were up to, and she didn't want to scare off Darrel with that thought.

Darrel's expression was somewhere between impressed and disapproving. "But where are you getting the money from? I heard the Foryx are no longer bounty hunting."

"I'm going to loot some carts."

"With your bad leg?" Darrel raised his eyebrows and crossed his arms. Ebony narrowed her eyes. How did he know? She thought her limp had almost gone. "Nothing gets past me." Darrel smiled. "Who managed to shoot an arrow into the legendary Demon in the woods?"

Ebony scowled. "A guard."

"What were they guarding?"

"The government headquarters."

Darrel's arms dropped to his side as his jaw dropped. "What *have* you been up to?"

Ebony looked him up and down and pursed her lips. How much trust could she place in him? After a moment's thought, she raised her chin and said, "If you want to help our cause, then meet me in the sparring yard in five minutes. We have carts to catch."

With that, she entered the hut and closed the door behind her.

"Why don't you come in?" a voice said.

Ebony jumped. "Sorry, Sam. I didn't think you'd

be in here."

Sam was lying on his bed, staring at the ceiling. "In my own hut?"

"You're normally out and about," she replied with a shrug, then sat on the end of his bed. "You okay?"

"I've got a dilemma."

"Anything I can help with?"

Sam sighed. "I fear for you, heading out alone into the woods with your injured leg, but I know I can't stop you going, and I don't want to. If I go with you, you'll think that I think you not capable. You *are* capable." He paused. "So do I act on my instincts and protect you or do I trust your judgement and sit here fretting?"

"I'm not going on my own."

"What?" Sam pulled himself upright, his back leaning against the wooden wall. "Who's going with you?"

"Darrel," she said, then instantly regretted it. Sam frowned and turned his eyes away, his shoulders slumped. "It's not that I chose him over you, Sam. He wants to be part of our cause, so I thought I'd test him. Besides … you're right. I shouldn't go looting alone with this injury. I need help." Sam didn't reply. "I trust Darrel. Well, I trust that he'll keep me safe. I don't yet trust that he will help us. But we have to test him somehow."

Sam huffed in response.

"Sam, I know what I'm doing. I'll be fine."

"Of course you'll be fine. You're Ebony Wick!" He gave her a small smile. "I trust you. I'm just a bit jealous, that's all."

"Jealous? Of what?" She gave a light chuckle but frowned at Sam's sincere expression.

"Darrel knows you better than I do."

"That's not true."

"He's a better friend."

"No. He's not," she said, shaking her head. "You gave me a home and people I actually trust. What has *he* given me?"

Sam gave her a long, searching look. "You have an

amazing capacity to forgive, Ebony Wick."

Ebony looked at her feet, feeling his lingering gaze. "Yeah … well, I actually came in here to get my bow and arrow."

"They're under the bed." Sam gave her a soft smile and stood up to leave the hut.

"Sam—" she said, and he stopped in the doorway. "How is Jackson getting on with our resident Snatcher?"

Sam took a moment to reply, as if carefully forming his next words. "Jackson's getting some good inside knowledge from him … but he's still not entirely sure the man is trustworthy."

"So he's still tied up in a barn?"

"We're keeping him fed and watered. We're treating him well."

Ebony nodded and Sam softly closed the door behind him. If she had learned anything in life, it was to stay far away from a Snatcher. She was perfectly happy to leave the others to it. In the meantime, she would get on with what she was good at.

Minutes later, Ebony emerged wearing her dark outfit, her dagger in her boot, and her bow and arrows on her back. She grinned. It had been too long. It wouldn't quite be the same without Hicks, but it was good enough. And this time, she'd have a horse. She strode towards the training yard, where Kai and Darrel were waiting with two saddled horses.

"You ready?" Kai asked as she approached.

"Ready? I'm excited!" Ebony beamed.

Darrel rolled his eyes, then jumped up onto his own horse, a blonde mare. Ebony's was a dark stallion. She stroked his mane before mounting and trotting out of camp.

"Didn't know you could ride," Darrel said as they left the wooden huts behind.

"Sam taught me."

"Ah, one more reason to like Sam."

Ebony ignored him and rode through the trees

towards the only track that led out of the Dwellings. They were further South than she was used to, but they had horses, so they could carry more than she'd ever been able to loot before. And they'd need them today. They tied the horses up off the road and out of sight.

"So how do we do this?" Darrel asked.

"You've never looted a cart before?"

Darrel shrugged. "Never needed to."

"It's simple, really. Take out the driver, threaten anyone else. Kill them only if they attack you first."

"This won't help the rumours, you know."

"What rumours?"

"You know—about the Demon in the forest."

Ebony stilled. If he was going to work with the Foryx, then he'd have to know the truth. Part of it, anyway. She took hold of his wrist and pulled him round to face her, her eyes a serious, dark crimson.

"There *is* a demon in the forest, Darrel. But it isn't me."

"What are you talking about?" he whispered.

"I've seen it, Darrel. More than once. So has Sam. So has Hunter."

Without another word, she trudged through the trees and found a large bush to hide behind. Darrel followed and gave her a quizzical look, but she put a finger to her lips as the sound of hooves neared. Her heart began to race with adrenaline, and she beamed. She had missed this. Pulling her bowstring back, she let loose, and for the first time ever, she hit a moving target.

The first driver cried out as he fell to the ground, the horses rearing up on their hind legs and whinnying. The cart behind almost crashed as the second driver dropped with a thud. The doors of the two carriages burst open and guards spilled out, swords at the ready. Ebony counted six in total. They glared into the trees, surrounding the two carts, ready to defend them with their lives. As Sam had said, Ebony would need to get her hands dirty to get what she wanted.

She let loose more arrows and men began falling,

one by one. The final three began striding towards Ebony as she nodded at Darrel. The pair launched themselves out of their hiding place and the clanging sound of metal rang through the treetops, birds squawking in alarm. Ebony's leg throbbed and her knee buckled more than once. Dodging a sword, she sank her dagger into the guard's ribcage and watched him drop to the floor. *Swords are useless*, she decided. Her dagger was light and she was nimble—well, almost. Her knee buckled and she winced. Rubbing her injured leg, she watched as Darrel dispatched the final two guards and came to help her back onto her feet.

Ebony slowly approached the whinnying horses and calmed them. She and Darrel tiptoed up to the cabin windows of the first cart and lunged, weapons drawn. But there was no one inside. They moved onto the next cart and found a young guard cowering behind a large sack. Without a second thought, Darrel drove a sword through his neck, then heaved the body out into the trees.

Ebony had been told that the carts would be heavily loaded, but she hadn't expected *this*. She gaped, then caught Darrel's eye through the opposite window of the cart. They both chuckled and gazed at their loot with wonder. The cart was jam-packed with sacks full of glimmering silver and gold bars. Ebony had never seen so much money! How were they going to get all of this back to the camp? Two horses wouldn't nearly be enough.

"Know how to ride a cart?" she asked Darrel.

"Should be easy enough."

"Think we can get them back to camp?"

"Through those trees?"

"We'll have to go slowly. And we'll have to fetch our horses on the way."

Darrel climbed up onto the driver's seat. "I'll give it a go."

After dragging the driver's bodies into the trees, Ebony climbed up onto the driver's seat—Hicks' seat—and began leading Darrel back to the wooden village, hearing the clank of precious metal behind her. She collected the horses as they rode past, tying them to the side of the cart.

Pride and triumph filled her chest as they returned. Word spread quickly, and soon enough, they were surrounded by impressed faces and a beaming Anna.

"Knew you had it in you!" she called to Ebony, who had dismounted her horse.

Anna got to work untying the steeds, including those they had claimed, and led them back to the stables as Darrel and Ebony began to unload their loot into the common room.

"This is amazing!" Sam said as he approached, his grin stretching from ear to ear. "Now we just have to work out how to store it and change it into money."

"I can do that," Darrel said, emerging from the other side of the cart, a large fabric sack in his arms. "I know a crooked accountant in the South Dwellings."

"I knew you'd be useful for something," Sam said.

Darrel looked affronted but didn't reply. "I'll take

the first load into town tomorrow by horse, if you'll lend me one," Darrel continued. "If I sit around in a camp doing nothing one minute longer I'll go crazy."

"I know that feeling," Ebony murmured.

"If you betray us—if you take any money for yourself or tell anyone our secrets ..."

"Sam, I traded in secrets not too long ago. I know you'd kill me without hesitation."

Still wary, Sam helped them unload the cart and offload it into the common room. Twenty large sacks of shimmering gold and silver. This would fund a rebellion—if they could trust Darrel to play his cards right.

By the time the cart was empty and the new horses put away, dusk had fallen and the mess hall was getting busy. Darrel joined Anna for dinner—she seemed to have taken a liking to him, leaving Sam and Ebony to their favourite quiet corner.

"I shot a moving target, today," Ebony said.

"You're getting better every day," Sam replied with

a smile before spearing a sausage on his plate.

They spent the next hour swapping stories of the Snatchers, and Sam filled her in on the back stories of various Foryx members. The Foryx clan had all sorts, but they weren't like the Bounty Hunters. There was no hierarchy, just a standard moral code: look after your neighbours and they'll look after you. Some of the members still made their money in town, but their numbers were dwindling due to the Snatchers. They were fraternising with outlaws, the Snatchers said, which made them just as bad.

The night grew dark, and Ebony agreed to stay at Sam's again, but she would take the floor and he the bed. She didn't trust the wooden frame that held him up at night. The material beneath … it was so soft, she felt like she could fall through it. Hard, reliable floor was much better for a good night's sleep.

24

She was in the town square. The Common Market had been burnt to the ground and was grey with ash. Shadows moved past her, hardly noticing her presence. The sky was dark, like a storm was about to strike. Sam had said she could explore the town, so she searched for her usual haunting grounds: where she used to sell her wares; the burnt-down building Myla had almost died in; the site of her old orphanage. It was the Dwellings in every detail, except it was dead.

She found the meeting place of the Black Jade gang down a dark alleyway that wasn't much different to the real thing. Except at the end of it, she could see a figure. A real, solid figure with golden hair. The woman turned away.

"Wait!" Ebony shouted and ran after her—yet she wasn't running, she was ... gliding.

She followed the woman down alleyways and across squares, only ever catching a glimpse as she turned a corner. She had seen her once before. How could she forget the woman's golden hair shining against the blackened city? At last, the figure came to a stop at the dead end of a long street.

"Who are you?" Ebony asked as she approached.

The woman reached forward and grasped both of Ebony's shoulders. "You shouldn't be here."

"Who are you?" Ebony said again. "Why don't you look like the rest of the Shadows?"

"How have you come here? You shouldn't be here," the woman said and placed her palm on Ebony's chest. The world went black and two red orbs shone out of the darkness.

Ebony woke on Sam's floor, gasping.

"Hey, hey, it's okay. You're back now," Sam said. He rolled off his bed and sat down beside her, stroking her hair until she relaxed. "You're in Rundlewood Forest in the wooden village. You're in my hut."

It took a moment for Ebony to recall her surroundings, but she eventually sat up, leaning against her elbows. "I saw the woman again."

"What woman?"

"The woman with golden hair."

Sam's brows creased. "I've never seen a woman, let alone golden hair. The whole place is black and grey with ash."

"Yes. All of it except her."

Sam frowned. "Don't know who that is."

In the back of Ebony's mind, a thought occurred—or was it more of a feeling? The woman ... she couldn't possibly be. The Mother had left this world hundreds of years ago. But a voice in her head said, *Your dreams aren't of this world.* Ebony shook her head and ran her hands through her messy morning hair. She stood up and redid her plaits, Sam watching her silently, a worried look across his face.

She realised it had been a long time since she had prayed to the Mother or painted herself with symbols. "I'll see you later, Sam," she said, and without another word, she left him dumbfounded and closed his door behind her.

The day was only just dawning and smelled fresh after rainfall. Almost tripping over her feet, she made her way over the bridge and back to her small camp, but she couldn't shake the feeling that she was being followed. She was imagining it, she was sure. It was just a remnant of that dream … that experience.

She stripped off her clothes and knelt at the edge of the river, scraping up the muddy clay. But which Spirit should she protect herself from? Fire? Death? Darkness? On one arm she painted protection symbols; on the other, she painted swirling summoning charms for the Spirits of light, warmth, and peace. On her chest she painted a diamond to protect herself against dark water spirits. And then she plunged in. The water was so cold, her bones ached, but it was fresh and cleansing. She stretched her arms out and lay back as the river slowly pulled her downstream and the blue sky above drifted past. Birds flew through the trees above her and the spring wind played on her skin. Her eyes shone gold and her heart felt warm. This was peace. This was joy. In her mind, she spoke the Fae words of joy to the Mother.

May the Mother, the Sister, the Daughter bring me joy. May the skies, earth, and water hold my joy.

She then began to swim back to her camp, and the river didn't hold her back. It almost helped her on her way. When she returned, her camp was transformed, every surface glittering with light, like the stars had fallen and graced her home. She stilled, treading water, her heart thumping. They had attacked her home and killed her friends. Well, 'friends' was a loose term when it came to the Bounty Hunters.

One or two Fae was fine ... but why were they all here? Without taking her eyes off the Fae Gathering, she heaved herself out of the cold water and stood shivering in a patch of warm sunlight. She needed to get to her tunic, which was hanging above her campfire. She took a step back as a large, buzzing ball of light lifted from the forest floor and flew towards her.

"W—What—"

The Fae landed on her arms and shoulders. Her words were taken from her as she watched them weave between her feet and sit on her wet hair. Their light was warm and dried her damp skin, and with it came a rush of energy that soured through her mind and body. She felt different, like she wasn't Ebony Wick. She didn't fear, she had no anger. Something told her that the Fae had come in peace. They clung to her sides and lay on her bare feet, swarming her like golden clothing; a figure of glittering light, its eyes shining pure gold. In that moment, she was one with the Fae.

Two fairies hovered before her. The king and queen. "Our deepest regrets," they said in unison. "We ask for forgiveness from the Mother, the Sister, the Daughter. We ask forgiveness from you."

Ebony knew the words to respond but didn't respond.

The ball of light lifted from her body and Ebony

rushed back into herself, her fears and anger intact. She wrapped her arms around herself and glared at the king and queen before her. *What just happened?* Two fairies delivered her tunic, which was warm and dry, and she slipped it on. The king and queen hovered before her, waiting for her to finish the ritual of forgiveness.

"You attacked my friends."

"They attacked us first," King Alvero said.

He wasn't wrong.

"My friend died that day—because of you." Ebony felt goosebumps cover her arms, remembering the carnage they had caused.

"We cannot pick favourites in war," Alvero said.

Ebony shook her head and frowned. The Fae may have attacked the Bounty Hunters, but it hadn't been unwarranted. She had warned them, but they had ignored her. They'd deserved the wrath of the Fae.

"If I grant forgiveness, will you stand down? Forget the war. You won already."

"We will not harm your people while the Shadow is in their midst. We will trust you to come to us in your time of need," Coralia promised.

Was choice did she have but to trust their word? She sighed. "I grant forgiveness, given by the Mother, the Sister, the Daughter. I grant forgiveness to you." Did she truly mean it?

With that, the Fae rose and, as one, a glittering mass of light, they disappeared into the trees, leaving Ebony shivering in the cold spring breeze, her wet hair dripping down her back. On the other side of her camp, a figure appeared.

"Who were you talking to?" Sam asked as he approached.

"Umm, the Fae came to apologise for attacking my friends," she said as she sat before the unlit fire, a haunted look in her eyes.

"And you forgave them?"

"I did."

"You don't sound very sure."

"I said the Fae words of forgiveness … but they didn't feel true."

"They did kill some of your friends."

"Those people ignored my warnings. They disrespected the Fae and their religion. They deserved what they got."

Sam took a sharp breath in. "You have to teach us how to respect them. They won't touch us if you're around."

"No, Sam. They won't touch us if *you're* around. You bring the Shadow with you."

Realisation dawned in his eyes. "When they attacked the Bounty Hunters … they wouldn't come anywhere near me."

"I think they fear you. But they trust me."

"What did they mean 'in your time of need'?"

Ebony shrugged. "No idea. They often speak in riddles."

"Why … why do they treat you differently to everyone else?"

Ebony shook her head and raised her eyebrows. "Maybe because I'm the only Dweller who ever cared for them and their way of life?"

Sam narrowed his eyes. There had to be more to it than that. He took a deep breath. "I wanted to check you were okay."

"I'm okay now," Ebony said with a smile, a deep feeling of calm and peace resonating through her. "The Mother has given me peace. But I want to spend today alone. Is that okay?"

Sam frowned but nodded. "Yeah, of course. But Jaymes wants to see you to discuss your outfit."

"My outfit?"

"Yeah, for the festival."

"The what?"

Sam frowned. "Did I not tell you? We're celebrating the Spring Festival tomorrow."

"I thought only the Southerners celebrated stuff like that."

"Some of us *are* Southerners."

"What does it involve?"

"Oh, nothing, really. Drinks, food ... some people dress up. A bit of dancing ..."

"*Dancing?*" Ebony spat. Sam's eye flicked around the clearing, doing his best to avoid her steely gaze. "I don't dance, Sam. I *can't* dance."

"Have you ever tried?"

"Yes, I have. They made me learn in the Clink," Ebony stated, hands on her hips. "I was never any good."

"I can't imagine you took it very seriously."

Ebony raised her eyebrows and gave him an admonishing look.

"Jaymes will be very put out if you don't go, and it's a tradition for the Foryx ... so you'll be disrespecting us or something," he said in one long, garbled sentence while looking at his feet.

"I don't have anything to wear."

"Jaymes isn't just good at healing people, you know. He has something for you already."

"Do I really have to go?"

"Yes." Sam smirked. "I'll be there to protect you," he said with a grin.

Ebony narrowed her eyes. "I'll be fine."

"I can't protect you from Jaymes, though. That's all on you. He'll be expecting you at Galen's hut late afternoon tomorrow, just before festivities begin."

Ebony shuddered. She hadn't worn a dress since the days of the Clink when they'd forced her into those awful pinafores. She didn't dare think what Jaymes might have in store for her.

"Good luck," Sam said with a chuckle before heading into the trees.

Dancing. Ebony grimaced. She sat down by her fire and tried to recall the feeling of peace that the Mother had given her.

25

"The Spring Festival? That's what he called it?" Jaymes shook his head with disappointment. "He isn't a Dweller. He wouldn't know our customs."

"They're not *my* customs," Ebony replied. They were in Jaymes and Galen's hut, which was just as hot as ever.

Jaymes looked at the floor. "I know. And it's not right that Common Dwellers are treated that way."

"Isn't it? I've managed to get by fine so far without attending a single party."

"It's called the Firelight Ball and it marks the coming of new life, change, new beginnings."

"It's a *ball*?" Ebony eyed the exit, wondering if she could get to it before him. She'd happily take an angry mob of Snatchers over a *ball*.

"In the South, it's one of the biggest celebrations of the year. Of course, here, it isn't quite so much of a ball, as such … no ball rooms, partying outside …" Jaymes sighed as he thought back to the splendour of his past life and the grandeur of the largest houses in the Dwellings. "But if you want to make use of our kitchens, our common room, our contacts … if you want to work with the Foryx, then you must honour our customs."

Ebony huffed. "Sam said you have an outfit for me."

Jaymes beamed and his eyes glistened. "I do indeed." He turned around and began rummaging in a wardrobe by the door. When he turned back, he was holding a long swathe of dirty white fabric hung on a wooden hanger.

"That's my dress?" Ebony frowned, unimpressed.

Jaymes looked at her like she was stupid. "This is just the material that protects the dress," he said, as if it was obvious. "This dress was my mother's. I've had it for a long time, but I've never had anyone to give it to before. Well, I say 'give it' … you'll have to give it back." He pulled the protective fabric away, revealing the most beautiful dress Ebony had ever seen, not that she was one to care much about dresses. It looked as if it had been intricately sewn together with spider's webbing, woven with vines, and decorated with golden-edged leaves. It swept the floor gracefully.

"I'm not the right person to wear this," Ebony breathed. It looked like the type of dress that someone like Mary Donahue might wear.

Jaymes glared at her. "Of course you are! Oh, I almost forgot!" He pulled out a box from under his bed and opened it to show Ebony a glittering pair of golden shoes. Jaymes didn't let Ebony inspect herself until the dress was fitted properly, the back tied with crisscrossing emerald ribbons. He finished plaiting her dark hair, then took a step back to look at his work.

He shook his head, smiling. "You're wasted in the Commons."

He opened his wardrobe door to reveal a long mirror. Ebony's jaw dropped. She looked like a different person—like a Southerner. The dress fit her perfectly and almost seemed to make her glow. "It's …" She didn't have the words.

"I know." He gave a small smile.

"Nobody will recognise me," she said.

Jaymes smiled. "Might be quite fun to see their faces!"

Ebony smiled mischievously.

"One last thing …" Jaymes added, and from his wardrobe he handed over a bundle of folded material, dark blue in colour, tied with a red ribbon. She took it from him and stroked the soft velvet texture.

"What is it?" she asked.

"It's for you. To keep, I mean. It matches your blue ring," he said, holding her hand out to inspect it. "Simple but lovely."

Ebony untied the ribbon and let the material slide from her hands, revealing a long, dark cloak and hood.

"Your black cloak is so old and worn. I thought you might need something warmer."

Ebony didn't know what to say. The cloak was beautiful.

"There's also a hidden pocket in it," James explained. "For any objects you might like to keep close." She knew he was referring to her dagger.

"Th—Thank you," she stammered, her eyes a dark teal colour.

"You might want to wear it now—it's a bit chilly outside."

Jaymes draped the cloak round her shoulders, and Ebony grinned at her reflection. Never in all her life had she felt so … beautiful. She retrieved her dagger from her boot and hid it in the cloak's pocket. She never felt safe without it.

A little while later, the pair emerged from the hut, Jaymes wearing a dark green coat and tails with dark grey breeches and a white cravat. He took Ebony's arm, leading her towards what was normally the training arena. They approached a throng of Foryx members, all dressed in their finery. Long tables had been set out, laden with food and decorated beautifully, ivy and greenery festooning the white tablecloths. Ebony had never seen anything so grand. She stopped walking, her feet refusing to take another step. She didn't belong here. She was a Commoner, not of the South or West or North—she wasn't welcome. That was what she had been told her whole life. Her palms felt sweaty, and the cloak felt as if it was glued to her skin.

"Ebony?" a voice said. Sam emerged from the crowd just as she shrugged off her cloak and handed it to Jaymes.

The whole world seemed to come to a standstill. Ebony could swear every eye was on her. She was overdressed, she had overdone it. She looked silly in such finery. She didn't belong here. Her face grew hot, and she looked away from Sam. Slowly, the world around her came back to life, but her heart only thumped louder as Sam approached.

"I'll see you in a bit, Ebony," Jaymes said quietly

and left her, a sitting duck in a foreign land.

She looked up at Sam, who was still gawking at her. He wore a dark red tailcoat with black breeches and waistcoat, decorated with delicate silver thread, as if the flowers of the night had devoured him. He looked, quite frankly, dashing. A band struck up, but Ebony couldn't see where they were.

"Will you dance with me?" Sam asked, offering her his hand.

"Do I have to curtsy?"

Sam laughed as she accepted his hand and led her through the crowd, their friends slowly choosing their partners for the first dance.

"I haven't done this for years, Sam. I hardly know what to do."

"Don't worry, just follow my lead. Remember, I'm not a Dweller. I'll be copying everyone else most of the time."

The music started before Ebony had a chance to

escape, all the men lined up opposite the women. Luckily, she vaguely remembered this dance from her time in the Clink. *Two steps back, two steps forward, right hand up beside the face, and touch the partner's hand.*

"The dances in your homeland are different?" she asked as she swapped sides with him and repeated the same movements.

"Everything is different in Shalo. Nothing is this beautiful," he said. "You would stand out like a rose amongst thorns in that dress."

Hold hands and step twice to the right, then twice to the left. "Is that a compliment?"

Turn left and walk forward three steps, back three steps, then forward again. It was all very precise.

"You said you couldn't dance," he said as they linked arms and turned in a half circle, repeating the steps to the right this time.

"I don't remember this bit. I have no idea what comes next."

He turned to face her and put one hand on her hip and one on her shoulder. He was so close she could feel his warmth. "Two steps back," he instructed her, "then forward. Then right, then left."

She did as she was told, careful not to trip over her own feet. She found she was enjoying it more than she'd expected she would, but her stomach began to grumble as the day grew dark, and she was sure that was unbecoming of her and not fitting for such a grand occasion. Sam led her to one of the tables and they stood by a platter of delicious cheese puffs. Ebony had had put her blue cloak back on, feeling the chill of the night air on her arms.

"See, it's not so bad, is it?" Sam said with a smile.

"I suppose not. But it does seem odd to be celebrating when we're in the midst of a rebellion."

"Our spy is working wonders, and we've got money to fund our cause …"

"Have you heard more from Erin?"

"I have."

"And?"

"I fear you won't like her methods."

"Tell me, Sam."

"She has had to resort to harsher persuasion tactics for some of the Snatchers. Not all of them need money so desperately. They're loyal to the Custodians until their family's safety is questioned."

"Whatever it takes," Ebony said with a sigh.

"Erin's words exactly. But it's working. We have infiltrated the Common Custodians and mutiny is within our grasp, so says our girl. We have a lot to celebrate."

Ebony smiled. He was right, of course. She was safe and free—as free as she could be with the Snatchers still in charge. She had food and water and warmth. What more could she want? Ebony's eyes shone as gold as her dress, and she beamed.

"I know this dance, too," she said as the band struck up once again and, this time, she led Sam into the fray.

Beside her, Anna danced with Kai, and she could

see Darrel dancing with one of the girls from the kitchen. As quickly as the dance began, it stopped.

A scream shot through the crowd and the dancers froze, their eyes drawn to the band. Ebony had to stand on tiptoes to see what everyone was looking at. A figure in a dark cloak … a man. His arm was around the violinist's throat, a dagger in hand. A hush settled across the yard.

"We have your spy, Samuel Sanker," the man called, and all heads turned to Ebony and Sam. Ebony recognised that voice. A path seemed to clear, giving them a direct few of the stage. It was now surrounded by men in dark cloaks, Rynn at the front—the Bounty Hunter that Ebony had once lived alongside. Sam dropped Ebony's hand and stalked towards the intruders, Ebony hot on his heels. She reached for her dagger as she walked, hiding it underneath her cloak.

"What do you want?" Sam asked.

"We have your spy. Call it off or she is dead," Rynn snapped.

Sam gazed around the crowd of confused onlookers. "Can we speak somewhere private?" he hissed.

"No. Call off the mutiny or your girl dies."

"Who are these men?" called a voice from the crowd.

"He's called Rynn," Ebony explained. "He was a Bounty Hunter once, but now it seems he is working for The Black Jade gang."

"What? How do you know?" Kai stepped up beside Ebony, glaring at the intruders.

"I recognise some of these men," she replied. Was Gren with them? Was he even aware that this was happening?

Rynn sneered at her. "We infiltrated the Snatchers before you. You have three hours to call it off."

Ebony shivered. It all made sense now. The rebellion had been too easy … because the Jades had sown the seeds long back. A knot twisted in her stomach. The Black Jades knew where she lived. They had former

Bounty Hunters working for them and now they had Erin and the Snatchers under their control. No wonder Sam hadn't been able to persuade the Jades to join his cause. They already had a cause of their own.

Rynn's man removed the dagger from the violinist's throat and took a step back.

"Meet us in the Snatcher training grounds," Rynn said, and the gang followed him into the trees. Sam swore under his breath and spun on his heel to face Ebony.

"Up for a rescue mission?"

"Always. But I can't go in this." She held up her arms, indicating her dress.

"Ah, yes. We need to change. Meet back here in five?"

Ebony nodded as Sam turned to address the crowd. "Everything's okay, it's under control. We'll get our girl back."

Ebony left him answering questions and heard to musicians strike up again as she reached Jaymes' cabin.

She had hoped to wear this dress a little longer, but Erin's safety was more important than her vanity.

"Wait, Ebony! Wait!" Jaymes called as he caught up with her. He grabbed her wrist, panting. "What happened? I couldn't hear him from the back. Where are you going?"

"Erin has been caught. We have three hours to rescue her, but I can't go in this dress. It's impractical. It's also your mother's."

"I'll tell Harris to fetch your weapons—just wait for me. You'll need help getting out of it."

He ran back to the party as Ebony found his hut and began attempting to part ways with the dress. But Jaymes was right. She couldn't reach the ribbons on her back and found herself contorting and grunting, trying to get out of it.

"Stop, stop," Jaymes said as he entered. "You're going to damage it."

Ebony stilled as he pulled the ribbons loose. He helped her step out of the dress and she practically launched into her trousers and old jacket, feeling herself again. Jaymes picked up her black cloak with a grimace.

"It keeps me hidden," she said and shrugged it on. She left the hut as Jaymes called, "Good luck!" from behind her. He would no doubt be rejoining the festivities. Harris, Sam, and Darrel were waiting for her by the tree line, Sam in ragged breeches and a dark cloak much like her own.

"You don't have to go, Ebony," Darrel said, his hands on her shoulders, ignoring the scowls from the other two. "This doesn't have to be your fight."

"Yes, it does. Sending Erin in as a spy was as much my idea as anyone else's. And I used to be a Jade," she admitted. "They've been trying to track me down all year. Now they know where I am, the wooden village could be in danger. I have to stop them. Whatever it is they're trying to do, I have to stop them." Darrel took a step back, and Ebony caught a glimpse of pride on Sam's face. "Go back to the party, Darrel," Ebony said, and he actually did as he was told.

Harris reached into various pockets and extracted her daggers, which he handed over. He also had her bow and quiver slung over his shoulder. When she was fully equipped, she nodded to Sam.

"I should come with you," Harris said.

"No. You should stay here and protect everyone. The Jades know where we are now," Ebony said.

Harris nodded. "I hope Erin is okay."

"She'll be fine," Sam reassured him. "She's a tough lass. We just need to get her out of there before it's too late."

"What are you waiting for, then?" Harris turned on his heel and returned to the party.

"Ready?" Sam asked.

"Ready," Ebony replied.

26

The sounds of the party faded behind them as they headed for town. The Common Custodians were trained in the South Dwellings and sent on missions to the Commons. Rynn had said to meet them in the training grounds. But how were they going to stop a rebellion? It could be out of Erin's hands by now.

They stuck to the shadows, barely visible in their dark cloaks. They didn't say a word to each other as they stole through town. Somehow, Ebony knew what Sam would do at each turn, reading his movements and expressions as they went. They knew each other well enough now.

At last, the training grounds were in sight: a large square lined with targets and straw men, surrounded by grey brick buildings: barracks and weapons storage. The Snatchers rarely used horses—it was too difficult to manoeuvre them through the twisting alleyways of the

Dwellings. They could hear the clang of swords inside one of the buildings. What was going on? Were the Snatchers still training this late at night?

Creeping around the back of the barracks, they found a broken window, smashed from the inside. Sam helped Ebony through, then pulled himself in after her. They were in a long, empty corridor lined with torches, but the ringing of swords was almost deafening. They crept up the hallway and peered around the corner. Pandemonium. Guards fighting guards, men in black cloaks trying to pull them apart. Swords clashed and fists thumped. Were they too late? They seemed to have stumbled upon a battle.

Men charged around the corner, swords drawn and bloody, and cried out as they saw Ebony and Sam crouching under a lit torch. Ebony leapt to her feet, pulling Sam up beside her. His sword was drawn in an instant and he began to duel an angry Snatcher.

"Intruders!" one of the Snatchers called. Ebony sidled up behind him and cut his throat before he could shout another warning. But she was too late. A stampede of men came charging around the corner—she could hardly tell if they were fighting each other or aiming for her and Sam. Perhaps they didn't even know themselves? Ducking and diving, she wove her dagger through the mob, aiming for a dark corner where she could fire her bow.

Thwack. The world went dark as her head slammed against the cold stone floor.

She lay on the floor in the Snatcher's barracks, but it was empty and blackened. There was no ceiling, and the walls were crumbling around her. She pulled herself to her feet, feeling as light as air. She could see shadows drifting past her beyond the broken walls, hardly noticing her presence. Was it night time or was the sky always that dark? She turned, fully expecting to see a Snatcher charging towards her, but the place was empty. She walked around the corner where, minutes ago, there had been a battle raging. The door to the barracks was hanging from its hinges, and next to it stood a golden-haired woman, her light blue dress billowing, though there was no breeze.

Ebony strode towards her—or was she gliding? But the woman turned away.

"Wait!" Ebony shouted and ran after her into a courtyard. The woman stopped and turned. "Why do I keep seeing you?" Ebony said as she approached. The woman reached forward and grasped both of Ebony's shoulders. Her eyes were fierce.

"Where is the Sister?" the woman asked.

"Who?" Ebony stepped backwards, out of the woman's grasp.

"You shouldn't be here, Daughter."

"I'm not your daughter."

"You are the *Daughter."*

"What do you mean?

The woman huffed with exasperation. "The Mother," she said and pointed to herself. "The Daughter," she said, pointing to Ebony. "But the Sister ..."

Ebony froze. The Daughter. Of the forest. This woman was the Mother, *and she thought* she *was the Daughter of the forest? She had to be mistaken. The Daughter had died many years ago.*

"You shouldn't be here," the woman said and placed her palm on Ebony's chest. The world around her fell away, and all she could see was darkness ... no, not just darkness. Two red orbs. Eyes ...

Ebony lurched upright, her head throbbing. All around her were bodies, lacerated and torn apart. The corridor was silent. Had the battle ended? She began to shake. Where was Sam? She turned around but all she could see was a corridor littered with the dead. From outside came a blood-curdling scream. She launched to her feet and turned the corner. There was the door, attached to the hinges and wide open. But no woman stood before it. She ran through the exit into a dark courtyard. The battle hadn't ended, it had just moved outside. Snatchers fought each other, with fists, swords, daggers, and whatever they had to hand. Whatever seeds Erin and the Jades had planted had grown into a full-on mutiny.

Where was Erin? The Jades had clearly thought they had more time. Would they kill her? She was likely already dead.

Something heavy slammed into Ebony's back and she almost tripped forward. An arm reached around her middle and squeezed. She tried kicking and elbowing in the ribs, but nothing would deter that grip. She kicked anything she could reach and eventually heard a yelp. The man's grip loosened, and she spun, dagger at hand. A snarling face glared at her, his sword at the ready. She gasped—he looked so similar to Alastor Bates, only younger and fitter ... but she and Sam had killed him.

"My brother told me a lot about you, Ebony Wick," the man said. "The Demon in the forest. But you're not going to get away this time."

Of course. This was Bates' brother, the new leader

of the Snatchers. Donavan Bates. Rumour said that he was even worse.

"You can try," Ebony replied and lunged at him with her dagger. She dodged his sword and slashed at his side, but he leapt out of the way just in time. She somersaulted and sprang back up onto her feet as Sam emerged from the crowd behind Donavan, his clothes red with blood. His eyes looked half crazed as he swaggered towards them.

Ebony tried slashing at Donavan again, but he was quicker than her. He pushed at her shoulder, and she stumbled backwards, falling onto her back on the hard stone floor. She winced and scowled at him as Sam appeared behind the man. Donavan screamed as a gash appeared across his face, splitting it in half. Sam hadn't even touched him. Blood gurgled out of his mouth and he sank to his knees. His body slumped beside her, and she pulled herself away, trying not to gag.

His face blank, Sam turned and reached his hand out before him. Men screamed and yelled as they fell.

Sam began shouting something, but she couldn't make it out. She stepped towards him, firing arrows into the fray.

"Kill them all!" she heard Sam yell.

No. He'd been taken by the Shadow. Her chest felt hollow. The Shadow was among them, seeing through Sam's eyes.

"Kill them all!" Sam repeated, his voice cold and clear.

"Sam, this isn't you!" She rushed up to him and tried to take hold of his face to look him square in the eye. "The Shadow is speaking. Come back to me! This isn't you."

Sam pushed her aside and his eyes shone a bright red.

"Sam!" She reached for his face again. "We have to go! It is too late for Erin. The mutiny has begun."

Sam looked at her like she was a stranger, his head to one side. Then he blinked and his eyes turned back to brown. He shook his head and sank to his knees. She pulled him back to his feet and dragged away from the courtyard, leaving the Snatchers to fight amongst themselves. "We have to go, Sam!"

"I'm sorry," he mumbled and gazed at the bodies strewn around them. "I'm so sorry."

"I know. But it wasn't you who did this."

"I'm back. I'm back now," Sam mumbled.

"Then let's go."

He seemed to hear her at last. He nodded and began to sprint for the trees. Ebony gazed around at the carnage. The Snatcher's training grounds had fallen silent, but she was sure more of them would appear in minutes. No Snatchers could follow them—they couldn't let their village be discovered by even more outsiders. Only hours before, they'd been happy. Safe. Now they were fleeing a mutiny and had an angry gang on their tail who could retaliate at any moment. Together, Ebony and Sam fled through the trees until they reached the river that lined the wooden village.

"You can't go back home like that," Ebony said, pulling Sam towards the water.

"Like what?"

"You're covered in blood."

"Oh." Sam paused to look at his hands, which had changed colour. "I'm so—"

"Don't apologise again, just clean yourself up," Ebony snapped. Sam nodded and the pair of them sat down by the stream. Ebony cupped as much water in her hands as she could before pouring it over Sam's head, doing her best to clear away the evidence of death.

"That will have to do," she said. She couldn't see much of his face in the dark.

"S—so c—cold," he stammered.

"Let's get going, then. We should try to go to my camp without being noticed. We'll stay there tonight."

Sam nodded and followed her meekly through the trees. The party was still in full swing, and, with a pang,

Ebony wished they were still there, dancing and oblivious. They managed to reach the wooden bridge undetected, but Harris came hurrying out of the shadows.

"Did you manage to get her back? Where is she?" he called as they crossed the bridge.

"Keep your voice down," Ebony snapped. "Nobody can see us right now. If they have followed us …"

"Who?"

"The Snatchers."

Sam's knees began to buckle, and Ebony caught him round the waist.

"What happened?" Harris asked, helping her to keep Sam upright.

"Mutiny. Shadow. Running." They were the only words Ebony had as she led Sam through the trees.

"The rebellion has already started?"

"It might even be finished by now."

"But the Black Jades … they won't be happy."

Ebony stopped in her tracks. "I know, Harris," she

snapped. "Snatchers are after us. The Black Jades are after us. Sam was taken by the Shadow again and is weak. I was knocked out. Please." She took a deep breath. "I will explain in the morning. But for now, we need to hide. And rest."

"The Snatcher we had tied up …"

Ebony huffed. Now was *not* the time. "What about him?"

"We found him dead. We think the Black Jades got to him."

"What? Why would they want him dead?"

"M—maybe …" Sam stuttered, leaning on Ebony for support. "Maybe he was one of theirs?"

"You think the Snatcher was a Jade spy?" Ebony looked at Sam's haggard face, then back to Harris.

"That would explain it," Harris said. "Maybe he was a liability and knew too much?"

"So they kill him?"

Harris shrugged. "It's possible."

"They weren't so ... brutal in my day." Ebony could hear Sam's teeth chattering, so she continued leading him back to her camp.

"Talk in the morning," Harris said, before turning away and leaving her in the dark.

When they'd reached her camp, she bundled Sam into her den and covered him with blankets. He was shivering and hardly seemed to know where he was. She lay beside him, hoping her body heat would help warm him up. She stared into the darkness, the events of the night replaying over and over in her mind. Then she remembered her dream. She had been in the barracks, right where she was knocked out. She had seen the golden woman, who had said she was the Daughter—the Daughter of the Forest. Was the woman the Mother? No. It wasn't possible. Just another bad dream. She closed her eyes and let the darkness flood her mind.

The next morning, Ebony, Sam, Kai, Harris, Cooper, Jackson, and Anna gathered by Ebony's campfire. Harris told them again how he and Jackson had found their captive dead and they all agreed that he had probably been a Jade spy. Ebony then told them all that had happened at the Snatcher's training grounds the night before.

"Sam, you can't keep letting it in," Kai said.

"I can't help it."

The group seemed reluctant to discuss the Shadow; a nightmare that they would far prefer to pretend was just a tale. The reality was too terrifying, too haunting.

"This morning I went to the docks to meet Erin, as I normally do," Cooper piped up. "None of you bothered to inform me that she wouldn't be coming." The group murmured their apologies, but Cooper waved them aside. "A member of the Black Jades met me instead. He had a message for you." The group waited with bated breath. "Erin is dead. The mutiny worked out in their favour."

"What is that supposed to mean?" Ebony asked. "They wanted us to *stop* the mutiny."

"The Jades are in charge of the Snatchers now that

Donavan Bates is dead. In fact, the Snatchers don't really exist anymore, or so he said. The Jades will be patrolling the streets now, and what they say goes. And they say Samuel Sanker and Ebony Wick can never set foot in the Dwellings again."

Sam chuckled darkly. "The Snatchers said that about both of us a long time ago and we've managed fine."

"He really meant it," Cooper pressed.

"So did the Snatchers. So the gang aren't angry with us?"

"They said as long as they don't see your faces in town, they won't attack our camp."

Ebony sighed with relief. "Darrel can still go into town. We can get work without leaving the trees."

"The gang will never be as disciplined as the Custodians were," Kai said. "Their reign won't last long."

"And then what?" Anna asked. "Who takes over from them?"

Ebony shrugged. That wasn't her problem. Her

goal had been accomplished; the Snatchers were no more, though the outcome wasn't exactly how she had imagined it.

"The Commons goes back to how it was before. Lawless." Harris frowned. "Hadn't really considered this bit."

"We'll get by. We always do," Sam said with a reassuring smile.

27

Ebony raced her horse through the trees. She loved the feeling of wind in her hair, though it often made her hair knotty. It wasn't too long ago that she had ridden a horse for the first time. She had been scared of them back then, but now she respected and adored the magnificent creatures. They gave her freedom, a feeling she was in dire need of. A smile stretched across her face, her eyes glowing a golden brown. When was the last time she had felt so ... alive? She knew when, but she didn't want to think about it. Images of Henry came to mind. She could hardly remember his face anymore. He would forever be young in her mind.

She shook her head and pushed the horse harder, faster, branches scratching against her arms and legs. Her horse whinnied, and she slowed to a trot before dismounting. She was in an unfamiliar part of the woods, and the light shone through the treetops like fingers reaching down to touch her.

Tying her horse to a tree, she said, "I won't be long, I promise," and disappeared into the trees. In a week, it would be the Spring Equinox—the biggest celebration in the Fae calendar. At this time of year, the Fae would all mysteriously disappear, leaving the woods silent. She used to circle her camp with flowers and berries and offer bowls of sugared water to the fairies upon their return. But she doubted they'd come to her this year, close as she was to Sam and the Foryx Clan. But she had decided to decorate her camp anyway. It wasn't like she had anything else to do. Now that they weren't spending their gold and silver on a rebellion, Sam was cooking up ideas for how they could improve the village. He'd been meeting with the gardeners, the cooks, the smiths—asking them what they might need. Darrel had happily agreed to buy all the goods they needed in town. He was being paid more than Hunter had ever been able to give him.

With a borrowed sack on her back, Ebony began

collecting flowers, lush branches of green leaves, and as many berries as she could find. The sun shimmered on her dark hair, and she relished its warmth on her face. She took a deep breath of contentment before returning to her horse, who was waiting patiently. In a pack on his back she had stored some apples and cheese. She fed one apple to her horse, who crunched happily, and then sat down against a tree trunk to eat her own lunch.

The trees were alive with birdsong, the sky blue and clear. She sat on a patch of ground highlighted by the sun's rays and lifted her head, her eyes closed. This was bliss. She was perfectly comfortable against the bark, and slowly her body grew slack. The half-eaten apple rolled out of her hand and onto the forest floor.

He stood before her—her old childhood friend, the same age he had been when he had died in that fire. Ebony rubbed her eyes.

"Where am I?" she asked. It was almost jarring to hear

her own voice in such a quiet place.

"You have made the right choice," the boy said. It wasn't quite Henry ... and yet it looked so much like him. "Follow me," he said, then turned back towards the palace of black turrets. Ebony tentatively followed; there was no force making her walk anymore. She could turn round if she wanted. She could forget the boy. But why was Henry here before her? What was he leading her to?

She climbed the stone steps before her and eventually reached the large, gothic doors that swung open like a breath of wind. Henry beckoned her to follow him inside, into impenetrable darkness. She took one step forward ... then another ... the darkness inside that tower was absolute. And before her were two red eyes, watching.

She yelled as she sat upright, the bright, sunlit forest flooding her mind. How long had she been asleep for? Her horse looked at her with curiosity. He bowed his neck and nudged her with his nose. Her heart was thumping. When she next dreamed of that place, would she enter that darkness? Something told her she would never come out. She stood up and shook her limbs, goosebumps covering her skin.

It wasn't real. It was just a dream. She was back in reality now under the blue sky, bathed in sunlight. She stroked her horse's mane and inhaled his musty scent, then untied him and climbed back on.

"Back home," she said.

She didn't stop when she got to the wooden village but made a beeline for her own camp. She tied him up again and went about setting up her Equinox decorations; a large circle of flowers, berries, and greenery around her camp. The dreams wouldn't reach her here, protected by the Fae ritual. She hoped they wouldn't.

"What are you doing?" a voice asked.

Ebony yelped and spun on her heel to see Sam watching her from the trees.

"Spring Equinox," she mumbled, not daring to

look at him. Would she see those red eyes shining from inside him? He was connected to the Shadow.

"Are you okay?"

"Yep. Fine," Ebony lied.

"You dreamed about it again, didn't you? The Shadowlands."

Ebony froze. "I took control, Sam. But now I think I regret it."

"You regret it? But … you could explore that city."

"But what's in the tower? Did you follow the boy?"

"What boy?"

Ebony shivered despite the warmth of the day. "You know … the boy that comes out of the tower and beckons you inside."

"I've never seen a tower there. Only a silent city of shadows."

"So who's the boy, then?"

"I don't know." Sam shrugged. "Sit down, Ebony. You're safe. You're not dreaming anymore." Ebony did as she was told. She and Sam sat side by side in front of her unlit fire. "Now, tell me what you're doing with all these flowers," he said, taking her hand and gazing at her blue ring. She shook him off and looked away.

"It's the Spring Equinox next week, so I'm decorating." Sam raised his eyebrows. She clearly hadn't answered his question. "At the Spring Equinox, we create large fairy rings, representing the circle of life. They circle our lands and protect us and the festivities. My fairy ring isn't very big ... because I don't have many lands."

"What are the festivities?"

"Well ..." Ebony faltered and looked at her hands. "I don't actually know. The Fae have never shared it with me. But they'll start disappearing from the woods now and return in a week or so, buzzing about the celebrations."

"Where do they go?"

"The Fae realm. But only the Three can go there."

"The Three?"

"The Mother, the Sister, the Daughter of the forest,"

she explained like it was obvious.

He raised his eyebrows. "So do you want to make a fairy ring around the whole of the Foryx Camp?"

Ebony looked up at him with surprise in her eyes. "You'd do that for me?"

"Of course. This is your home too."

"It would take us ages to collect enough flowers and lay it all out."

"I'm sure Anna would be happy to help."

Ebony didn't know what to say. "You really mean it?"

"Yes," Sam laughed. "The Fae respect you, so you must respect them, as must we. We will learn from you."

"Okay." Ebony said and beamed.

Sam touched her cheek with his hand, and she rested her face in his palm, his warmth turning her eyes a rich purple. "I love that you feel so comfortable with me." He took her hand again, and she didn't shake it off this time.

"How do you know I feel comfortable?"

"Your eyes are a dead giveaway. They turn purple when you're content and safe."

He was right. She *did* feel safe with him. It didn't make any sense, especially since she knew he was connected to the Shadow. But he was warm and calm. He was loyal and trustworthy. He understood her and let her be herself. As her eyes turned gold, he pulled her close and wrapped his arms around her.

"I will never hurt you, Ebony. You know that, right?" he said in a quiet voice. She nodded and her stomach fluttered as he stroked her hair. All too soon, he pulled away. "You matter to me, Ebony Wick."

"You matter to me too," she said, gazing into his kind face.

Sam smiled. "We'll decorate the camp tomorrow," he said. "But first, I want to show you something. Come with me." He stood up and held his hand out to her. She accepted it and allowed him to pull her up. He wound his arm across her back and led her through the trees.

Silence fell between them, and the further they walked, the more curious she became.

"Where are we going?" she asked.

"You'll see."

"Sam, I don't like surprises."

"We're nearly there."

They reached a large barn, similar to the one she had been in last year ... she jumped away from him, her eyes swiftly turning from gold to brown. "What are we doing here, Sam?"

"I just want to show you something inside. You'll be safe, I promise. No fire," he said with a cocky smile. "Trust me," he whispered as he held out a hand.

She tentatively took it and let him lead her through the barn doors, which he closed behind them, shrouding them in almost darkness.

"Sam ..."

"You're ready, Ebony. You took control, so now you're ready."

"Ready for what?"

He let go of her hand and reached forward like he was pulling something from the air.

"Come to me," he whispered, his voice cold. She looked at his face, which had turned pale and sharp, like he had been sick for months.

There was someone else in the darkness with them. She could feel it. A presence, oppressive and heavy.

"At last," a voice whispered. "You're ready." The voice was rasping and cold, like wind whipping at a windowpane.

From across the barn, something began to move. *Wake up.* Ebony shouted in her mind. She must be dreaming. *Wake up. Wake up! This can't be real.*

The red eyes moved, growing larger, coming closer.

"S—Sam. What are you doing?"

"Samuel Sanker is under my control," the voice rasped slowly. "He cannot hear you."

Ebony's heart thumped in her chest so hard

she thought it would break free. A figure moved closer, writhing in shadows. A figure made from smoke and those glowing red eyes. A scream caught in her throat as it steadily approached, gliding across the barn floor.

Help me. Mother, Daughter, Sister. Help me.

"I have been waiting so long for this." The voice filled her mind and sent a chill through her bones.

She tried to speak, but her throat didn't seem to work. Her breathing was short and sharp. It was there. Right before her. It was speaking to her.

"You have felt drawn to Samuel Sanker, haven't you? Do you know why?"

Because he's a good man … he's just possessed by a Demon, she thought. But it was right. She had always felt drawn to Sam, even when she'd hated him.

"You are drawn to *me*, not Samuel Sanker. I will never hurt you, Wick. You matter to me."

Ebony flinched. Sam had just said those words to her in her camp. Had he been controlled by the Shadow?

Had *Sam* hugged her earlier or ... had he been ... possessed?

"Sam is a lost cause. But you can save him if you come under my protection, under my wing."

She had a thousand questions that this *thing* could answer. Why her? Why Sam? It slithered closer and she could see the outline of its pointed, swirling fingers. A cold as hard as ice flooded through her, but her arm was burning. With a yelp, she looked down. Around her wrist was a writhing mass of shadow, gripping her, pulling her forward.

Help me! Mother, Daughter, Sister! Help me!

The barn doors crashed open, flooding the barn with light. Warmth flooded through her as she shadow let go, and without a second thought, Ebony fled.

28

She didn't look back. She didn't think for one second what might happen to Sam if she was lost again. Terror filled her core and her legs took her, branches flying past and whipping at her cheeks. Her chest burned but she continued running, leaving that nightmare behind.

The image of that figure wouldn't leave her mind. That was the *real* Demon in the forest. The stories had been true all along. But people had thought it was Ebony. If they had known the real Demon ... Ebony was just a girl with red eyes and a quick dagger. She wondered if even Hunter had felt the same fear that coursed through her heart as she ran, fled, flew through the trees. The birds squawked in alarm as she pushed through endless low-hanging branches. She vaguely recalled a fairy joining her at one point, speeding along beside her, but she paid it no mind. All she could focus on was distancing herself from that *thing* as much as possible. That and keeping the scream from escaping her chest.

Her legs burned, her chest ached. She wanted to cry but her eyes seemed to be frozen with horror. At last, she reached the wooden village. She couldn't stay there. She had to keep running. As quietly as she could, she stole into the stables and found herself a brown horse. She pulled herself up onto the steed, riding bareback. The horse understood her urgency and fear, and they cantered into the trees, away from the village, Ebony grasping his mane.

She had to get away from the Shadow. Her heart hammered and her hands shook. Just a bit further—further still. They fled with no direction—anywhere but that barn.

They careened to a sudden stop and the world spun around her as the horse bucked and whinnied. He flung her forward and she flew off its back. She somersaulted, desperate to grab onto a branch—anything. SLAM. She smacked into something solid, and the world went dark.

She jolted upright and took a minute to catch her breath. Where was she? The day had fallen to twilight, but she was surrounded by tall stone walls ... it was a ruin. She was in the middle of an old ruin, the mossy ground strewn with old rubble. The walls stretched so high she couldn't see the top of them, and the bricks had something drawn on them. Fae symbols. Every single brick of this ruin had a Fae symbol etched into it, most of which she didn't recognise. How had she got here? The horse was gone.

Behind her was a small stone archway. She shivered. She'd had enough of archways. Standing up onto shaky legs, she crept towards the exit and hesitantly took a step out. It led into a large field where there were more ruins. Some were larger than others. Some had ceilings still and even some of their internal structure, while others only had the walls remaining.

In the centre of the field sat a large tree—an old, gnarled yew, its thick roots splayed across the forest ground underneath its magnificent bows. The leaves of the tree ... Ebony blinked and rubbed her eyes. The branches were glowing, twinkling. Realisation dawned on her. That was the light of the Fae. But where were they and how had she got here?

She caught sight of a small fairy approaching, its silver skin catching the Faelight. It hovered before her and seemed to inspect her.

"You wake," it said.

"Where am I?"

"Come," it said. Ebony hesitated. "Come to the tree." It placed its hand on its chest, signifying 'friend', then beckoned her to follow.

Ebony did as she was told and began to walk towards the yew in the centre of the field. Her body felt weak. She needed food and water. She stood underneath the large tree and looked up into its twinkling branches.

"So it's true," a voice said. King Alvero flew towards her, Queen Coralia in tow. "You came through the Fae door."

"The what?"

"The entrance to Faelynn. Our lands."

Ebony gasped and scanned the field of ruins. Their lands?

"Few can enter the Fae door."

"What's the Fae door?"

"The archway you flew through yesterday."

What archway? How long had she been asleep for? It didn't feel like she had slept at all. Her head was heavy and hazy with exhaustion.

"I—I was running from … something."

"The Shadow," Queen Coralia confirmed.

Ebony nodded. "I'm sorry. I didn't mean to run through an archway. I didn't even see it."

King Alvero smiled. "You are welcome here." Ebony heaved a sigh of relief. "This part of the forest is protected. We are safe behind the Fae door."

Did that mean she was safe here too?

"Why am I here?" she asked.

"You flew through the door and ... into a wall. We carried you to the old infirmary."

"I flew? Oh." A memory ran through her mind. "I was bucked off my horse. I hit my head ..." *My mother's ring.* She checked her hand, to find her blue ring still firmly on her finger, then reached up to rub her head, which had a large swollen welt on it. Wincing, she asked, "What is this place? I mean, I know you said it's your lands ... your home. But what was it before?"

"The Mother's Abbey," Queen Coralia replied in her lofty voice.

"The Mother? As in the Mother of the Forest?" Ebony openly gaped. "She had an abbey?"

"We will explain in time," Coralia replied. "For now, welcome to Faelynn. Welcome, Daughter of the Forest."

Also by M. J. Glenn

On the Edge, Book 1 in The Dwelling Hunter Series

Available from Waterstones.com

"The writing is flawless and the detail is impressive."

"M.J. Glenn presents a powerful story of independence and loyalty in the first of her Dwelling Hunter series."

"A very well written YA fantasy adventure with plenty of action and a strong female heroine."

After a childhood of chasing fantasy creatures round rural Sussex, it's no surprise that M.J. Glenn's first published book series is set amongst the trees of Rundlewood Forest. In reality, she now lives in rural Suffolk, where she runs Softwood Self-Publishing, supporting a global network of independent authors through their own publishing journeys.